BLIZZARD!
Alan began to realize that the woman to whose rescue he was hastening might die in spite of his efforts—and that he and his guide might die even before her! The wind was cold and searching, piercing through all those garments that he had thought so superfluous when he started. His mind raced through the experiences he had read of explorers at the poles.

And then they came to a great drift looming out of the gloom, a drift as high as their heads, and extending interminably . . . it seemed an impassable barrier . . .

Tyndale House books by Grace Livingston Hill.
Check with your area bookstore for these best-sellers.

THE SUBSTITUTE GUEST

LIVING BOOKS ®
Tyndale House Publishers, Inc.
Wheaton, Illinois

This Tyndale House book
by Grace Livingston Hill
contains the complete text
of the original hardcover edition.
NOT ONE WORD
HAS BEEN OMITTED.

Printing History
J. B. Lippincott edition published 1936
Tyndale House edition/1991

Living Books is a registered trademark of Tyndale
House Publishers, Inc.

Library of Congress Catalog Card Number 90-71915
ISBN 0-8423-6447-1
Copyright © 1936 by Grace Livingston Hill. Copyright renewed
1964 by Ruth H. Munce.
Cover artwork copyright © 1991 by Corbert Gauthier
All rights reserved
Printed in the United States of America

IT was the day before Christmas and it had been snowing hard all day.

They began in the early morning, shortly after seven, large feathery flakes sliding down as if they were only playing. They soon grew larger, swirling fantastically, like children taking hold of hands, chasing one another through a fairy world, now this way, now that, whimsically, with no regular meter or rhythm.

In just no time at all the ground was covered, and then the snow settled down to business, imperceptibly changing into fine stinging grains, slanting down with swift accelerated measure, beating into every crack and cranny, packing firmly into an impenetrable mass. The wind rose gradually, drifting the falling particles into solid walls of stubborn whiteness. Before noon it became apparent that the intention was something more than just a winter snowstorm.

Children came rollicking out with their sleds, bundled in gay scarlet or green or blue, reveling in the snow, shouting to one another with muted voices that seemed amazingly to have lost their resonance, deadened in this strange padded atmosphere. Till even their young ardor was baffled by the increasingly bitter cold, and the pitiless slant of whiteness that shut them from one another, and one by one they drifted from a suddenly frightening world, into the warmth and brightness of the fireside, to careful mothers who kissed their little cold wet faces, dried their smarting wrists and folded them in warm garments with comforting embrace.

But the snow went steadily on.

Alan Monteith drove gaily into the first of the storm, wending his way between the largest of the lazy flakes, a bit thrilled at the thought of snow for Christmas. He was still young enough to thrill over snow.

Not that Christmas meant so much to him any more. Christmas was a home day and his family were all gone except a married sister who was touring Europe on her wedding trip. Christmas didn't seem like Christmas in an apartment hotel with only a city office for alternate. Oh, of course he had friends, and there were plenty of social engagements. He was on his way to one now, a colossal house party in a fabulously expensive castle on a vast estate ninety miles or so away. But it didn't suit Christmas, not in the least, not his inherited traditional Christmas. There would be excitement and hilarity, there would be amusement and a wealth of unique variety. There would be luxury of eating and drinking and apparel, but it would not be Christmas, not real Christmas.

Still, there would be Demeter Cass! Would that make up for the lack of a real Christmas? Demeter with her hair like ripe wheat, her strange sea-green eyes under long golden lashes, and her red, red lips. There was a lure of mystery about Demeter. It was not merely the beauty of the flesh either. She had intellect, and an uncanny insight into men's minds. Was she psychic? A siren without doubt. Yet, couldn't she be tamed? There was thrill and lure in the thought of taming a beautiful creature like Demeter, so-phisticated to the last degree. But could one ever hope to build up a happy future around a girl like Demeter? A future that would have in it an old-fashioned Christmas somewhere? Or were Christmases, the kind that used to be when he was a child, gone forever?

He wove his way among the city traffic skillfully, where late Christmas shoppers were even so early in the morning thronging the streets for a last frantic dash after forgotten gifts. He brought up before an office building, parked his car hastily, and took the elevator up to the tenth floor, walking down the marble corridor to a door that bore in gold letters the inscription: "Malcolm Sargent, M.D."

He marched in, past the white-garbed nurse who presided at a desk to guard the noted doctor, greeted her pleasantly and tapped at the inner door like one privileged.

"Doctor alone?" he asked the nurse casually.

"Yes. It isn't quite time yet for patients," she smiled, "and he's expecting you."

Monteith was one of the favored few who walked in at all hours and found a welcome.

The door was opened almost instantly.

"Well, you are prompt!" said Dr. Sargent cordially. "Did you get it through all right?"

"Of course!" said Alan. "Didn't I tell you I would?"

He settled down into the chair offered and pulled out an official-looking envelope from his inner pocket, handing it over to his friend.

"Well, I am relieved!" said the doctor. "When I heard about that uncle on his way back from California who had to sign to make it legal I thought my plans were all up! Did he get here in time, or what did they do?"

"He arrived yesterday afternoon and was tickled to death to sign. Pleased as punk that they got their price. I tried to get you on the phone to relieve your mind last night but couldn't. But say, what was the great rush? You're surely not expecting to move into a new house for Christmas, are you?"

The doctor smiled as he took the document out of the envelope and looked at it delightedly as if it were a treasure long desired.

"Not move in," he said happily, "but I'm expecting to put this deed in Natalie's stocking Christmas morning. It's her Christmas gift. You see, she's been keen on this house for about two years now, always wanting to drive by it, always saying she would like to build one just like it if we ever got wealthy enough to do it. She hasn't an idea, either, that it was even for sale, so it will be a complete surprise. A real Christmas gift!"

"Some Christmas gift!" said Monteith with a bit of a sigh and a wistful look in his eyes. "Any woman ought to be contented with that!"

"Well, I know she'll be delighted," said the doctor with satisfaction, touching the envelope again as if the mere handling of it gave him keen delight. "You see," he went on, "it isn't as if I were giving her something I wasn't sure about. She went through the house when they had some club committee meeting there and she raved about it for days afterwards, telling me of this and that advantage it had over any other house she'd ever seen.

"Well, Alan, I'm all kinds of grateful to you for getting this deal through before Christmas. It's going to make my Christmas perfect. You know, being able to hand over the actual deed to an article instead of just telling about it, makes all the difference in the world. And besides, I wanted to have something special this year. It's our tenth anniversary this month. Ten years since we were married and went to live in a four-roomed cottage on Maple Street! This year means a lot to me!"

"Well, I certainly was glad to be able to help," said Alan. "Christmas isn't what it used to be for me. All my folks are gone, you know."

"I know," said the doctor sympathetically. "Natalie and I were speaking about it the other day. You were just a kid in college when we were married. If we were only going to be at home we would want to have you with us. But Natalie's people wanted us to come to them this year. They are still living at the old farm, and I don't suppose they'll keep it much longer now. They're getting too old to stay alone so far away from everywhere. I imagine they'll come and live with us, now that we have a real house."

There was a ring in the doctor's voice as if the anticipation was a pleasant one.

"You're fond of them, aren't you?" said Alan wistfully.

"I certainly am," said the doctor heartily. "They've been all the father and mother I ever knew, you know. Mine died when I was too small to remember."

"It must be great to feel like that about them!" said Alan, trying to speak cheerfully. "You're leaving soon?"

"Yes, I have just two patients to see after my office hours and I'm taking the noon train. It will get me there a little before midnight. Just time to fill the stockings. Father will be down with his car to meet me! Natalie and the children have been there for a week. Maybe I haven't had a hard time arranging things here so I could leave! It seems all the doctors want to get away for Christmas this year. But I've got it fixed at last. I wired Natalie last night I was coming. And now having this deed to take along is going to make my Christmas perfect!"

Suddenly the telephone interrupted.

"Just a minute, Alan!" The doctor turned with an annoyed glance and took down the receiver.

Alan watched the keen sensitive face as the doctor listened.

"Yes! *Yes?*" his tone growing sharper. "You say she is worse? Broken? *What* is broken? Oh, the bottle of medicine I brought you last night? You don't say! That's bad! Wasn't there *any* of it saved? Not even a few drops? What a pity!"

The doctor's voice had grown exceedingly grave.

"What's that? Do without it? No! Not on any account! I would not answer for the consequences if you tried that. But isn't there any of the first bottle left? It wasn't quite gone when I was there yesterday. Let me speak to the nurse a moment. Hello! Hello! Is that you, nurse? How is the patient? Yes? Yes? Temperature? *No!* Not on *any* account. She *must* have the medicine! How much have you left? Let's see! That would carry you through till six o'clock! Well, isn't there someone there you could trust to come down and get it? I don't see how I could possibly come up. I'm leaving on the noon train, and my man is off on a three-day vacation. Just left. No, you couldn't get that at the ordinary drugstore, it's not a common drug. You say you haven't even a servant to send? Oh, not one who can drive. Where's the chauffeur? Gone on his vacation too, has he? That's bad! Well, I'll see what I can do. I'll try to get somebody to go, or I'll come myself. Yes, you can depend on having it by six o'clock. What do you say? Snowing? Oh, well, I'll find somebody to come."

The doctor hung up the receiver and turned dazed hurt eyes on his friend, the radiant look all gone from his face.

"Now can you beat that?" he said blankly. "I ask you, can you beat it? Everything all planned to go off on the noon train, even that deed here in time, and now this has to happen. I might have known things were going too slick to last. They let a fool pet dog get into the sick room where my patient is desperately ill, and he jumps up on the bed and backs against the bedside table and knocks off a bottle of very important medicine that I took the trouble to go all the way up into the mountains to take to them last night so they would have enough to last while I am away. Isn't that the limit? And it is absolutely necessary that medicine shall not be interrupted. They have only enough left from the first bottle to last till six o'clock. And of course I won't be able to hire anybody for love or money to take some more to them, not today! Not the day before Christmas!"

"Well, but surely you can hire a messenger boy," said Alan.

"It's seventy miles away, man, and up a mountain! How would a messenger boy on a bicycle make out? They say it's snowing up there, too. And the woman is in a critical condition. There isn't a chance for her life if she doesn't get the medicine in time. I couldn't expect anybody I hired to realize that, or care enough to carry them through difficulties.

"The woman is one of my best patients. Why they ever went up to that forsaken place at this time of year is more than I can tell, but her daughter is married and lives up there and they went to visit her three weeks ago. Then Mrs. Watt was taken sick. They let her get pretty sick before they sent for me last Wednesday. They thought she was dying and the local doctor wasn't sure what was the matter with her. I've been up three times since, was up yesterday evening, got back at two o'clock this morning. It's some jaunt. I went up to see if it was safe to leave her, and now I suppose instead of carrying out my Christmas plans I've got to go up again. That's what it is to be a doctor! Have to disappoint Natalie and the kids! But I wouldn't feel happy in my mind if I didn't go. You can't trust just everybody with an errand like that, the day before Christmas. Well, perhaps I'll get back in time to take the midnight train, and reach the farm about ten tomorrow morning."

He touched the bell on his desk and the nurse appeared capably at the door.

"Miss Rice, prepare another bottle of that prescription I took up yesterday to Mrs. Watt. They've broken that one. Put it in one of those foolproof boxes so they can't break it again. And then get Western Union and wire Mrs. Sargent that I can't get the noon train. I'll try to make the midnight if possible."

"Wait, Mac," said Alan Monteith, springing up eagerly,

"don't send that message to Natalie! Why can't I take that medicine for you? I'll swear on my life that I'll deliver it in good order before six o'clock. I'll take it as a sacred trust. I guess you can rely on me, can't you?"

"Rely? Well, I rather guess yes, but I couldn't think of letting you upset your plans for this. It's just all in the day's work for me, and you were on your way somewhere, I know. I wouldn't have you go out of your way for anything. No, Alan, it will be all right. Really it will. I'll get there before the day is over, and that's all they can expect of a doctor."

"Look here, Mac, I'll take it hard if you refuse me. I don't care a picayune for the fool house party I'm going to. It's the only excuse for a holiday that presented itself, and I wasn't at all sure I was going until a few minutes before I started."

"But I can't have you bearing my burdens and upsetting all your plans. There's probably at least one lady involved in the case who will never forgive you. No, Alan, I can't have you going off on a pilgrimage for me, traveling miles out of your way."

"There is no lady involved who has a right to care, and I don't in the least mind a pilgrimage. And how do you know it is so far out of my way? Where is it, anyway? Show me!"

Alan pulled out a map from his overcoat pocket and they both bent over it.

"Why, it's practically on my way!" said the young lawyer, straightening up. "Of course I'll take that medicine, and you needn't worry a minute. Get it ready for me, Miss Rice, and I'll start right away. There is no reason in the world why I shouldn't have it there early in the afternoon."

"I'll have it wrapped in five minutes, Mr. Monteith," said Miss Rice crisply. Then to the doctor: "Mr. Patterson is waiting, Dr. Sargent."

"Send him right in!" said the doctor. Then he turned to Alan.

"I'll never forget this of you, Alan. It's an even bigger thing than getting the deal through in time, for Natalie had counted so on my coming Christmas Eve. I just know I shouldn't let you do this, but somehow I can't resist it. You're sure you are not spoiling some delightful plan?"

"Not in the least! I haven't any delightful plans, I told you. I'm not so keen on this party, and don't care when I arrive there. And I'd go twice as far to have you spend the whole of this Christmas with Natalie and the children. I'm glad to have a part in it."

"Well," said the doctor, with a suddenly grave face, "you're having a part in something far more important than that, you know. You're helping to save a life. I'm serious about that. It is a matter of life and death with my patient. And I may as well tell you the truth about it, there's scarcely another man I know I would trust at Christmas time to take an important matter like this over. Especially with a snowstorm coming on. Almost anybody would say, 'Oh, well, I've done my best. A few hours won't matter.' But I know you will put a thing like this first. Of course, I don't anticipate any such necessity. I imagine this is only a flurry of snow. However, I'd take all precautions. Have you got chains on your car?"

Alan laughed.

"Oh, that's not necessary, Mac, it's only snowing a few lazy flakes. It won't amount to anything. Just a flurry to give us a white Christmas. The sun will probably come out by noon and melt it off. Anyway, I don't like chains. I always say if you are careful you make out better without them."

"I don't know, Alan. Up there in the mountains the storms come up in a hurry sometimes. Better take your chains along."

"Well, I can easily get some on the way, if I see it is

starting to drift. Good-by. Give my regards to Natalie."

There was a quick handclasp, Alan took the package of medicine and left.

"Remember you are to spend next Christmas with us!" the doctor called, and then turned to his patient and closed the door.

Out of the city traffic at last Alan Monteith whirled away into a really white world, for the snow seemed to have been very industrious during his brief stay in the doctor's office. The ground was already covered with a fine white blanket, and the flakes were settling down with a steady plunk, though still large and frolicsome.

The car dashed briskly on into it. He had the road mostly to himself and flew along into the whiteness with a kind of exultant thrill. It was nice to have it snowing. It seemed more like Christmas. How he used to love it when he was a kid!

His thoughts sped on ahead to the Christmas that was before him. So different from the Christmases of the past.

Would Demeter Cass be as alluring as he had found her the two or three times that he had met her? Would there be a sweeter human side to her, perhaps, that he had not learned yet, as well as the gay worldly side with which she had dazzled him?

He acknowledged to himself that she was his real reason for having accepted this invitation. He had wanted to come into closer contact with her, and find out if her charm was real or only superficial. And perhaps he recognized also in a vague way that Demeter had been at the bottom of his invitation, for the people who were giving the house party were only casual acquaintances of his.

Thinking about Demeter Cass, recalling the exact shade of her strange fascinating eyes under those long golden lashes, eyes that were neither blue nor green nor gray, but yet had lights of all those colors that she seemed to be able to turn on at will, he drove on through the whiteness and straight past the signboard that would have directed him into the way his errand called him. For someone the night before had run into that signboard and snapped off the pole that held it, and it was lying face down upon the ground entirely snowed over. There was not a sign of even the broken stump of the pole.

On he swept up the mountain side, and out a wide road that would have overlooked a valley if the air had not been so filled with whiteness that the valley was obliterated.

After he had been going thus, up and up the gradual ascent, he noticed that there were very few dwellings now, only long stretches of woodland well blanketed with snow. The silence all about him was almost appalling. One could imagine he heard the snowflakes whispering. At first he had been engrossed with his thoughts, but presently he began to grow uneasy. The silence was almost sinister. He had not been watching the mileage but it seemed a long time since he had seen a route sign. Surely he would soon come to a road branching off to the left as he had been directed! Was it possible he had missed it? His windshield wiper was working away gaily, but keeping only a small space of clear vision ahead.

When at last he emerged from the woods and looked across the world it seemed made of great mountains of snow, with an atmosphere of feathers everywhere. There was no sign of the sun coming to pierce the thickness of it and guide him on his way, and the road seemed too narrow to turn about. He must go on.

At last he came to a signboard, a crude, weatherbeaten affair, capped and veiled in snow. He got out, wiped the snow off, and peering close managed to make out the name of a town of which he had never heard, announced to be fourteen miles away.

He stumbled back into his car to study his map, but could not find the town mentioned by the signboard.

The road was narrow here, with an abrupt sheer descent

off to the left. He dared not try to turn about here nor to back down the mountain in this weather. He must go on till he came to a crossroad or a service station. What a fool he had been not to take the doctor's suggestion and get his chains before leaving the city! He had a strong conviction that he had missed his turn and was now going in the opposite direction from his destination. If the house party were his only goal it didn't matter what time he got there, nor if he ever arrived perhaps, but that medicine must get to the patient as soon as possible and set the family at rest about it! Yet he must run no risks.

About two miles farther on he came to a house with a gasoline pump in the front. There seemed to be nothing else in sight but the snow was so dense it was impossible to tell whether there were more dwellings.

The desolate old man who came out to wait upon him informed him that he had no chains to fit his car, no chains to fit any car, and only three gallons of gasoline left, with no likelihood of any more arriving today.

Alan took two of the gallons of gasoline, which was all the old man would sell him. He said someone might come along without any, and one gallon would take him to the next service pump.

The old man, however, could tell him where he was, and gave him very clear directions how to find his turn when he reached the foot of the mountain.

He had come forty miles out of his way! Forty miles to retrace before he could make any progress! The whole expedition took on a serious aspect. However, what was forty miles? He could at least turn around here.

So he turned and went slowly down the mountain, going cautiously, for the visibility was even worse than when he had come up.

The snow had subdued itself into finer grains, but a wind had come up and the road was drifted in places so that the car wallowed and rocked as it crept on. Alan realized that he had something far more important to attend to than strangely changing green-gray eyes under golden lashes. This was a serious journey, and a determined storm. Life and death hung upon his arriving, and he must press on as cautiously as possible.

It seemed hours that he was creeping down that mountain, watching the gauge anxiously to see if he was going to have gas enough to get to the next service station, but at last he came to the foot and recognized under its burden of snow the old tumbled down shanty that marked the crossing where he was to turn. He drew a breath of relief, glanced at the clock on his dashboard and plunged into the new road. The next filling station was four or five miles from this turn, the old man had said. Could he make it on so little gas? There was nothing to do but go on as long as it lasted.

At last he recognized a pump ahead, and a village street with houses.

It was half past two when he left the brief shelter of that filling station, and still with no chains, wallowed on.

It was half past three when at last he reached the village of Collamer to which he had been told to come to get directions for the castle on the mountainside where the medicine was needed.

Chains? Yes, they had chains here. They had oil and water and gasoline and air and advice. They advised him by no means to attempt to climb that mountain today. They told him of a drift between the village and the regular mountain road that made it impassable. They said the only possible way was to go on twenty miles and return by another road that took the back way up to the mountain home which was his destination. Of course even that road might be closed by now! They wouldn't go if they were in his place.

Alan shut his lips grimly and said it was a matter of life and death and he was going. So they put on his chains for him and shook their heads after him before they turned to succor the next floundering car.

It was more than a mile out of sight of the village that the engine suddenly coughed and sent out a series of weird rappings, clack, clack, clack! An alarming sound in the white stillness, with that garage so far away and the snow in many places now almost two feet deep. How on earth had so much snow fallen in so short a day?

In dismay Alan drove on, but the clacking grew louder and more insistent, and suddenly with a great pounding sound that seemed to echo Alan's groan, the car stopped short with an awful shudder like something that had suddenly died, and slumped in its tracks.

Alan looked about him. A perfect mountain of snow arose on both sides and ahead of him. The steady, persistent fall of the snow was slantwise now, in little fine even lines, impenetrable as if they were opaque. Now and again a gust of wild wind would snap at the snow, and toss it hither and yon, in wild orgy, clearing a space here and there for a second, and flinging blinding whiteness in great eddies.

With a sinking heart he looked about him, wondering if he would have to go on foot all the way back to that garage to get help. He was no mechanician, and if he had been, no one could work on a car in that blinding storm and cold. It would have to be towed back to the garage for repairs probably. If there were only some place he could go to telephone for a man to come and get him! He must get on with that medicine. It was quarter to four now, and at six the medicine would be needed. Death would be waiting to snatch its victim, the woman whom he had pledged his honor to save!

He opened the car door and stepped out into the depth of snow, trying to peer about.

There was a house on his left. He could make out the outline of a long low roof capped deeply with snow, an old farmhouse. Lights! There were lights in the house. Colored lights! A Christmas tree! His heart leaped up with joy. People who had a lighted Christmas tree might have a telephone. But first perhaps he would better look at his engine and get a general idea of what might be the matter.

He wallowed forward and lifted the hood, peering helplessly down as the snow gleefully hurried inside, but his inexperienced eyes could not tell what might have happened. Neither his expensive education, nor his inherited legal mind could help him in this predicament. He closed the hood quickly and turned toward the house. He was suddenly aware that his shoes were wet, and the snow was inside them, making quick work with his ankles and feet, and that the wind was icy and biting. His hands were already numb with cold, for he had foolishly taken off his gloves when he looked at the engine. How quickly cold could get in its work, even through an imported overcoat! How cruelly the snow stung his face, and tangled in his lashes so he could not see.

But the house was there, and he was headed toward it. There must be a front walk somewhere, though his uncertain feet could not find it, but with head down against the wind he struggled on, and now as he ventured to look up again he saw the door ahead, and a girl's face pressed close to the snow-rimmed window, looking out.

The wind tore the breath from him as he groped toward the door, but then just as he came blunderingly up to the porch the door was opened and a strong arm reached out and pulled him into sudden warmth and light and cheer! It seemed like stepping out of horror into Paradise!

2

THE Devereaux family had been up since before dawn.

Of course dawn in December did not break early, but it seemed exceedingly early to them all, they were so filled with excitement, almost as if all four of them, father, mother, son and daughter, were just four children.

It was to be a special Christmas, the first since the children had finished college and come home to stay, the parents fondly supposed. They were all thrilled with the joy of it. Not even a sullen sky which the day reluctantly parted to let in a somber gloom, could dampen their ardor.

"It looks as if it were going to snow!" said Father Devereaux hopefully as he wound the warm woolen muffler over his ears and about his throat, and buttoned his big coat to the chin.

"It sure does!" echoed Lance, stamping his feet into his galoshes and stooping to fasten them. "It wouldn't seem like a real Christmas without snow!"

"Wouldn't it be just perfect to have a white Christmas!" flashed Daryl. "Oh, suppose it should snow enough to make sledding! How grand that would be!"

"It may," said the father with another glance at the drabness out the window. "A few flakes can do a good deal in twenty-four hours if they really get down to business. And that sky looks like business, or I miss my guess!"

"Well, you'd better get going then," admonished Mother Devereaux. "It will be a lot easier lugging a big tree home before the snow gets started. A blinding snowstorm doesn't make pleasant traveling."

"Oh, we'll get home before that, Mother!" laughed the son. "We're only going up on Pine Ridge. It's not so far."

"Oh, that's good," said the mother, drawing a sigh of relief. "Your father said you might be going up on the far mountain."

"That was only in case we don't find the right tree on Pine Ridge, Mother," said the father, twinkling. "Daryl has given her specifications for height and width and we're not coming back till we can fill them." He gave a loving smile toward the daughter.

"Yes," said the son, "we're going to have the swellest tree we can find. But don't you worry. I'm sure there are plenty of trees on Pine Ridge. I've had my eye on one ever since fall, if some other fellow hasn't beaten me to it. But if we should be late don't you worry. We're going to be tasty in our selection."

He gave his mother a resounding kiss as he took the package of sandwiches she gave him and stuffed them in his pocket. "We ought to be back in good shape around noon, or maybe before."

They started out into the keen penetrating gloom, and the two women stood at the door and watched them away, then turned back to the bright kitchen and attacked the mountain of work they had planned for the day.

"Well," said the mother briskly, "we can get a lot of work done with our men out of the way and be ready to enjoy them when they get back. You do the breakfast dishes, Daryl, while I mix up the doughnuts, and then you can fry them while I roll out the crust for the pies. I think we ought to have plenty of pies, don't you? Young folks always like pies." She drew a deep breath and set her lips firmly in a pleasant line. "Will mince and pumpkin be enough or would you think an apple pie would be good to have on hand, too? This weather they keep indefinitely, of course."

If her daughter had been watching her closely she might have sensed that there was something a bit forced in the very pleasantness of her smile, as she brought out the memory that there were to be guests before the day was over. But Daryl was absorbed in her own thoughts. There were starry points of happiness in her sweet eyes as she lifted them to meet her mother's.

"Mince and pumpkin will be plenty, I'm sure," she answered gaily. "Don't the new curtains in the living room look beautiful from here!"

She stood in the dining room door looking across toward the living room windows and her mother came to stand beside her for an instant, feeling the thrill of joy at the sweet companionship of the day.

"Yes," she assented. "They are lovely and sheer. I was afraid they were going to look cheap, but they don't. I like the way you've looped them back with just that broad band of the stuff; and that spray of holly nestling in gives the right festive touch. The mantel looks lovely, too, with that bank of holly and laurel. Why, Lance laid the fire in the fireplace, didn't he? I don't see when he had time."

"He did that while I was pouring his coffee," laughed the sister. "He didn't intend to have anything weighing on his conscience to keep him back when he is ready to go to the village for Ruth Lattimer."

The mother smiled indulgently. There was nothing troubling in the thought of Ruth. She was a dear girl whom they all knew and loved. It was going to be nice to have Ruth with them. But then the shadow crept into her eyes again as she hurried back to the kitchen to do her mixing.

The two flew around at their work in a pleasant silence till Daryl had the dishes marshaled into the kitchen and was making short work of them. The fat was beginning to sizzle in the kettle, the dough was lying in a soft puffy mass on the molding board, and a bright cutter was forming it into rings ready for the frying.

Daryl hung up her dish towel, carried the pile of plates and cups to the pantry, and came over to test a bit of the dough to see if the fat was hot enough for the frying.

The mother looked up and smiled, with that little pool of worry back in the depths of her brown eyes. She thought the smile covered the worry, but it hovered out in her voice too as she spoke:

"What time is Mr. Warner coming?" There was something formal in her voice and the girl felt it and looked up.

"Why won't you call him Harold, Mother? He wants you to. You don't need to hold him at arm's length that way."

The mother flushed.

"Well, I can't seem to get used to it. I've seen him so little," she apologized hastily. "You know in my day people didn't call each other by their first names until they were well acquainted. But what time is he coming? Will it be before lunch? I don't think you told me."

"Oh, no," said the girl, "he has to stay in the office till noon, and then it's quite a drive."

"Driving, is he? I didn't know he had a car."

"No, he hasn't, but the company is lending him one. At least he has one for his work, and he said they wouldn't care if he used it on off days."

There was silence for a moment while the mother considered this.

"I wouldn't think it would be wise to do that without asking," she said, speaking her thoughts aloud, and then wishing she hadn't. "Suppose something should happen to it while he had it out for pleasure."

"Why, he'll probably ask, of course," said Daryl a bit loftily. Then after a brief tense silence: "You don't like him, do you, Mother?" Her voice was brittle, reproachful, as if the edge of her joy had suddenly broken off.

"Why! I never said that, Daryl!" said the mother hastily, shocked at being suspected in her innermost soul. "Why child! What have I done that should make you think that? I don't really know him well enough to be sure whether I like him or not. I'm sure I never suggested such a thing as that I didn't like him."

"No, but you don't!" said Daryl, with tears in her voice. "I felt it the minute you first looked at him. I've felt it both times he was here. And I can't understand it! Everybody likes him! Simply everybody! And he's so good-looking!" Her voice was almost a sob.

"Yes, he's good-looking," admitted Mrs. Devereaux, "he's very good-looking. Perhaps that's the trouble. He's almost too good-looking to be true!" She tried to turn it off with a laugh, for after all she mustn't say anything she would have to live down, but her voice faltered, and the depths of trouble shone out clearly from her eyes.

"Now, Mother!" said Daryl in a vexed tone, her own eyes suddenly filling and making them look like great blue lakes. "You would find something to worry about in that. The very idea of you not liking Harold because he is too good-looking. How perfectly silly!"

"I know," said the mother, turning her troubled gaze on her child again, "it wasn't that, of course. It was just that I love you so, dear child, and I want to be sure your friends are—all right!"

"But why shouldn't he be all right? What is there about him, Mother, that made you think he wasn't?"

"Nothing!" said her mother, yearning toward the look of trouble and indignation in her girl's eyes, "nothing whatever! I just felt as if he wasn't—quite—our kind!"

"What do you mean, our kind?" flashed the girl, on the defensive at once.

"Well,—I don't know—" said Mrs. Devereaux. "I rather got the idea, I guess, from some things he said when he was talking with Father, that he was out in social life a lot, and that his business threw him among a rather fast lot of men. Daryl, he doesn't drink, does he?"

The girl's face flushed suddenly red, and a flash almost of fear went shivering through the blue of her eyes.

"Why, no, of course not!" she said haughtily. "At least, I know he has taken it occasionally out at a dinner or somewhere that he thought he had to, but he doesn't care for it at all, and he never accepts it when he is out with me!" she added proudly. "He just doesn't order it. He says I'm very good for him, Mother! You needn't be in the least afraid of anything like that. He understands perfectly how I feel about drinking, and he says it's nothing to him at all, whether he drinks or whether he doesn't drink! He says that he never wants to do anything to worry me."

A misty look came into Daryl's eyes as she remembered the look in the ＿ ʼʼng man's eyes when he had told her this.

The mother watched her, more fearful than ever, yet saw and understood that misty look too, and yearned to her child again.

"Dear Father in Heaven! Grant that it may be so!" her heart breathed.

"Oh, Mother! You are just spoiling this perfectly wonderful Christmas time!" Daryl suddenly said with a quiver of her young lip.

"There, now, child! Put this all away!" the mother said quickly. "You got it all up out of whole cloth! And of course I'll like him if he's all right. And of course he's all right or you wouldn't like him. I'll be very fond of him when I know him better. Don't I always like your friends? And besides, why make such a fuss about it? You're not engaged to him or anything, not yet, anyway! You're just friends!"

"Yes, of course," said Daryl, relief beginning to over-spread her face, "just friends!" but there was a twinkle in the corner of her mouth where a dimple lurked.

"But awfully good friends!" she added with the starry look coming back into her eyes.

"Yes, of course!" said the mother, suddenly drawing her girl into her arms and smothering a sigh in her sweet young neck as she kissed her tenderly.

And just at that moment the fat got itself ready to boil over, and the experimental doughnut came to the top as black as a doughnut could possibly be. The ensuing rescue diverted the conversation for the time being, and when calm had been restored the two loving women dared not broach the subject again.

Daryl at least, forgot it, and her joy bubbled over in song now and again, as she sifted powdered sugar over the great platter of beautifully brown crisp doughnuts, while she cleaned the fine old family silver, and got out the best long tablecloth to look it over for possible breaks, counted out the napkins, and arranged everything in order in the sideboard so that the dinner tomorrow would be assembled with the least possible effort. And now and again she would drop into the living room for a minute to ripple out some notes on the piano, and trill a bit of a song, some favorite of her mother's, or a snatch of something she had learned out in the world. It was all one joyous Christmas medley of happiness, and the wonderful Christmas wasn't spoiled after all.

So Daryl went back to the kitchen to assist in the solemn ceremony of stuffing the great turkey. It was the one that Father had raised with such care, till it almost seemed a part of the family.

As they worked they planned out what things should be done at what hours so that the necessary work in the kitchen should not hinder the joy and good-fellowship in the living room.

"Ruth wanted to be here this morning to help us, but they had to go and put the Primary Christmas party this afternoon and she had to stay and get ready for that," said Daryl as she worked away rubbing breadcrumbs fine as fleece, and then rubbing them into the sweet butter that Mother had made from the cream of their own cow. Daryl was thrilled not a little to be at home helping with all the homely pleasant duties, preparing the delicious delicacies such as the world outside could never achieve even with all its luxury and glamour.

The morning sped rapidly, and the two were so busy with their work that they did not notice when the first snowflakes fell, and it was the mother who discovered it first after all.

"Daryl! It's snowing!" she announced, suddenly pausing as she lifted a pie out of the oven and set it on the table. "It's been snowing sometime. See, the ground is quite white already!"

"Oh, isn't that just grand!" said Daryl, going to the window to look out. "It's really going to be a snow as Father said, not just a little flurry! Oh, it will be the realest Christmas we've ever had!"

The mother looked at her compassionately and smiled, covering her own forebodings.

"Yes!" she said. "A white Christmas! But I do wish our boys would get back!" She looked at the clock uneasily. "If they only went to Pine Ridge they ought to be here pretty soon."

"If you ask me, I think they went farther. I know Dad had it in mind to get a really wonderful tree this time, one that we would always remember. Don't look at the clock, Mother, and don't worry! They'll take care of each other, and there's nothing really to happen to them. Let's just enjoy this morning together! It's so gorgeous to be together, getting ready for Christmas!"

The mother's heart leaped up to that call with a thrill. She would put aside all cares and worries for the future and just exult in her girl and being together with her for that morning. Times would come, she knew only too well, when she would need to remember that precious look from Daryl, and those words. She must treasure them as armor against the desolation that would be sure to come in the future.

So she put her worries in the background, and they were just two girls together, getting ready for a joyous occasion.

As the morning went on the kitchen began to take on the air of being ready to feed a hungry army. Crisp brown loaves of bread were cooling across their iron pans, pies in a fragrant row stood on a broad shelf by the window, and the turkey, full to bursting, was just getting its waistcoat buttoned across its breast.

"The hardest things are done now," said Daryl, as she measured out the sugar for the cranberries.

"Yes," said her mother with satisfaction. "I'm glad I made the fruit cake several weeks ago. It's always nice to use between times during holidays. I think we have plenty so that the work can be kept at a minimum while our guests are here. And the lunch is all ready as soon as our men get home." She looked complacently toward the kettle of old-fashioned bean soup on the back of the range, getting itself cooked without any fuss or trouble to anybody. "The soup with bread and butter and applesauce and coffee will be all we'll need. And for dinner tonight there will be the scalloped oysters. I can whip those together while you are talking to the guests and pop them in the oven with the potatoes to bake. We want everything to move along as if there were no such thing as work to be done, don't we?"

"Oh, Mother! You're simply great!" said Daryl, casting a loving look at her. "It's such fun to be having a real house party. And it's going to be so much nicer than any of the city house parties because we have your cooking and a real home!"

"You're a good girl! Here you might be fretting because you didn't go to that house party your college roommate had and instead you're rejoicing over our plain little home party!"

"Nothing good about it, Motherie! I really like it better. But look! Look at the snow! Why, it's getting to be almost like a blizzard!"

"Yes, I've been seeing it for the last half hour! I do wish your father would come!" said the mother apprehensively.

"Oh, they'll be all right, Mother. They'll just enjoy it. You know they are not children, and they aren't so far away. They'll come pretty soon. Come, aren't you done? You look tired. Suppose you go and lie down a few minutes now while you can, and I'll dust the living room."

But the mother would only lie down for about five minutes on the dining room couch, and then she was up and looking out the window again.

"They ought not to have gone so far!" she said, real worry in her eyes now. "Just for a tree! It isn't worth it."

"Oh, Mother! Don't get frightened. Why, there isn't more than six inches of snow on the ground. What could happen?"

"I know, but it is getting worse all the time. If anything happened to them, how could we find them?"

"Now, look here, Mother, you know that is silly! They are men, strong men. What could happen? They aren't going to cut down any ancient pines that might fall on them. And there they come now! See! And oh, look at the tree, Mother! No wonder it took them a long time! Isn't it a beauty?"

The mother's face relaxed and she turned quickly and began to get the lunch ready to put on the table.

"They'll be very hungry," she said, with happy eyes glancing out of the window again as she saw her two men tramp into the yard dragging the great feathery tree between them.

Daryl went out with a broom and helped them brush the snow from the tree branches, and then they brought it in.

"Oh, why don't you leave it out on the porch until you've had something to eat?" protested the mother.

"No, we want to set it up and be done with it," said Lance eagerly. "We might as well get it over while we are still all snow. Daryl, get a lot of newspapers and spread them out over the carpet till we get done broad-casting snow. Then we'll clean up and be ready to eat."

So there was a happy rush in the house again, and presently the tree was up in all its beauty, steadied by invisible wires strung across the room. Its fragrance filled the house. They could see it from the dining room as they sat down to eat, and it seemed as if the very spirit of Christmas had come to them from the great out of doors.

"Where are the lights?" asked Lance. "I'll put them on after lunch."

"They are on the piano in those boxes. I thought we would make the tree all silver and lights this year. Don't you think that will be pretty?" asked the girl.

"Lovely!" said the mother. "I never cared for a great array of baubles. The lights give plenty of color."

They were enjoying the bean soup and applesauce, as only tired, hungry, happy men can enjoy plain food well cooked, and there was such a pleasant light of love in all their faces that it was a scene worthy of a painter's brush.

"Well," said Father Devereaux, folding up his napkin and shoving back his chair, his eyes proudly resting on the beautiful tree, "we got her here, didn't we, son? Say, Mother, isn't that the most beautiful Christmas tree you ever saw?"

"It certainly is," said Mother Devereaux, her eyes following her husband's gaze.

"Say, Mother, do you remember the first Christmas tree we ever had, just after we were married?" He reached out and put his hand gently down upon her small wiry one, both hands that had worked so very hard through the years, yet warm as ever each to the touch of the other.

"Do I remember it?" said Mother, turning a beaming look toward her old partner. "How could I ever forget it?" and her hand nestled in his clasp.

The children gave them a quick wistful glance. They were old enough to appreciate the love between these two, far enough along in their own life-stories to wonder if anything so precious and lasting could be in store for them.

"Well, we've had a great time up in the woods, Lance and I, and I sort of think we enjoyed it all the better for the snow, though I will own it did get a bit heavy for me toward the end. I'm not as spry as I once was. Now, what's to be done next? When do our guests arrive?"

His eyes traveled around the group. Lance, who was cleaning out the applesauce dish was too busy to answer, and Daryl flushed and hesitated, dropping her gaze suddenly. It was the mother after all who had to answer.

"Why, Daryl says Mister—Harold, I mean—is driving and can't get here till late in the afternoon. I suppose Lance means to go for Ruth, Don't you, Lance?"

"No," said Lance, putting down the empty dish. "At least I didn't arrange that way because I wasn't quite sure what time Dad and I would get home. You know I took my car down last night to the garage to have them fix a leak in the pump, and Ruth was to go to the garage and get it as soon as she got done with that kids' party she is running at the church. She won't be through that till half past four or I'd go right now and get her. I don't like the idea of her driving through all this snow alone. I'll see how things get done here. Maybe I'll foot it to the village and drive her back myself. It's ridiculous her having to stay for that party. I don't see how the kids can get there in this snow anyway."

"Oh, children don't mind snow!" said the father, peering around to look out the window. "You know how you always used to go everywhere in it."

"I know!" sighed Lance. "And I suppose it wouldn't do any good even if I did go after her now, for she wouldn't leave till the hour was over, even if there was only one kid there. She'd make him have a good time. That's Ruth!"

"Yes," said his father, "that's Ruth! And that's why you like her, because she's that kind of a dear faithful girl!"

"Well, yes, I suppose it is," admitted the young man reluctantly, "but you know it makes me hot under the collar sometimes to see how they all let Ruth do everything, and she doesn't even belong in this town, just does it out of the goodness of her heart. They wouldn't bother for half the good times she gives those kids. She's just a slave to whatever she undertakes."

"Well, that's a pretty good way to be," said the father. "But I guess after a while you'd better walk down and drive her back. This is really a storm, you know, and she's a dear girl. I wouldn't want her to get stuck in a drift."

"Yes," said Lance, getting up quickly with a businesslike air. "Well, I'll bring in plenty of wood for the fireplaces tonight and then that will be done. I'll lay the other fires, too. Want one in each spare room, don't you? I would. It'll be chilly getting up in the morning without a fire, and a chap from the city will feel it even more than we would. Then I'll fix the lights on the tree and Daryl can go ahead with her decorations."

"Yes," said the mother firmly. "Fires laid in both rooms."

"Well," said Father Devereaux, rising slowly, reluctantly, and stretching his tired limbs, "I'll just go out to the barn and see how Chrystobel is getting on. She'll be thinking it's night with all this storm, and expect to be milked pretty soon. And I suppose the hens have gone to roost already."

"Better explain to them that tomorrow is Christmas, Dad. Tell 'em they'll have a good dinner, and find plenty of corn in their stockings," laughed Lance as he swung out through the kitchen shed to where the woodpile was, and presently they heard his ax ringing cheerfully.

Daryl thrilled to the joy of the day and their own dear home, and wondered shyly how it would all impress Harold when he came. She smiled quietly to herself at the glib way Mother had called him by his name, after almost mistering him after all. But she had said "Harold," and she would surely like him when she knew him, of course. Everybody liked Harold. He was very popular wherever he went. Then she got up and whisked the dishes into the pan and out again to the shelves in a jiffy and was ready to work on the tree.

Lance was already at work on the lights.

"It really is a blizzard, isn't it?" she asked a little anxiously. "You don't suppose the roads will be blocked so badly that Harold will not be able to get through?" Her tone showed an anxiety she did not want to own, and her brother gave her a quick keen glance.

"Well, I don't know, Darrie. It might be. You know the wind is pretty high, and I wouldn't be a bit surprised if the drifts were high in the open country."

"Even on the highway?"

"Yes, even on the highway, if the wind happens to veer the wrong way. You know it's been snowing for a good many hours, and it doesn't take long for snow to make a big barrier of itself when it has the wind at its back. What time did he start?"

"Why, I don't know. He said he doubted if he could get off before noon." Her eyes were troubled, and Lance had a sudden thought that she looked like their mother with that anxiety in the depths of her blue eyes.

"I wouldn't worry," he soothed. "He would likely have telephoned you before this if there was any doubt of his coming through. Just don't think about it. It'll all come out right."

Daryl flashed a smile at him and brightened.

"Of course!" she said.

"Of course!" said he. "Now, that's that. You can go ahead and put on your silver threads and pretties and I'll go out and milk Chrystobel. I think Dad is planning to get ahead of me and I don't think he should. He got pretty well puffed before we got home this morning, and I think he ought to rest."

Lance lowered his voice and nodded toward his father who had come in from his consultation with the hens and cow, and was taking a bit of a nap in his easy chair near the dining room couch where Mother had already fallen asleep.

"Yes," said Daryl in a soft whisper, "do, and I'll strain the milk and you can get ready to go for Ruth."

So Lance went to the barn and Daryl, thinking pleasant thoughts, went on threading the noble branches of the tree with silver. Outside the snow thickened and pelted down with added vigor, but Daryl resolutely kept her back turned to the window till she heard Lance come in and then she went quickly to the milk room to help him with pouring the milk through the strainer into the shining pans that stood waiting.

There was a window directly behind the broad shelf where the pans stood, and its outside sill and overhang were deep and heavy with snow. Daryl couldn't help looking out and was aghast.

"Oh, Lance. It's awful, isn't it?" she said, appalled. "I don't see how anybody can drive in that! I don't see how even Ruth is going to get here! Our Christmas is going to be all spoiled!" Her tone was full of dismay.

"Ruth will get here!" said Lance firmly. "Don't worry about her. And our Christmas isn't going to be spoiled. It's going to be great. Be your age, Daryl, and rise above this. Everything is going to be fine!"

Daryl looked at him dubiously.

"Oh, yes?" she said dejectedly.

"Well, it will, you'll see! There! There goes the telephone! You go! I'll finish this!"

Daryl hurried into the other room, but came back almost at once, her face excited, her eyes bright with worry.

"It was Ruth," she explained. "She was afraid you were coming after her, and she says you mustn't. She says Bill Gates has just telephoned over from the garage to the church to tell her that your car is finished, and that he is sending it over to the church for her, but she is not to start till he gets there with the snowplow. He has been ordered out with the plow and they are coming up this way in about an hour. She is to follow right after the plow, and he will look after her."

Lance set down the empty pail with a troubled look.

"It's almost four o'clock," he said. "I think I ought to go for her."

"No, she doesn't want you to. She says there's no sense in your having that long hard walk for nothing, and she will be here soon. Go talk to her. She's on the wire yet."

Lance hurried to the telephone. After he had hung up, Daryl, as she returned to the front of the house, heard him calling up Bill at the garage.

"Well, Bill says he'll be here in less than an hour," said Lance, coming back, "so I guess she will be all right. She made me promise not to come. But I'll be on the lookout and if they aren't here on time I'll go anyway. Now, come on. I have a few minutes' reprieve. Where's the stepladder? I'll put on a few icicles at the top. Turn the lights on the tree, Daryl. Gosh, listen to that wind! I certainly will be relieved when R—when—our guests get here!"

"Yes," said Daryl in a small tired worried voice, and cast her anxious glance out the window.

It was just at that moment that Alan Monteith came to a sudden stop in front of the house, and the tree lights flashed out to meet him.

"Oh, there he is now!" cried Daryl with a lilt in her voice, and rushed to press her face against the window pane.

"How do you know it isn't Ruth?" said Lance, descending the ladder with a bound and coming to look out over her shoulder.

"It's a man!" said Daryl excitedly. "He got out! See! My! I never realized how tall Harold was! Go open the door, Lance, and tell him to come in the driveway. The snow is so blinding he won't be able to find the walk."

"Open the door, nothing!" said Lance in a suddenly aloof tone, "don't you know if I'd open the door all outdoors would rush right in and freeze us? Wait till he's up on the porch and then we'll haul him in. He's supposed to be a man, isn't he? Well, I guess if he has come this far he can make it up to the porch!"

Daryl's joy shriveled within her at his tone, and then she rallied to thrill over the thought that Harold had really come! In all this storm he had come, to be with her!

They watched the tall figure in the fading light, bending over his engine, then saw him shut the hood quickly and turn struggling toward the house.

"Poor devil! He's having a hard time at that!" said Lance, relenting.

Daryl's heart had time to leap up again with relief at her brother's friendly tone, and then the door flung wide and the storm burst in, with a great swirl of wind that tore through the hall and into the living room like a hurricane, swinging the branches of the Christmas tree, and making the crystal prisms on the candle sconces over the mantel shiver and tinkle fearfully as it searched the corners of the room and swung out into the dining room, waking up the two sleepers in sudden alarm.

Just an instant. Then Lance reached out and pulled in the baffled creature striving to gain a foothold on the drifted porch, and slammed the door shut. With a sound like a sigh the noise ceased inside and the house settled to its usual warm peace again, with the firelight on the hearth and the Christmas light from the tree.

The man shook the snow from his eyelashes, shook the snow from his coat to the linoleum of the hall, took off his battered snowladen hat and stood forth—a *stranger!*

3

DEMETER Cass arrived at Wyndringham Ledge on the mountain at mid-morning, while the snow was just beginning its gay whirl.

Snow! of course that was right for a festival season like this. One almost expected it to be on order when one thought of Christmas parties in the mountains. But there was something serious and sinister in the look of the sky in spite of the gaiety of the flakes, that Demeter did not like. Such a storm was only interesting when there was a large party, a wide open fire, plenty of music to drown the sound of a possible wind, and banish the thought of cold and suffering and peril outside.

Demeter had arrived early, contrary to her usual custom, partly for her own ulterior motives and partly because she had a curious foreboding that if she didn't go early she wouldn't be able to get there at all. There were so many reservations in the voices of servants around the holidays, and her chauffeur was no exception to this rule. He wanted to spend Christmas with his family. It was most annoying. If a man was a chauffeur he ought not to expect to spend Christmas with his family, ought he? He was a chauffeur, not a man, to the mind of Demeter Cass. For Demeter Cass was a self-centered creature, with very few thoughts for others. But because she saw a certain look in her chauffeur's eyes, and a familiar set of his jaws that told her he would go anyway, whether she allowed it or not, she gave in and started on her way early, that he might take her to her destination, and then get to his as best he could, returning for her after the holiday.

She had tried to induce Alan Monteith to accompany her. She had done her best for a whole evening to convince him that she needed his protection on the journey, but he had told her that he was not sure that he could get away to go at all yet, as he had an important law matter that must be arranged before he could leave the city. So she had gone on her way alone, through the increasing storm, with her grim chauffeur silently driving in the front seat.

It was not that she could not have had other company, for Demeter Cass was not usually begging for company, but it did not suit her plans just now to have anyone hindering her movements. She had planned out a campaign for this holiday and wanted to be sure just how the land lay.

So she arrived at The Ledge three hours ahead of even her host and hostess, the Wyndringhams, and had the castle and its servants to herself, incidentally getting her pick of the guest rooms, and establishing herself so thoroughly that any contrary plans of her hostess would be futile.

Restlessly she roved from room to room. She hunted up the butler and, narrowing her green eyes keenly, asked him: "Has the count arrived yet?" When he replied in the negative she commanded, "Let me know as soon as he comes!" Finally she went to the telephone, a frequent employee of hers.

First she called up Alan Monteith's apartment, and after a long wait with prolonged ringing was answered by the janitor of the building.

No, Mr. Monteith was not there.—No, he was not coming back until after Christmas.—No, he had not left any address where he could be called.—Yes, he had said he was leaving the city.—No, he did not know how far.— No, he did not know who would be likely to know his whereabouts unless they had some message at the office.— The party had better call the office. His partner might be there.

Demeter Cass called Alan Monteith's city office, and was answered by Alan Monteith's secretary who had come in to attend to some mail that must go out that morning. Yes, she said, Mr. Monteith had been in the office that morning early, but had gone and would not return until after Christmas. "Who is calling, please?"

Demeter Cass was clever. The secretary might or might not know her voice, but she gave her no satisfaction.

"Just a friend of Mr. Monteith who is a fellow guest where he is going," she answered in honeyed tones. "I reached here an hour ago and discovered that I had left a small leather case at home that I very much need, and I was wondering if Mr. Monteith would be so good as to stop at my home and bring it for me, in case he has not started yet. I understood that he was not leaving the city till somewhere near noon."

She understood nothing of the kind of course for Alan Monteith hadn't mentioned noon. But she had nothing on the secretary; she knew her voice. She had heard it often enough to know it.

"I'm sorry, Miss Cass," she said cooly, "I really don't know whether Mr. Monteith has left the city or not. He certainly has left his office, and I would not know where to look for him."

"Oh, really?" said Demeter Cass in hurt tones. "That's most unfortunate for me! It was my jewel case I left behind, and you know one really needs one's jewels at a place like this."

"I suppose one does," said the secretary dryly, smiling to herself. Her employer was much too nice for this selfish lazy intriguing woman.

"I hate to send my chauffeur all the way back in the storm if I can possibly locate anyone coming up who could bring it."

"I suppose you would," said the secretary coldly. "Sorry I can't help you."

"Well, I suppose there's no use," sighed Demeter Cass, with no notion yet of giving up, for she was a clever little detective. "You don't know whether Mr. Monteith had an errand before he left the city? There wasn't any place at all where he might have stopped off for a few minutes? What did he come to the office for this morning? Don't you know? That might give me some clue to follow. Excuse me, but this is a very important matter to me. Do you know what he came for?"

The secretary was getting angry, yet she dared not show it. She had no right to rebuke Alan Monteith's friends or acquaintances. She tried to answer patiently.

"He came for some papers he had left in the safe. It wouldn't help you in the least, Miss Cass. He was stopping for just a moment to leave them with a man who was taking a train this morning. He wouldn't be there now. He was in a hurry!"

"Oh, really?" Demeter's voice brightened. "And who was the man? He might happen to know where I could locate Mr. Monteith. Just tell me his name and I won't bother you more. I can see you are impatient to hang up. I shall be sure to let Mr. Monteith know how helpful you have been."

There was cold rebuke in the voice and a hint of something vindictive. The secretary drew a deep breath and tried to steady her voice.

"It was Dr. Sargent, Miss Cass. Dr. Malcolm Sargent. But I'm quite sure it wouldn't do you any good to call Dr.

Sargent for Mr. Monteith told me that he was leaving for the west this morning. He must be gone by this time. It was fully two hours ago that Mr. Monteith left here."

"Thank you!" said Demeter Cass acridly. "I shall be *sure* to tell Mr. Monteith how helpful you have been."

There were angry tears in the secretary's eyes as she hung up. But what could she do? Miss Cass often came to the office to see her employer. He looked after her legal business for her. And of course there couldn't be any harm in giving Dr. Sargent's name. He would be gone anyway.

But Demeter Cass lost no time in calling Dr. Sargent's office.

Dr. Sargent was gone, but the nurse, Miss Rice, was still in the office. She answered with her usual quiet courtesy. Yes, this was Dr. Sargent's office but Dr. Sargent was not in. He had left on the train a few minutes ago for the west. Yes, Mr. Monteith had been in that morning, but only for a very few minutes. He had left over two hours ago. Why, yes, she did happen to know his immediate destination. He was taking some medicine to a very sick patient in the mountains for Dr. Sargent. He was on his way somewhere else but she didn't know where. Yes, she could give the name of the patient, but Mr. Monteith would hardly be there yet. It was a three-hour drive.

Demeter Cass thanked the informer graciously, representing her necessity for contacting Mr. Monteith as most important, and hung up the receiver with a glitter of triumph in her eye.

So, Alan Monteith had delayed himself to go on a fool's errand for some doctor or other, when he knew perfectly well that she had gone ahead early, and would be there with several perfect hours to spend alone with him if he chose to come. Well, he would do foolish philanthropic things like that! It was vexing but it was like him. Perhaps he wouldn't be half so attractive if he weren't like that. And then of course everybody had to have some faults, and she felt sure she could cure him of that if she chose to exert herself.

So Demeter Cass waited a little while and then she called up the castle on the other mountain where a woman lay fighting death and waiting for the medicine that was to bring her help.

A servant answered the telephone. She had never heard of Mr. Monteith. She consulted the other servants, but none of them knew him. Dr. Sargent? Oh, yes, Dr. Sargent came up yesterday to see a sick lady; but they had never heard of Mr. Monteith.

Demeter Cass was persistent. She asked if the doctor was not to send some medicine, and at last she got hold of the nurse, and learned that the medicine was to come, but they did not know who was bringing it, perhaps Dr. Sargent himself.

At intervals during the remainder of that restless boresome day, Demeter Cass retired to the telephone booth and called up the home where the woman lay between life and death, to know if Alan Monteith had not arrived yet, but the answer was always, he had not arrived. Demeter looked out on the snowy world that seemed more and more a menace to her plans, and drew her delicate brows in a frown. Then by and by she called again, and yet again, till the sick woman's husband grew annoyed and alarmed by turns, and still the medicine had not come.

But Demeter was cunning. She had not left her name nor her location. She wanted to talk with Alan herself, not to leave him a mere message. She wanted to make sure she got *him*, and that he was coming. She suspected him of being able to evade her if she only left a message. If he did not want to come he might pay no attention to her request to call her up.

So Demeter turned her main attention to what she should put on for the evening, in case he did finally arrive.

But Alan Monteith was not thinking of Demeter Cass

just then. He was standing in a long homelike room, with big beams in the ceiling, a great fire blazing on the hearth, and a Christmas tree draped with silver fringe and twinkling lights, that had their counterpart in miniature, in tinkling crystal prisms over the mantel. He was looking down into a girl's eyes, astonishingly lovely eyes, fringed about with the longest, darkest, curling lashes he had ever seen. They seemed like great blue stars shining out through the depths of the pleasant room, twin stars that somehow were a part of Christmas, the tree, and the lights and the prisms and the firelight flicker. He blinked the clinging snow from his own eyes, and stared down at her for the instant, not yet breathing easily after his wrestle with the storm.

"I'm sorry to intrude," he gasped, with a winning smile that tried to take in the others in the room as well as this lovely girl. "I'm a pilgrim on my way and something has happened to my car. I couldn't make out in the blinding snow, what is the matter. Would you mind if I telephoned to a garage and asked for help? I'm on a very important errand, and my time is short."

"Sure, you can use the telephone," said Lance, "but I'm afraid it will be slow work getting anybody up from the village. They're crazy-busy, I imagine. A man is coming out in about an hour, though, with a snowplow. Better sit down and warm up till he gets here."

"Oh, I couldn't wait an hour. I must get on as quickly as possible. It is most important."

"All right. I'll get on my togs and go out and have a look."

"Oh, I couldn't think of taking you out into the storm," protested Alan. "I'm so sorry to intrude. If you'll just let me telephone."

"Sure, go ahead! There's the instrument. Call Gates' Garage. Number's 92. But I'll get my high boots on and be ready."

So Alan Monteith went to the telephone, and the family in the shadows of the room furtively watched his broad shoulders, and trim shapely head, silhouetted against the window. They liked his courteous troubled voice, and pitied him in this interval of their waiting for their own guests.

But the stranger turned from the instrument with a real anxiety in his voice.

"He says they can't spare anyone now. They have trouble enough. He says he doesn't know how long it will be. And I must get on at once!"

He seemed to be talking more to himself than to the family in the shadowy corners of the room, but Lance appeared fastening his leather jacket.

"I guess we'll need a torch," he said, taking down a long powerful-looking flashlight from the hall closet shelf. "Come on. We'll see what's the matter. If it's fixable I'll do my best."

"You're awfully good!" said Alan. "I can't bear to be making all this trouble. If it were just for myself I shouldn't allow it, but—"

They were outside now with the door slammed behind them, and suddenly Alan Monteith's words were snatched from his lips and cast from him into the roaring seething storm.

Lance plunged across the drifted lawn, seeming to know by instinct where to set his foot for a sure step, and they arrived wallowing and lurching at the side of the car.

Lance got in and turned on the ignition. Grimly he worked for several minutes, trying to start the car, listening to its helplessness with experienced ear. Then suddenly he turned off the switch and shook his head at the unfortunate stranger.

"No good!" he shouted in his ear. "You've stripped the teeth from the gears in the differential. That's easy to do with chains on in a snow like this. Come on in and we'll see what can be done."

Alan gave a startled hopeless look at his car, and then turned and plunged after his new friend, wondering what he should do next. As he wallowed through a drift because he hadn't kept close to his guide he had a sickening sensation of fierce cold hands gripping his thinly clad ankles. Snow in his shoes. Why hadn't he stopped to put on his galoshes?

The two fought their way back in the teeth of the wind and arrived at last in shelter once more.

"Now," said Alan, shivering with cold as he stood exuding snow onto the clean linoleum-covered hall, "would you mind saying over again what you told me out there? I couldn't be sure what you said."

Lance grinned.

"I said you had stripped the teeth from the gears in the differential. That's easy to do with chains in a snow like this. Tearing, grinding sound in the rear when it stopped, wasn't it? I thought so. Well, that's the story. It's like this, you know," and Lance put up his fingers and illustrated the stripped gears. "But the question is what can I do for you? You can't get that car fixed in a hurry, and not out there in this storm anyhow. It's got to be towed to a garage, and I haven't even got my own car to help tow you. You'll have to wait till Bill Gates gets here. Where was it you were going? You'd better stay here all night. This storm is something fierce, and getting worse all the time."

Alan shook his head.

"It's impossible. I'm carrying some medicine to a woman who will die if she doesn't get it. I gave my word of honor. I've got to get it there by six o'clock. The doctor said he wouldn't answer for the consequences if she didn't have it by then."

"That's different!" said Lance suddenly grave. "Of course you have to go. Where is it?"

"It's to a sort of castle on a mountain. There's a Mrs. Watt there very sick. It's her son-in-law's home. The name is Farley."

"Not Tom Farley's big stone castle on the cliff!" exclaimed Lance with startled eyes. "Man alive, you couldn't have got there even if your car hadn't broken down. Not in a car! It's ten miles, around by the river road, but I just heard a few minutes ago when I was telephoning that there's a drift twelve feet high there at one place, that shuts the pass off entirely. They are utterly shut off up there except from this side. There's only one way to get up there now—and I'm not so sure of it—and that's by the trail up the mountain, and you have to take it on your feet."

Alan looked into the other young man's eyes and seemed to read just what that would mean. His face grew white and stern and he looked down for an instant and then up and straightened his shoulders, setting his lips.

"Then I'll have to take that way!" he said. "I staked my life on it and it's that woman's life or mine it seems, so here goes. Show me the way and tell me how far it is."

He ended with a brave smile.

Daryl in the shadows of the dining room was watching him, comparing him with another, wondering what Harold would have said if confronted by such a demand.

They were all watching him, the mother and the father from the other room, and looking with startled eyes at their own boy, a frightened question in their hearts.

Lance looked at him steadily for an instant and then he answered quietly:

"It's only three miles up the mountain on this side, but it's a hard climb up the cliff. I'll go with you, of course."

"No!" said Alan decidedly, "I couldn't let you. This is my challenge, not yours. Just tell me the way and I'll find it."

"You couldn't possibly find your way alone, you a stranger. I've been born and brought up climbing all over the place. I know every nook and cranny. If anybody can find the way in the dark I can. I've camped up there since I was a kid!"

"But I can't let you run this risk. It is my duty, not yours!" declared Alan with finality.

"Look here, man, don't you know that the same thing that makes this a challenge to you, makes it binding on me also? There's a life to be saved up there, and we're going to save it. Come on. We mustn't lose a minute of daylight."

"Yes," said Father Devereaux, stepping into the light of the fire, his white hair like a halo about his sweet strong face, his fine eyes shining with something almost like exaltation. "Yes, both of you must go, of course, but you'll have to put on good warm clothing before you start. This friend here is shaking with the cold , and can't you see his feet are dripping wet? You couldn't survive a mile in this storm like that. Lance, take him into the spare room and give him some good warm clothes, long woolen underwear, two pairs of wool stockings, high boots, you know what he needs, and you've plenty of them."

"Why, I've a few things for sports out in my car," said Alan, suddenly remembering. "I was prepared for winter sports."

"Never mind those things!" said Lance sharply. "We haven't time to wait to unpack the car. Leave it where it is till Bill Gates gets here. Dad, you'll have him unload it and bring the things in, won't you? Got your keys, man? Better leave them here. Where's your medicine? In the car?"

"It's right here in my inner pocket," said Alan soberly, handing over his car keys. "I don't know what to say to thank you all, and I feel like a criminal letting your son in for this awful climb——" Alan's voice grew husky with feeling. "I'm Alan Monteith. Here's my business card. Not that it matters of course, now."

"That's all right, son, don't worry. This is a call of course. We'll put you both in God's hands."

"And I'm Lance Devereaux," said the other young man with a quick clasp of the stranger's hand. "Come on now, we've got to doll up. Mother, you going to give us a cup of coffee to start on?"

"I'm making the coffee," said Daryl quietly. "Mother's gone up to the kitchen chamber to get some more warm woolens."

"Come on, then!" said Lance, starting toward the stairs.

"Take Mr. Monteith into the guest room," said Daryl, coming forward and flinging open the door of the room that was all ready for Harold Warner, and her brother saw as he looked that the fire he had laid there was touched off and the room was bright and warm. He flung his sister an inscrutable look and then gave her a blinding smile of appreciation that warmed her heart all during the hours that followed.

"Get those wet socks off, Alan," said Lance, coming in with a rough Turkish towel, "and rub those ankles till they burn. It won't do to start off on this expedition with cold feet. There. I guess you can wear those things. I'm about your size. Anyhow we aren't being choosy about our costumes just now. Haste is the main thing. I'll beat you to it!" And Lance with a grin strode up to his own room to array himself with swift fingers.

Then the telephone rang in the little hallway just beside Alan's door, and he could not help hearing most of what was said. He was dressing in strange woolly garments as swiftly as his cold shaking fingers could manipulate them, but he could not help listening eagerly with a wild hope that perhaps the garage man had somehow come to his rescue, impossible as that seemed.

The voice at the other end of the wire was one of those high-keyed, raucous voices, which sometimes on the telephone broadcast themselves more widely than they intend. Every syllable uttered could be clearly heard in the guest room by the guest who was working so frantically to array himself for his daring expedition.

"That you, Darling?" the voice said.

"What? What did you say?"

"I shaid 'Darling!' Isn't that your name, Lovely One? Didn't you shay Daryl meant Darling? Well, there you are!"

"Harold! What in the world do you mean, talking like that? Stop kidding me, and tell me where you are? I've been so anxious about you!"

"Angshus about me, Darling? That's awfully sweet of you! But why angshus?"

There was a puzzled pause and then Daryl's troubled voice. "How strangely you talk, Harold. What's the matter with you? Where are you? When will you get here?"

"Me? I'm at Bayport. Called up to say hello."

"At Bayport? What are you doing at Bayport? Oh, have you had an accident, Harold!"

"Acshident? No, I haven't had acshident! I'm at a housh party, Darling, at Bayport, my boss' summer home. My boss' daughter brought me down in her limousine, and she wantsh you to come, too. She said I might ashk you. She shuggestsh you take a taxi over, ur ef you can't get a taxi justsh shay the word and we'll drive over fer you. Joy ride. Shee?"

"Harold!" Daryl's distressed voice was raised sharply. She had forgotten the nearness of the stranger. "What *is* the matter, Harold? Aren't you coming to spend Christmas here?"

"No, Darling. No, I can't! Had a previoush engagement. No, it washn't previoush, it was premature. No, that isn't the right word either. But you know what I mean. The boss' daughter asht me, an' buishnessh alwaysh comesh firsht, you know."

"But, Harold, you promised. You said it was our Christmas. Our first Christmas together!"

"Did I shay that? Well, mebbe I did—" The voice trailed off uncertainly and then began again. "Yesh, maybe I did shay that but I didn't mean it. I meant shecond Chrishmus, ur mebbe it wash third—!" The voice trailed off again.

"Harold!" Daryl's voice was full of tears and horror. "You've been drinking!"

"What, Darling? Yesh, jusht a dear little bit of a drink! Couldn't help it, you know. Boss offered it. Boss' daughter shaid I must. Buishness, you know. Wouldn't wantta loosh my job. You wouldn't want me to loosh my job. But, Darling, ef you'll jusht take a taxi and come over I'll promish to say no." The uncertain voice broke into song: "Have courage-my-boy to—shay—noo!"

Daryl suddenly hung up the receiver and when Alan came out of the spare room a moment later she was still standing there, her face white as death, her great eyes wide with sorrow. His heart almost stood still with its sympathy for her. But, oh, he must not let her see that he had heard that conversation!

Lance appeared on the scene almost simultaneously, and Mother Devereaux with a sweet brave look in her eyes called them out to the table to get the coffee.

As they sat down Father Devereaux appeared from the kitchen and standing by the table lifted his hand and looking up said:

"Father, we commend these two dear boys to Thy care as they go forth into Thy storm and cold on their errand of mercy. Keep them, guide them, and bless them. Bring them safely back to us without mishap if it be Thy will, Amen!"

Alan with quickly bent head listened to every word and felt suddenly as if God were in that house. That was what made it so different from other homes he had been seeing lately. God was there!

He lifted his head and looked at the quiet old man, tall and strong, white-haired but glory-faced, and marveled.

Then the talk dropped to the immediate needs of the hour.

"Son," said Father Devereaux, "I've got some paraphernalia for you. Here's a rope and you are to put one end around your waist and the other around this friend's waist, and you are not to lose each other. Mind! Your lives may depend upon that. I don't want to frighten you, but it is well to take precautions. We don't want either of you lost in the snow."

"Yes, sir," said Lance between swallows of coffee, "that's a good idea! We'll do it."

"And here's another coil of rope," went on the father. "When you come down the mountain it will be dark. You can sling this around a tree, and each take an end, and go down to the length of your tether, and then pull one end loose and sling it around another tree. In that way you will be able to keep your bearings better, and get back if you get off the trail. Understand?"

"Yes, sir. I understand, sir. You know we used to do that when we were kids out camping, Dad. If it's only clothes-line it's very light. I'll sling it over my shoulder. And I've four flashlights and some extra batteries. We'll be all right."

"Yes, and now just one more thing. Here are these two little candle-lanterns that you and Daryl used to have when you were children. Mother's fixed them up with candles, and a string on each handle. When you are on your way up and come to the narrowest place by the cliff there, we want you to tie these lanterns to the trees on the side farthest from the cliff, then light the candles and close the lantern shades so the wind can't blow them out. They'll probably burn till you get back to them. The candles are good and thick. Now, is that giving you too much to carry, son?"

"No, Dad, and we're packing a couple of the light snow shovels, at least for a ways. We might need them at the turn of the road before we start up. We may have to abandon them but we'll fling them where we can find them when the snow melts off. We'll carry them as far as we comfortably can."

"Good idea, but you mustn't climb with too heavy a load. You'll find it heavy walking. Now go, and God be with you!"

The benediction seemed to Alan to be a tangible thing that hovered over them as they went out into the thick white gloom of the fast approaching evening. Alan looked back as they turned into the road and caught a glimpse of the lights on the Christmas tree, and the silver rain from its branches, and the girl's white face pressed against the window pane, stark and white and suffering.

Then he turned sharply into the road and followed the steps of his guide. The rope which they had tied about their waists was a light thing in itself, but a comfort even as they started, plodding knee-deep in the heavy snow, each step an achievement. It was going to be no easy expedition, he saw, and a strange startling possibility suddenly presented itself to him there in the still whiteness. He might never come back alive!

At the turn of the road he looked back once more. He could barely see the glint of the lights from the tree now, for it was not dark enough for them to carry far, and the visibility was poor. But he gazed as long as he could, for it seemed he was leaving a house where God presided. And yet, God had come along with them, out into the storm. His storm, His snow, His cold, the old man had said.

He could not see the face of the girl now, but it was there, he knew it was there watching them out into the white peril, and there were tears, perhaps, upon her face. But she was strong and brave. He could see that. They were all strong and brave. It was their nearness to God that made them so. It was this that sent their son out to accept the challenge for this errand.

Now he could no longer see the house, the whiteness was too dense, and the snow stung his eyes so that he could scarcely keep them open, even bundled as he was, and so he turned almost blindly to plod on into the storm. He had staked his life, and the hour was moving on toward six. Would they make it in time? Would they ever come back alive, or would there be three lives lost instead of one?

4

RUTH Latimer had been too busy all day to look out at the snow. She had come from her boarding house to the church during the early stages of the storm, and being shut within stained-glass windows she had no realization of what a few apparently idle flakes of snow could do in a few brief hours.

Ruth was the daughter of a Christian missionary, who with his wife had died during their early ministry, when Ruth was a tiny child, and she had been sent home to her grandmother. But now the grandmother was gone, also, and Ruth was practically alone in the world, with only a very small income. She had come to Collamer in the fall to teach in the public kindergarten, had become acquainted with the Devereaux through attending the same church, and the three young people had seen quite a little of one another. It had been a great joy to Ruth to be invited to spend this first lonely Christmas since her grandmother's death in a real home instead of a boarding house, and she cherished every minute of the anticipated visit. So it had been a disappointment to discover that the ladies of the church had arranged to give the little children's classes in

the Sunday School their Christmas treat on the day before
Christmas, and of course they expected the teacher to be
present, and to help in the preparations. For Ruth was not
only teaching the kindergarten in day school, but also had
charge of the youngsters in the Beginners' department of
the Sunday School.

So instead of going to the Devereaux house early on the
day before Christmas as she would have liked to do, and as
they had asked her to do, she had to go over to the church
to help prepare for the children who were scheduled to
appear at half past two for a couple of hours of undiluted
happiness.

Ruth had packed a small suitcase and taken it with her,
taking the precaution to ask her landlady for a couple of
sandwiches so that she would not have to stop and run back
for her lunch, as the boarding house was at some distance
from the church. Lance had said his car would be brought
over for her to drive straight to his house from the church,
so that she would have to waste no more time than was
necessary.

But when she arrived at the church, fearing lest she was
a little late, she found that none of the other ladies, and no
other teachers were there. The janitor had just come, and
the church wasn't very warm yet. She had to keep her coat
on while she worked.

She had brought several games, and a lot of material for
a good time, and for the first half-hour she busied herself
arranging that. Then on the long blackboard that ran the
length of the room, she drew a picture of Bethlehem to use
with a story she was going to tell the children. She made it
much more elaborate than she had intended, sketching in
a hint of glory in the sky, and angels hovering above awed
shepherds and sleeping sheep. She lingered over the picture
to make it realistic because there seemed nothing else to do
until the women came who had planned this party and had
merely asked her to assist.

But the morning went on and no women came. Presently the telephone rang and Mrs. Bartlett, who was supposed to be at the head of this affair, told the janitor to tell whoever was there to go right ahead without her. She had been delayed and couldn't tell how long it would be before she could get there. She didn't wait to talk with Ruth. When the janitor told her Miss Latimer was there, she said with a relieved sigh: "Oh, well, then, everything will be all right. Tell her to just go ahead and do whatever she thinks best. I'll be there as soon as I can!" and hung up.

Ruth listened to this message from the janitor with dismay. Just what had they intended to do? She couldn't carry out plans that she had never heard discussed.

She rushed to the telephone and called Mrs. Bartlett, but found she had left for the train to the city. She had gone to shop for a few forgotten Christmas things.

Ruth's heart sank. She called up another woman, but got no answer. Probably she, too, was shopping. She tried two of the teachers and one was away for over Christmas, and the other in bed with tonsilitis. But the families of both declared they were sending down their contributions of cake and candy according to promise, and that the ice cream would be sure to be there, for Mrs. Bartlett always ordered it.

So Ruth went back to the big empty room where the affair was to be held and looked about her speculatively. It was going to be up to her, was it? Very well, she would do what she pleased.

She enlisted the janitor and rearranged the little tables and chairs, so the main part of the room would be empty for games, marshaling the tables in a circle with the little chairs behind them, for the refreshment part of the affair.

Then the cakes began to arrive, and there were dishes to get out, and spoons, and lovely Christmas paper napkins that one of the delinquents thoughtfully sent. It really was rather interesting to have all this provision and do just as she pleased with everything. She wished that she dared telephone for Daryl to come and help, but she knew Daryl was expecting another guest and would be needed at home getting ready for the next two days. Besides, how would Daryl get there? The car was in Collamer at the garage, and Lance had gone into the woods for the Christmas tree. So she worked away alone, folding napkins, placing little games, balls and simple puzzles, ringtoss, balloons to be blown back and forth from opposite lines. It was going to be fun, only how could she do it alone? Perhaps when Mrs. Bartlett came she would think of some other girls who would come to help.

But time went on and Mrs. Bartlett came not. Presently came Mrs. Bartlett's chauffeur with two enormous cakes and a lot of cookies and a great clothes basket full of toys wrapped in bright paper. There was also a message that the lady herself had been delayed in the city and would not get out until late in the afternoon, and that Miss Latimer *and her helpers* were just to carry on!

Ruth laughed aloud when she got that message, and didn't even stop to eat her sandwich, she had so much to do.

The ice cream arrived, though she hadn't had time to miss it yet. The men who brought the things came in with snow on their shoulders and hats, and snow on the packages they brought, and they said it was a bad day, but Ruth scarcely heard what they said.

And then at last everything was ready and the kiddies began to arrive, muffled to their eyes, and so heavily garbed they had to be undone like bundles.

"I didn't think I ought to bring Jimmy out in this weather," explained one troubled mother stamping the snow from her galoshes, and unwrapping Jimmy from an enveloping lap robe. "He's got an awful cold, and I don't suppose this weather'll do him a bit of good, but he cried something awful to come to the Christmas party! So his pa said fix him up and he'd bring us down!" She undid him, and he stood forth in all the glory of a new red suit, his mother eyeing him proudly.

That was the first intimation that Ruth had of how bad the storm was, and she went to the outer door and looked out aghast. How could the children get there! No wonder Jimmy's mother had been dubious about bringing him! Probably Jimmy would be the only child that would come; that would make it harder for her than if she had to entertain a lot of children.

But it was surprising how many came! Those kiddies were not to be cheated out of their Christmas party, not they. Most of them had bullied or coaxed or harried their unwilling parents into bringing them. A few of the older ones, mostly boys, and tomboy girls, arrived by themselves, laughing and stamping snow, with knees and ankles sopping wet, and rubber boots wet inside. There was plenty to be done, drying them up and taking care that they didn't catch cold. Fortunately a few mothers and a father or two remained and helped quite materially.

The party began in great shape. Ruth sent the children scurrying across the room in rows first, to pick up peanuts that had been laid down at intervals, and the exercise warmed them all up. Next they went to the other games for a time, till they were all out of breath, and glad to sit down. Then she grouped them in front of the blackboard and told her picture story. After that, one by one, each was blindfolded, and gravely walked ahead with a stocking solemnly grasped in his hand, to hang it upon the cotton chimney place, and they had great laughs over the crooked walk of the little pilgrims.

Then they all sat down in the semicircle at the little tables to eat their ice cream and cake.

The helping mothers and fathers were serving now and Ruth, while she filled the paper stockings from the pile of bundles concealed behind the cotton fireplace, reflected that it was almost over and she would soon be free.

At last the weary happy children were being stuffed into leggings and rubber boots and the mothers were telling her what a wonderful time the children had had, and how they thanked her for the beautiful picture lesson. They said they never would forget it and they thought the children would always have a better idea of what Christmas meant, and they intended to follow up the lesson.

Ruth scarcely heard them. She was thinking that it was almost time for her to go. Then she followed them to the door and saw with horror the denseness of the storm. It seemed impassable and she came back in a panic. She telephoned to the garage almost in terror. Perhaps, after all, she would have to spend the night here in the lonely church!

Bill Gates was very nice. He told her the car was ready and he would send it around, but that she mustn't think of driving it out to the farm till he got around with the snow plow which would be in a few minutes now.

She turned away and stared at the gloomy window that was covered so thickly with snow.

Lance would think he had to come for her, of course, if he were back from the mountain with the tree. Oh, suppose he wasn't! Suppose he should get lost on the mountain in the snow! But that was nonsense, of course. Lance was a man and could take care of himself. Still, she must prevent him from walking all that way to the village to drive her back.

So she called the Devereaux house, and had that breathless moment with Lance, reassuring herself, so happy to know he was safely home, and happily unconscious of the more perilous call that was on its way to him.

Ruth hurried back to help the janitor wash the spoons and ice cream saucers, and be ready to go when Bill Gates came, her eyes happy and her cheeks rosy at the thought of what was before her. As she worked swiftly wiping dishes and putting them away, she thought how she would arrive at the farm, and Lance would be out in the storm to meet her, and perhaps swing into the car and drive it into the garage for her. He would have a path all shoveled up to the house and they would go in to the light and warmth, and Christmas would begin! Lights and the tree and the open fire, good things to eat and loving friends all about! It was going to be wonderful! She was tired, but very happy. And she needn't worry a bit about driving in the storm, with the snowplow close ahead of her, and Bill Gates to call to for help if anything went wrong. Christmas had begun in her heart already.

It was slow progress after the snowplow, however, and a bit roundabout, because Bill Gates was obliged to look after certain spots in the borough before he went out on the highway, but eventually they crept out toward the farm, and Ruth, keeping her car close in the wake of the snowplow, and worrying her windshield wiper to make it do a little better with the blurring driving snow that blinded her way, finally arrived in sight of the glinting colors on the Christmas tree that nobody as yet had thought to turn off. If she had known that a mile and a half ahead of her at that moment Lance and an unknown stranger were struggling along, shoveling their way through a drift higher than their heads, at the worst curve of the road below the mountain trail, she would certainly have plowed ahead herself, no matter what the risk, and tried in some way to help them out. But she didn't know.

Bill Gates, however, knew the possibilities of the drifted driveway, and he ran his big plow a little ahead of the Devereaux gate and stopped, jumping off and running back to her as she was about to venture the turn.

Father Devereaux was out with the coal shovel from the furnace, endeavoring to make the entrance a little safer for her, but Bill Gates wasn't taking any chances. He made Ruth shove over, and himself took the wheel, turning the small car with extreme care, and slowly plunging it through the billows of snow that had furrowed themselves up since the storm began. Father Devereaux hurried ahead to open the garage door, but Bill Gates stopped at the kitchen door, and lifting Ruth out bodily before she realized what was happening, he bore her up the steps and set her down at the kitchen door, under the porch roof comparatively out of the storm. Then he drove on into the garage and housed the car safely before he hurried back to his snowplow.

It wasn't the reception she had hoped for, but she was glad to be here at last. What a terrible storm! How had any of those children got to the church at all? She hoped in passing that they were all safely home. Then she wondered where Lance was and why he hadn't hurried out to greet her. But of course the storm was so loud he might not have heard her arrive. Still, wouldn't he have been watching?

The sleet was biting her face and she tried the door, found her way into the kitchen shed, and so on into kitchen and dining room. Nobody seemed to be about. Had they all gone upstairs? Then suddenly in the dimness of the corner of the dining room she saw Lance's mother kneeling by the old rocking chair praying quietly.

She paused a moment startled. She knew that Lance's mother was a wonderful Christian woman, and took everything to the Lord in prayer, but she sensed an unusual atmosphere. Of course Mrs. Devereaux had not heard her come in. The wind was roaring so around the house that it drowned all but very clear sounds. And darkness was settling down about the house. There was only the soft light from the Christmas tree in the living room. After an instant Ruth went softly by the kneeling figure on into the other room, and then she saw Daryl standing by the window with her face pressed against the pane looking out into the blinding snow. Daryl must be watching for her, and the snow was so thick that she had missed her.

She stepped over softly and slipped her arm about Daryl's waist.

"Daryl, dear!" she whispered. Daryl turned sharply toward her and she saw that there were tears glistening on her cheeks.

"Why, Daryl, darling! What is the matter?" she said, her heart filled with sudden alarm. "You've been crying! Christmas Eve! What can be the matter?"

"Oh, Ruth! Everything is so mixed up!" cried Daryl softly, trying to brush the tears away and hold her head up bravely. But her lips were quivering and her eyes were full of trouble.

Ruth unfastened her snowy coat and dropped it on the floor behind her, putting out her arms to Daryl and folding her in a loving hug.

"What is it, dear? Tell me, please," she said softly.

Daryl yielded for an instant, and then her face coming in contact with the snowy particles on Ruth's hair, she lifted her head.

"Oh, my dear! I'm letting you stand here in all your wet things! But you don't know how glad I am you have come! I was worried about you, too. I telephoned the garage and when they said you were on your way in all this awfulness I just trembled. It seemed to me there were just too many things to worry about all at once. I'm glad you are here safe and sound. Here, let me take your hat, and sit down till I pull off your galoshes. I thought if Lance should get back and find you lost that would be the last straw. Thank God you are here safely!"

"Lance?" said Ruth with sudden fright in her voice. "Where is he? He didn't start out after me after he promised me he wouldn't, did he? *Where* is he?"

"He didn't start after you," said Lance's sister with a catch of her breath like a sob, "but he's out, he and a strange man. They've gone on foot to take some medicine up the mountain to the Farley house on the cliff, where there is a woman who will die if she doesn't get it by six o'clock. They've been gone half an hour, and it's the longest half-hour I ever lived through!"

"But why did he go on foot, Daryl?" asked the distressed Ruth. "Oh, if Lance hadn't left the car down in the village for me he would have had it here to use! But he knew I would be here in a short time. Why didn't he wait and take it?"

"No, Ruth, it wouldn't have done any good. They had to go on foot. The river road to the cliff is impassable, a twelve-foot drift. No car could get through. They had to take to the trail."

"But if the car had been here they could at least have driven to the foot of the trail. Why didn't they wait?"

"They couldn't wait, Ruth. The woman is dying and every minute counted. And besides, Lance said the car wouldn't do any good. The snow was too deep, unless it was broken by the plow, or shovels. You mustn't blame yourself, Ruth. You did just what Lance asked you to do, and besides it had to stay in the garage till it was finished. It couldn't be used till it was fixed. Now lean back and rest, do, and I'll get you a cup of something hot. Would you rather have tea or coffee? You look tired to death! I know you have had a terribly hard day. If I had had any way of getting down there I would have come to help you. But forget it now, and just rest."

"Oh, I don't want anything to eat, Daryl, really I don't. Please tell me more about this. Who is the woman Lance has gone to help, and what is the matter with her? How did Lance hear about her? Did he know he had to go when he talked to me on the telephone?"

"No, he didn't. It was just after he hung up that the man came along."

"Man, what man?"

"A stranger! His car stalled right in front of the house. He stripped the gears or something. I didn't pay any attention to what they said about it, and he was on his way to take some medicine to the Farley house, said he'd staked his life on getting there by six o'clock and he had to take it even if he had to walk. He wanted to get his car fixed, or hire a car, and when Lance told him he couldn't get there in a car tonight in this storm, he just shut his lips and said he had to go anyway, even if he died in the attempt. Of course when Lance heard it was to save a life he said, 'Oh, that's different. Then I'll go with you.' So Father got them some ropes and lanterns and things, and Mother made coffee, and got flannel things for them, and they went right off. It was rather awful, seeing them go into the storm, and the darkness beginning to come down!"

"It is awful!" said Ruth, shuddering. "If you haven't been out in it you can't possibly know! I don't see how they can live long in it. Don't you think we ought to go after them? I wouldn't mind driving. I can't bear to think of him out there freezing to death perhaps!"

"No!" said Daryl, taking a deep breath. "They won't freeze to death. They are so bundled up they couldn't for a long time. No, and you would only get stuck in a drift yourself and have to be dug out, or walk back. By this time they've likely reached the foot of the mountain trail, and you couldn't climb the trail in a car. Besides, Lance would be furious. No, we've just got to wait and bear this till—till—they come back. Mother's in there praying. I guess maybe that's the best thing we can do."

"Yes," said Ruth. "We will! I've been doing it in my heart ever since your first word. But oh, I'd like to be doing something more! It's provoking to be only a girl at a time like this. You know perfectly well if we were out there struggling along in that storm Lance would come after us!"

"Yes," said Daryl, "but you know he wouldn't want you to come after him. Besides, it's impossible!" Daryl shut her lips and drew a deep breath of resignation.

"But it seems as if somebody ought to do something. Where is that friend of yours you said you were expecting? Hasn't he come yet? Perhaps he would go after them and make sure they are all right. It seems as if there would be more safety in numbers."

A sudden shade passed over Daryl's face. She caught a quick breath and said in a sad decisive voice:

"He's not coming! He telephoned!"

"Oh! Couldn't he get here? Well, that shows you how dangerous the going is. And up that mountain, too. It seems so awful! Don't you think we ought to telephone the police in town, or somebody? If Bill Gates knew about it he would go after them with the snowplow, I'm sure."

Daryl shook her head.

"Lance wouldn't want us to do that," she said decidedly. "And Bill Gates couldn't run the snowplow up the mountain! No, Ruth, if anything ought to be done Father'll do it."

"Oh, yes, you have a father," said Ruth, drawing a breath of relief. "What did he think about it? Why did he let Lance go?"

"He told Lance he must go, of course, and he prayed for them when they started out. Prayed for both of them. He's probably praying now."

They sat quite still for a moment or two thinking, while the room seemed to grow momently darker in the corners, and the firelight flickered and glowed. A stick collapsed with a soft plush sound and scattered lovely rose coals in the ashes, and then flared up golden and flame color again and went on burning the stick above.

"What was he like, the stranger?" asked Ruth suddenly. "Was he a Christian, do you suppose?"

"I don't know," said Daryl thoughtfully. "I didn't look at him much. He bowed his head when Father prayed. They were at the table to drink coffee before they left, and Father came and asked a blessing on them—" She paused gravely. "He had nice eyes. That was all I noticed about him. I was rather upset, you know."

"Of course," said Ruth sorrowfully.

Then suddenly Father Devereaux came in with Ruth's suitcase.

"Well, you got here safely, little girl, didn't you? Thank God for that!" he said cheerfully, setting down the suitcase and coming to shake hands. And Mother Devereaux appeared from the shadows of the other room just then and took Ruth in her arms and kissed her.

"It is good to have you here safely," she said gently. Ruth noticed that there was a calmness about her, and a peace upon her brow, and suddenly she took heart of hope. Of course, Lance was safe in the hands of the Lord! Why should she doubt?

"It's time we had something to eat!" said the mother practically. "Come, girls, let's get to work and get supper. It's getting on toward six o'clock and Ruth looks worn to a frazzle."

"Oh, Mother, aren't you going to wait till—till—?"

"Wait till the boys get back? Why, no, of course not. We're going to be sane sensible people and eat now when we need it. Then we can be free to wait on them when they come back hungry as bears."

"Yes," said Father, "they'll be hungry all right. But it will be some time before they get back, and it's much better to be busy and happy and not sit around holding your breath. We'll just put the matter in God's hands, and then trust Him. Mother, what can I do after I've mended the fires? Do you want that big kettle of soup brought in from the cold room and put on the fire?"

"No, we'll keep the soup for the boys. I've got scalloped oysters in the oven, and potatoes roasting too. They'll be done by the time we get the milk and butter and things on the table."

"Oh, Mother," said Daryl sorrowfully, "and Lance is so fond of scalloped oysters! It seems a pity not to wait for him."

"Soup will be better for him when he is tired. It's easy

to eat, too, and won't spoil by waiting. Get to work, girls, and let's have supper! It's Christmas Eve, you know!"

In spite of their heavy hearts, the mother put new life into them, for they remembered she had been talking with her Lord, and they felt her assurance and faith.

Father went out into the cold room and brought things in from the refrigerator before he took his overcoat off, and they could hear him singing in his sweet baritone:

> *"God's way is the best way,*
> *God's way is the right way,*
> *I'll trust in Him alway,*
> *He knoweth the best!"*

5

AFTER the first dash into the storm, which took his breath
and bit at his nerve and lashed his already weary body, Alan
Monteith seemed to get his second wind, and with his head
bent to the gale to shelter eyes and tender cheeks unused
to such blasts, he plodded after his guide with a feeling of
courage and purpose. Right here it wasn't unbearable. The
snow was deep, to be sure, and required long strides, and
high lifting of feet, but it was possible to make a slow
progress. After he had gone about a quarter of a mile he felt
that they must be almost at their destination and his hopes
grew high. He was making it after all.

He had no means of judging time, for he could not see
his watch even if he had time to stop and look, but he
plodded on hoping that in a few more steps they would be
climbing the mountain. But the relentless clothesline fastened around his waist drew him on, and his strength
presently began to flag. His limbs ached excruciatingly. He
longed to sit down in the snow, if only for an instant, just
to relax and take the terrible ache out of his back. But
Lance was so far ahead of him that the only way he could
attract his attention was by pulling the rope, and he was too

proud to halt the march and own that he could not keep up with the young giant ahead who was going on and on and on as if he wore seven-league boots. So he lifted his feet higher and strode on, though it seemed as if each step must be his last, and his breath began to come in quick short gasps.

He felt ashamed of himself to find that he was so soft. In his college days he had been a lusty football player, a fleet runner, strong of heart and sinew, longwinded and light as a feather on his feet. But he was two years out of college and he hadn't been practicing stunts just like this in his office since. He hadn't even had time of late to play golf, or get in a game of tennis. He was soft, that was it, and he might as well own it. But he did not intend to give up. Even if it lamed him for life he would keep up his end of this venture, and not hold back.

Then presently he stepped on some obstacle well hidden, lurched and stumbled to his knees, floundering about to get his balance again, and longing just to lie down in the snow and get a rest. He never knew that nerves and muscles could get as sore as this in so short a time.

But Lance was instantly at his side. Lance, who had been plowing and sowing and reaping all summer on the farm, and sawing and splitting wood for the winter; who had been keeping in the pink of condition by long nights of sound sleep, and long days of hard work and hearty eating, and whose young muscles knew not the word weariness. If this journey was hard for Lance he did not falter. He took it only as another hard thing that came in the day's work, and he was out to win.

Lance stooped and helped him to his feet, gave him a cheery word which he could not hear, and after an instant they started on again.

It was growing dark now, and Alan would fain have opened his flashlight, for there was something exceedingly gruesome in this ghostly walk in the thick whiteness of the storm with the darkness like a pall over all. But Lance, before starting, had told him not to waste his flashlight till it was absolutely necessary, and he would not yield to any weakness. He could not forget that this expedition was his, not Lance's. He must not in any way hinder the expedition by his own weakness or unpreparedness. He must keep up his end. So he toiled on in the white darkness, and wondered, would it never end?

And then they came to a great drift looming out of the gloom, a drift as high as their heads, and extending interminably, it seemed. Lance flashed his torch across it and it seemed an impassable barrier. He began to realize that perhaps the woman to whose rescue he was hastening might die in spite of his efforts and that it was not unthinkable that he and his guide might die even before her. The wind was cold and searching, piercing through all those garments that he had thought so superfluous when he started. He thought of how it would feel to freeze to death, and his mind went racing through the experiences he had read of explorers at the poles. He knew all this was ridiculous. He was probably not fifty miles from the warm, bright, gay house party where he had expected to spend this day and evening, certainly not more than three from the farmhouse he had just left with its Christmas lights agleam, and civilization all about him; yet civilization seemed as remote as if he had been in Alaska or Greenland.

But Lance was maneuvering his snow shovel out of its sling upon his back, and attacking the wall of snow ahead of him. So Alan wriggled his shovel around and got it free, conscious that it was good to get it off his back for a while.

Together they worked, burrowing through the drift, until at last they had tunneled a way out of the maze of whiteness, and a flash of the torch showed a dim outline of trees off to the side in two indistinct lines. Lance shouted that it was a road, their road, and with a sinking heart Alan plunged off into it after Lance, thankful for a guide-line about his waist that made it unnecessary to look where he was going. For now as they faced to the right the wind was directly in their faces again, and the sleet was more cutting than before, almost unbearable if one attempted to keep his head up and his eyes open. So he staggered on, wallowing in deeper snow, up to his waist at times, and almost losing his footing again and again. For this new road was rougher than the highway, and it was almost impossible to walk steadily.

The darkness seemed to bring with it a great dread, as if some monster were struggling with them to keep them from going on. Now and again the wind would howl as if the monster had them at his mercy and it was useless to try further. Then the wind would pass, and for a moment there would be surcease, and they could lift their heads and shoot their torches ahead, and go mounting up a few steps.

Lance signaled to him to use his torch now, for the way was up, and rough and winding. They kept close to the right now, holding to trees where the way was steep, and pulling themselves more than once out of a hollow filled so deeply with snow that it threatened to engulf them.

Now and again Lance would call a halt to rest, and sweep his torch upward, but there seemed no end to the high whiteness they were climbing. Would they ever get there? Would the medicine get to the woman in time? Hours, nay, eons, seemed to have passed since they started on this terrible journey, and still there was no sign that they would ever be done with it.

But at last Lance stopped by a tree and tied one of their lanterns to a sheltered branch far to the right of the road. Alan, turned his torch to the left, saw a sheer cliff below him and thrilled at its white declivity, crept closer to his guide, and hastened on, taking comfort in that little flickering light they had left within its frail lantern globe. Would they ever come back and meet that light again, and would it guide them aright? His head reeled and now he scarcely knew which way he was going.

A little farther up, Lance left the other lantern tied to another tree. They were traveling light now, for they had left their snowshovels at the foot of the mountain, cached at the side of a giant tree where Lance seemed to think he could find them again. But even so the way had been long and hard, and both young men were panting wearily when at last they attained level ground and Alan, exploring with his torch, discovered a looming castle ahead and gave a shout of joy. It did not matter that the shout was snatched from his lips and cast inaudibly aside by the gale that whistled over their heads as they came up from the woods which had partly sheltered them for a while. Alan felt they must be winning out, and though he could scarcely drag one foot after the other, they plodded on and suddenly came upon a driveway where there had been an attempt to shovel a path to the garage.

Alan almost felt he must sink down and kiss the roughness of that cleared space, as he stumbled into it, and cast weary eyes toward the looming building. He saw to his joy that there were lights in the windows. It was really a dwelling, and there would be warmth and light and a place to sit down, cessation of this pitiless driving of the snow in their faces, and a chance to breathe, a place where motion would be no longer necessary, at least for a while. Rest! Blessed rest! In his longing for rest he had almost lost sight of the object of his coming. Just to have reached there, supposing it was the right place, was enough to have attained. What he was to do when he got there seemed to have ceased to exist.

But now at last they were standing within a spacious hall where light streamed forth in blessed abundance, and a winding stairway of noble lines swept upward. It was warm there, blessedly warm.

Alan staggered into a chair and dropped down, his face in his hands. The sudden warmth and light dazzled him, and almost took his senses from him. There were parts of him that suddenly seemed dead. He hadn't been aware of it when they died; it must have happened somewhere out there on the mountain when they were so cold. There was a dull numbness in his arms and legs, especially his legs, and prickling sensations. He cradled his cold, cold face in his hands, and wished he might sleep then and there without waiting for further ceremonies. Then suddenly he began to be aware of Lance's voice explaining, and it all flashed over him.

He lifted his head.

"Are we there?" he asked half bewildered, and Lance's face as he remembered it back at the farm took form before his stinging eyes.

"Yes, we made it! Hear that?" said Lance triumphantly. "Listen to that!" And a great clock upon the stairs chimed out six long silver notes.

"You haven't got some hot coffee, have you?" asked Lance suddenly of the servant in uniform who stood before them. "I think my friend here has had a little too much cold, and he's bewildered."

Kind hands brought coffee hurriedly, and Alan drank and came to himself as the hot liquid penetrated his chilled veins. Then a white-garbed nurse appeared eagerly.

"You've brought the medicine?" she asked anxiously. "I didn't think you could possibly get here, but you have!"

Alan fumbled with the buttons of the alien garments he was wearing and found the little package he had come so far to deliver, and the anxious-eyed elderly man who had followed the nurse down the stairs, exclaimed fervently:

"Thank God! It's come!"

Then turning to Alan he put out his hand gratefully:

"Now, to whom am I indebted for this wonderful service in this tempest? It is nothing short of a miracle that anyone could make this place in a storm like this!"

"Don't thank me," said Alan, putting his hand in the old man's, "thank Devereaux there! I had the will to come, but

I would never have got here if he hadn't insisted on coming along to guide me."

But Lance only grinned when the old man attempted to thank him, and to say that he wanted to do more than thank, that he would never forget the service rendered.

"Oh, that's all right! It wasn't so bad when we got going, was it, partner?" and he looked keenly into Alan's face.

"But now, what can we do immediately for you to make you comfortable?" asked the old man solicitously. "You should get those wet clothes off at once and get dry and warm, and have something more substantial than coffee. You'll stay here tonight, of course, and tomorrow, if the storm doesn't let up, and perhaps by that time my chauffeur will be back and can take you to wherever you want to go."

"Thank you," said Lance quickly, "that's fine of you to ask, but I couldn't. I've got to get right back. Perhaps my friend here would like to stay, I can't answer for him. But I've got to get down that mountain as fast as possible. All I ask is that I may telephone home. My mother will be worrying, I suppose."

"Telephone, of course," said the old man graciously, "but tell them you're staying here till the storm is over. I couldn't think of letting you go out again. It's perilous!"

Lance grinned.

"Thanks, awfully," he said again, "but you know we have a thing called Christmas down at our house, and they'll be expecting me. I wouldn't miss it for all the perils in the world!"

The stately butler handed him the telephone that stood on a little table in the hall, and Lance called his own number, his eyes alight with eagerness, his face wearing the look of a conqueror. He had come through so far and he meant to get back, God willing.

The old man turned to Alan to whose face the color was returning since he had swallowed the hot coffee.

"But you'll stay with us anyway?" he urged cordially.

Alan arose with a lift of his nice chin and a smile, and shook his head.

"Thanks, but I couldn't," he said firmly. "I wouldn't let that man go down the mountain in the storm alone if it was the last act of my life. Not *that* man! He's wonderful! We hang together!"

Then Lance's voice broke in.

"That you, Daryl? Tell Mother we reached here safely, and we're starting back immediately! Ruth get there all right? That's good. Give her greetings from me. Don't let Dad go out in this storm and shovel. We'll tend to that tomorrow! Don't wait supper for us. We may be slow, but we'll get there. And *don't* send out any rescue parties after us! We're all right! O.K. So long! I'll say 'Merry Christmas' first in the morning!"

Lance hung with another grin, and began to button up his slicker, but before he had finished it the butler arrived with two plates on which was something inviting and steaming hot; and briefly, hastily, they ate, while the old man hovered around, took down their addresses, and heaped thanks upon their heads.

"And now," he said as the two handed their plates to the servant and started to go, "we've got some snowshoes here. Would they help? You could cast them aside if you found they hindered."

"Why, that might be a help," said Lance. "Ever on snowshoes, Alan?"

"Once or twice!" said Alan ruefully. "I guess I could make a stab at navigating that way. It couldn't be worse than my clumsy feet sometimes."

So they took the snowshoes and started on their wild way down the mountain. The storm met them at the door, tore their breath from their nostrils, and menaced them, but the blessings of the old man rang in their ears as they plunged out of the driveway into the deep snow, making, as nearly as they could guess, for the place where they had come over the top.

Three miles away, down that awful mountain, and over trackless wastes, was a Christmas tree with sweet-colored lights, a home waiting, and two girls with starry eyes. Would they ever make it on their weary limbs?

IT was while they were washing the supper dishes and Mother was getting ready the table for the two whom they were tremulously expecting, that she suddenly remembered the other guest that was to have arrived, and chided herself for not having mentioned him before. Surely Daryl would have missed her apprehension about him. And Daryl had been strangely quiet and troubled all the evening. It was not alone apprehension for her beloved brother, she must be concerned for the guest also, whom she had said would likely get here around supper time. And there hadn't been a mention of him. She had not seen Daryl even looking out the window since Ruth arrived. Could it be that she had forgotten him?

She cast a furtive, questioning look toward her girl, but could not be sure just what her expression portended. Was her look just a polite attempt to put aside all her cares and worries and entertain Ruth, or did it hide deep pain and worry? She could not tell. If it was acting she certainly was doing it well.

So the mother thought the matter over, and carefully arranged a casually pleasant look on her own face before she broached the subject the next time Daryl came to the china closet with her arms full of dishes.

"Oh, Daryl," she said, as if she had just thought of the matter, "Harold hasn't come yet. Didn't you expect him before this time? He may get here about the time the boys get back." Queer how she had slipped into saying "the boys," including that stranger, and couldn't quite take this other young man into so intimate a place. "Hand me another plate and cup and saucer. We'll need to set the table for three, of course. I've been so upset by all that's been happening that I can't count straight any more."

Daryl paused and looked at her mother, a stricken expression in her eyes.

"No!" she said shortly. "Harold isn't coming."

"Why, what do you mean, dear? Why isn't he coming? How did you find out?"

"He telephoned!" answered the girl shortly. "He's going somewhere else! His boss invited him and he thought he ought to go."

There wasn't a particle of expression in her face, just that stricken look in her eyes. It seemed as if she had come a long way and got used to the barrenness of it, since she knew.

But the mother's voice was all compassion and disapproval.

"He went somewhere else when he had *promised* to be with us! When he knew how much you had counted upon it? He deliberately did that and didn't let you know till the last minute?" Her eyes were flashing indignation.

But Daryl's voice was cool, as if she had schooled herself for this. As if these words were some that she had been feeding to her disappointed heart for several hours.

"I don't know that he deliberately did it," said Daryl with something hard in her tone, "it seems the other party just happened along and he was swept with the tide." There was something almost contemptuous in the way she said it. Her mother gave her a quick keen look. Did that mean that her girl had been suddenly disillusioned? No, nothing so final as that. A real disillusionment clears the sky usually and heals the hurt. Still—this thing whatever it was had but just happened.

"My dear!" said her mother tenderly, hesitantly, "don't make the mistake of being too hard on him. There may be more to it than appears on the surface. You must be fair to people. And then you know the storm is really very bad! Anyone would be excused for not going far in it."

"It's not so bad but that my brother went out in it, is it?" said Daryl, and now her voice was really bitter.

"Yes, but there was a very serious reason."

"Well, isn't a girl—a girl one is supposed to—care for, a serious reason? If she isn't, then what is she? Why should she bother?"

Her mother looked at her for a long moment and then she said slowly, thoughtfully:

"Well, I sometimes wonder!"

Then she roused herself and looked pitifully toward her child.

"Don't worry about it, dear! You know it may come all right in the morning! He may turn up bright and early when the storm is over."

Daryl looked at her mother gravely.

"That's nice of you, Mother, when you don't really like him. I appreciate it, but it wouldn't make any difference if he did. The damage is done."

"But, Daryl, dear! That's not fair to him! You mustn't be unforgiving. And besides, when he explains—"

"He couldn't explain it all," said the girl with tears in her voice. "He's spoiled Christmas, that's all, and it can't be fixed up. You don't understand, I know, and I don't want to talk about it tonight. But Christmas is *spoiled.*"

"One man can't spoil Christmas, Daryl! That isn't possible. Christmas is bigger than that. It is something heavenly and cannot be touched by things of the earth. My child, have you been thinking to celebrate the birth of our Lord Jesus Christ by arranging circumstances around yourself like cushions and settling down comfortably in them? And remember this, too, dear, if this friendship with Harold Warner is something that God has planned to crown your life with joy, nothing, not even a storm, nor some little lack of thoughtfulness, nor even some strong chain of circumstances can stop it. Not if it is of God! So you can safely trust your happiness with Him, who knows the end from the beginning. And if this friendship is not of God, Daryl, dear, you wouldn't want to try to get happiness where God had not planned it for you, would you? You would not want to go against God, would you?"

"I suppose not," said Daryl tonelessly.

"Well, then, dear, can't you just take it all and lay it in His hands and trust your happiness with Him?"

Daryl didn't answer quickly. Then she said slowly, wearily:

"Yes, Mother, but somehow I can't quite sense it tonight! I'm just awfully—shocked—I guess it is."

"But, my dear!" said her mother, "aren't you making a great deal out of his not coming tonight?"

"No, Mother!" The answer was grave and decided.

Her mother looked at her puzzled.

"Where is he, dear?"

"At Bayport!"

"At Bayport! But that isn't twenty miles away!"

"I know," said Daryl significantly.

"What's he doing there?"

"He's at a house party! His boss' daughter invited him."

"And didn't invite you?"

"Yes, she invited me after a fashion—I *guess!* He said she said I might come too. She sent word for me to take a taxi and come over!"

"My dear! And didn't Harold even suggest coming after you?"

"Oh, in a way. But as if I would go away from our Christmas and you for any party with a lot of strangers! *Our* Christmas!"

"But, my dear," said her mother anxiously, "if Harold is there?" She ventured fearsomely: "You know if you don't feel that way about him there is certainly something wrong."

Daryl faced about to the window and stared into the storm, saying nothing, her very back eloquent of distress.

Then the mother spoke again.

"You know unless you can be happy anywhere just because he is there, he ought not to be anything to you but a casual acquaintance. Something is wrong somewhere, dear."

But Daryl stood motionless, frozen into the very personification of sorrow. Then suddenly she spoke quickly, as if the words were drawn from her agonized heart by a force she could not resist.

"I guess there is, Mother. I guess that must be what's the matter!"

Her voice was quivering and full of tears.

Then the mother went swiftly and gathered her girl into her arms and drew her face close to hers!

"My precious child!" she murmured softly in her ear, "God has been very good to you to let you find it out before it was too late!" and she laid her soft lips on Daryl's hot quivering eyelids, and kissed away the tears that came slipping out in spite of the girl's bravest efforts.

Just a moment they clung together and the tears had their way, and then they heard Father Devereaux and Ruth coming from the kitchen where the last rites of the supper dishes had been performed. Father was calling them.

"Mother! Daryl! Where are you? Ruth and I have got the work all done, and now we want to keep holiday. This is Christmas Eve you know and we mustn't have long faces when the boys get back. Is everything ready to welcome them?"

Daryl sprang away from her mother's arms and up the stairs, calling as she went:

"Yes, Father, I'll be down in just a minute. I want to tidy up my hair a little!"

But the mother went and sat in the big chair at the side of the fire where her face would be in shadow, and tried to take this great thing which her child had told her, conscious that it might be God's way of answering her own agonized prayers about this friendship her girl had formed with the attractive young man of the world. Conscious too that it might mean a broken heart for her pearl of a girl. Gladly conscious, too, that Daryl's lips had responded lovingly, almost hungrily to her own kiss. Oh, her dear girl! To think a thing like this had to come to her to mar this Christmas that had meant so much to them all. To think her girl had to be entangled in a heartbreak. Dear God! Peril, peril, peril, everywhere! Storm for her boy out there in the snow on the mountain. And storm for her girl in the quiet home with the Christmas lights burning, and the home stage set for joy! Sin in the world and heartbreak and storm! And she had somehow dreamed that her children were to be exceptions to the general rule of life, and would not have to pass such terrible testings!

Then came Ruth and settled down at the piano, touching the keys lightly, playing sweet Christmas music: "Oh, Holy Night," "Angels of Jesus," "While shepherds watched their flocks by night." Ruth claimed she was not much of a player, but the notes seemed fairly to sing the words that night, and presently came Daryl with her violin and stood in the shade of the tree, with her back to the lights, and drew tender strains from her fine old violin. Then Father hummed softly, and Mother murmured a note or two now and then, and watched her girl furtively. What had happened to Daryl? Something more than what she had told, she was sure. It would not be like Daryl to make so much of the mere fact that Harold had not come through all that storm. There was something back of it yet that she did not understand.

But wasn't it enough that Daryl seemed to be somewhat disillusioned? Did she dare rejoice in that? Fearfully she thought over all Daryl's vague answers to her questions, and trembled on the border of relief, not daring to hope it would be permanent. Yet why could she not just rest back and trust and leave her child in God's hands? Why did she have to suffer these ups and downs, these fears and brief reliefs and fears again? "Oh, it must be lack of faith. 'According to your faith be it unto you.' Oh, Lord, increase my faith! Lord, give me more faith!"

But if it should be that her girl was to be released unhurt from this unfortunate friendship which she had regarded with such dread, what joy it would be.

The clock struck ten, and still they sang on, each one furtively watching the windows, listening through the sighing of the wind for sounds of the two wanderers returning.

When the clock struck eleven Mrs. Devereaux got up with an air of going about something she had planned.

"Where are you going, Mother?" asked Father Devereaux calmly.

"Yes, where are you going, Mother?" They both looked fearfully toward the windows.

"Why, I'm just going out to light my oven," she said cheerfully, as if she hadn't a thought otherwise. "I thought it was about time to put in some potatoes to bake. The boys ought to be getting home in a few minutes now, don't you think?"

"Well, I don't know," said Father in a slow leisurely tone, "perhaps it's a little soon, isn't it? Won't it be time enough to put their supper on when they get here? They'll have to clean up a little, you know." Although everyone knew perfectly well, having worked it all out in their anxious minds over and over again, that if the boys had made as good time getting down the mountain as they made going up they ought to have been here two good hours ago. However, they were all united in pretending to believe that it wasn't reasonable to expect them yet.

Mother Devereaux listened respectfully to her husband and then she smiled and said, "Well, it won't do any harm to have my oven hot." So she hurried into the kitchen. And if she lingered before she lighted the oven to kneel by her work chair in the dark corner of the kitchen and pray for her girl, and her boy, and the stranger who was out in the storm with her boy, no one but God knew. She came back into the living room just as quietly and calmly as she had gone, and sat down to listen to the singing again.

But when the song was finished Father said:

"It's Christmas Eve, Mother! Girls! Don't you think we ought to be planning where to hang the stockings? How would it be if I were to put up six hooks around the fireplace to hang them on? There's always so much fuss getting them hung, and the boys will be tired when they get in. Daryl, you and Ruth get the stockings together and sew some tapes or something on them to hang them by. Get one of Lance's for the stranger, and have it all ready. He'll probably be shy about producing his stocking. He won't likely be prepared for that ceremony among strangers."

"Oh, you think the stranger will stay all night, do you?" asked Ruth with a hint of dismay in her voice.

"Well, I don't see how he could well help it, do you, seeing the morning isn't so far away, and his car is crippled and has been hauled down to the village garage? I don't suppose he'd feel quite like starting out again so soon afoot."

Daryl whirled about and stared thoughtfully at her father, and then looked dubiously toward her mother.

"What about something to fill his stocking?" she asked aghast.

"Oh, that'll be easy enough. We'll hunt around and find some little things. You might be thinking about it now. It'll help fill up the time while we're waiting."

Brave Father, keeping up the courage of his little frightened woman household.

"What about Harold? You say he can't get here, daughter?"

"No! He's not coming!" Daryl spoke sharply. "Of course! We can give him Harold's things! I hadn't thought of that!" She said it in a matter of fact tone that did not deceive her mother, although it fell right in with what her father, bless his man soul, had been thinking.

"Why, sure! Of course that's the solution, if you think they'll be appropriate. Well, I'll just slip out to the barn and see how Chrystobel and the hens are doing. I don't know but I ought to take the oil stove out there and light it. Lucky the kitchen shed opens into the barn and I don't have to bundle up to go out doors. I know Mother here would raise the roof if I did." He turned a nice old grin toward his wife, and not one of his adoring women was in the least deceived. They knew he was going out to look at the storm, and see what was the prospect of the wanderers reaching home. He put on his overcoat surreptitiously, too, and they heard him stamping into his galoshes, but they pretended not to hear, while they bustled about getting stockings together and sewing loops on them. It was clever of Father Devereaux to think of that to occupy their time during that anxious waiting.

The little stir and bustle of everyday duties, no matter how trivial and unnecessary was a relief, the running up and down stairs for stockings and searching for scissors and thimbles and needles and tape. And where was the thread? Not in its drawer in the sewing table. Oh, in the kitchen where Mother had it sewing up the vest of the turkey! A little laugh ringing out bravely was managed now and then, just as if everything were quite normal and natural, and those two weren't out there in the tempest at least two hours overdue. Oh, God! Aren't you guiding them? Aren't you going to answer our prayers?

Daryl's heart cried out now and then in anguish. It seemed that everything had come upon her at once, and her life was ruined forever, yet as the hours went by and Lance did not return, his absence overtopped everything else. Her mind went back to the sane early fundamental things of her life, the safe sweet home things. And if anything should happen to Lance, how could life go on! Gradually her other anguish, the one that when it first smote her seemed to her the most terrible sorrow that could ever come to her, seemed less important, a thing to shrink from, to keep from thinking about, but not to compare with her anxiety about her brother which grew from minute to minute till somehow his peril seemed hopelessly her fault, though she knew it was not.

So she sewed tapes with trembling fingers on a pair of long stockings of Lance's. They had bright red and orange and green stripes about them, and he never wore them because they were so loud. She made silly jokes about them, whether they would fit the stranger, as she talked in a high unnatural voice, and tried not to look out the window nor hear the wind howling, tried not to see how fast the clock was racing. Near midnight now, almost Christmas morning, and the storm was worse than ever! Would her bright strong brother never come again?

But the mother in the shadows of the kitchen arose from her knees and went and stirred the soup. And the father coming in with a halo of snow about his white hair sang softly, clearly, with his sweet old voice:

"God's way is the best way,
God's way is the right way,
I'll trust in Him alway,
He knoweth the best."

"I've made the coffee," said his wife. "They ought to be here soon now, don't you think, Father?"

"Yes, soon now," said the old voice hopefully.

"Girls, have you got those stockings ready to hang?" called the mother. "Then you'd better come out here and get the bread and butter and things on the table. It won't be long before the potatoes are done, and the boys will be hungry when they get here!"

Daryl cast a frightened look at the clock. Three minutes to twelve, and Christmas morning would be here. Six hours the two had been out in the storm! It didn't seem as if there was a particle of hope that they could ever get home alive! Lost in the snow on the mountain! How could Mother bear it? How would they dare to tell her? She with her faith so bright and strong! Her coffee was sending out its savory odor. And there was a sweet homely smell of roasting potatoes, with their skins all brown and crusty!

The girls put the finished stockings in a pile and gave one look at one another, and then at the clock again. They had white lips, and wide sorrowful eyes!

It was just at that moment that two figures, one half bearing the other, staggered, almost fell, struggled painfully on again into the area where the Devereaux gateway had formerly been located, and two wavering flashlights searched the white impenetrable gloom.

The girls paused in the living room doorway instinctively catching each other's hands as they heard the clock give the preliminary *whirr* to striking the midnight hour, and then because it seemed something crucial, they stood still and watched it strike. One! Two! Three! So slowly and deliberately. It seemed to be striking on their hearts! It seemed like the tolling of a death knell instead of the ushering in of a joyous Christmas morning! They would never forget it. Nine! Ten! Eleven! *Tw-el-ve!*

Its last *whirr* blended with the roaring of the wind that seemed like the groping of a desperate hand outside beating and clutching for the doorknob. Then suddenly the side door of the sitting room burst open, and the two figures slipped, struggled, and fell headlong into the room, bearing the whole outside storm with them, cold and snow and bitterness! A glad wicked gale mocked them saying, "Here I've come back again! You thought you could keep me out, but I'm here!" And it swirled around the room, and hissed its hate against the hot oven door in sharp stinging snow, it slapped Mother Devereaux in the face taking away her breath, and flung upon the two girls in the doorway clutching hands and looking with frightened eyes at the two who had fallen on the floor. Then it whirled into the living room and raced with wicked glee into every cranny, billowing out the delicate muslin curtains at the windows, and the heavy draperies at the doors, swaying the crystal prisms on the candle sconces over the mantel, and tilting the Christmas tree irreverently, then rushed around again into the kitchen wildly. Till the strong old arms of Father Devereaux drew the two men inside and with a mighty effort closed and bolted the sturdy door.

Then out from beneath the heap of snow-covered arms and legs and heads a mittened hand feebly waved a lighted torch till it slipped down rolling crazily to loll on the floor, and a voice, weak but still undaunted, cried huskily:

"We made it, folks! MER–RY CHRIST–MUS!"

"Yes," said Mother Devereaux as she rushed to kneel at her boy's side, "I knew you would! I've got nice hot barley soup and coffee all ready for you."

"Good work!" said Lance feebly, and then faded right out of the picture.

7

THEY lifted the tall figure of the stranger and put him in Father's big chair, and they laid Lance on the dining room couch, and then hurried to minister to them. For having arrived the two seemed incapable of anything else. The heat of the room in their benumbed condition seemed to take away further ability to move or speak. Once Alan roused to explain in a weary tone:

"He fell and hurt his ankle—" but his voice trailed off vaguely again as if he had suddenly fallen asleep in the midst of the thought.

Father Devereaux brought pails and a tub of snow from the sheltered back porch. The girls rushed for warm blankets and aromatic ammonia, and then all hands went to work pulling off the frozen garments from the numb bodies, rubbing frosted cheeks and feet and hands with snow, applying restoratives at Mother Devereaux's directions, bringing warm woolen garments, till presently the two pilgrims were thawed out and able to talk.

They told their story briefly between sips of hot soup. They were being fed by the two girls, while Mother hurried the meal on the table that had been prepared just in the nick of time.

"You see," said Lance from his couch where his father was still rubbing his stiff hands and feet, "they loaned us some snowshoes and we got involved with those when it came to the trail down the mountain. The snowshoes and the trees didn't agree. They got in each other's way and we couldn't do much about it, and when we tried to kick them off and go on without them we found they were frozen to us, at least we couldn't undo the buckles with ice on the fingers of our gloves, so we decided to skirt the woods and come down by way of the fields, but that didn't work either. Our guide rope caught on the last tree we had fastened it to, and broke. We couldn't find the trail so we somehow lost our bearings and went a wandering over the country. Once we got involved with a creek. It didn't seem to be our creek, for it certainly didn't look familiar to me, and I didn't know whether we were going up or down it, so that didn't help much. Once we saw a bright light high up on the mountain but couldn't tell whether it was the house we'd come from, or another away across the valley. So there we were. How we came home or whether we are really home now or not we don't know. It may turn out to be just a dream, and maybe we are really still lying in a snowbank with the sleet in our faces, but if it is, it's a mighty nice dream, and me for the snowbank!"

"Yes," said Mother Devereaux gently, "I thought it would be about like that, and I was praying for you. I was asking God to guide you both home safely."

"Yes," said Lance happily. "I knew that! I told Alan once when we got close enough together to hear each other, and were resting a minute before we went on—that was after I turned my ankle and couldn't walk so well and Alan had to sort of carry me—I said, 'Don't give up, Pard! Mother's down in the corner of the dining room this minute praying us through. We'll get there yet!'"

Alan looked up with a sudden light in his eyes.

"I appreciate those prayers, Mrs. Devereaux," he said.

"I'm sure we couldn't have got through alone."

Mother Devereaux smiled lovingly at the stranger and patted his hand as she went by with the dish of crackly roasted potatoes.

"Yes, but, Mother, you don't know the half yet," said Lance, suddenly eager in his enthusiasm. "You don't know what a man I had with me. Why, Mother, after I stepped in that hole and turned my ankle I thought it was all up with me. I knew no one could reasonably find us before morning even if they sent out search parties in that tempest, and by morning I was sure we would be frozen dead. Alan here had been all in for a long time, and I didn't see how he was ever going to make it, not being used to the mountain the way I am, and then when I found I couldn't walk alone, what did he do but just pick me up and sling me over his shoulder and struggle on. He didn't know where he was going, and I couldn't see to tell him. And I'm no sack of feathers to carry, you know, but he just kept on as if he had new strength. I don't know how he ever thought he was going to find the way, but he would keep on. He wouldn't leave me behind, and he wouldn't take my suggestion of digging a snow hut and crawling in. He just plugged away, and somehow we got here."

"Well," Alan grinned, "I figured that if we kept on long enough we'd surely come to something somewhere, and I didn't want to go alone. I felt if you had courage to go out in that storm with a stranger up that awful mountain, that I surely ought to hold out to get you home!"

Ruth looked up from her post beside Lance's couch where she was feeding spoonfuls of soup as often as he would stop talking long enough to take one, and thought what nice eyes the stranger had, and Daryl murmured as she offered another mouthful of soup to Alan:

"I shall never be able to thank you enough for saving my brother!"

Alan looked up and caught the gratitude in those lovely

eyes and was startled at their beauty. Suddenly it seemed a wonderful thing to be sitting there in the old-fashioned armchair with that comfortable sense of warmth and well-being stealing over him, and that lovely girl ministering to him. It seemed to his weary senses that it was worth all the toil and hardship and cold and terror through which he had passed.

And now the meal was on the table, and the two young men declared they were able to sit up and act like men. But it was on very shaky limbs that they moved to their places.

Again Alan experienced that feeling of awe as the old man bowed his head and spoke to God.

"Lord, we cannot thank Thee enough for bringing our two boys back safely to us. We rejoice that Thou art a prayer-hearing and a prayer-answering God, and that Thou hast heard and answered us tonight. Bless this food to their needs and make us fit for Thy service. Amen."

It warmed Alan's heart that he should be included in the thanksgiving. "Our two boys!" As if he belonged, too! And he suddenly wished that he really did! What a circle to be in by right! It must be something like his mother's family whom he had never known. And then a sudden memory of the house party to which he was due that night came to mind, and his soul revolted at the thought. What a contrast it would be. Drinking and dancing and unholy riotous music! How had he ever thought he could go among them? Just for the doubtful companionship of one girl, whom he wondered if he really admired anyway? Somehow the stern realities of life and death as he had faced them all those hours out there in the storm had given him a new sense of values that he felt he never would forget! Values that he did not want to forget! This home, even the brief glimpse he had had, showed that there was still beauty and love and good fellowship left upon the earth, still a real spirit of Christmas to be found if one looked in the right place for it.

In the morning of course he would have to go on his way as soon as he could get a conveyance to take him. Even if he had to leave his car behind for repairs, and take to the train, but that way would not lead to the house party. He was certain of that now. Tonight had opened his eyes. But of course he must get out of here as soon as possible. He must not intrude upon their Christmas, kind as these people had been. He was conscious of a relief that Demeter Cass and her crowd could not find him tonight. He was lost out of their ken, and need not fear invasion even by the telephone. He would have time in plenty to think things over and find out just where he stood before he saw Demeter again; and tonight, at least what little was left of it, was his. Even with his weary body, exhausted almost to the breaking point, he was enjoying every minute of the time.

The meal was cooked perfectly.

"I don't see how you came to put the potatoes in at just the right time, Mother," said Daryl. "You acted as if you knew the exact minute when they would be needed."

Mother smiled.

"I just asked the Lord to show me what to do about it," she said gently.

"And you think the Lord gives attention to such little details as how long a potato should cook?" asked Ruth earnestly.

"Why, yes, dear," answered the mother, "if you put a matter, even a little matter, into the Lord's hands to guide you, and trust that He will, of course He will."

"Well, but suppose He didn't, Mother? What would you think then?"

"I would think I hadn't trusted Him," said the mother promptly.

"Leave it to Mother to provide an alibi for her faith," grinned Lance.

Alan caught the tender look in Lance's eyes as he glanced

toward his mother, and a great envy and hunger grew in his heart for a home such as this other young man had. No wonder he was what he was, a prince among men. It had taken him only a very few minutes out in that terrible tempest to show him that, and the hours they had faced death together had bound his heart to Lance's in a love that he felt would last forever.

And now of course the next thing in order was for him to go away, just as soon as it was light, and leave them decently to their own holiday without intruders. He sighed at the thought of going and somehow the Christmas time seemed suddenly a hundredfold more desolate to him than when he had started out in the morning. Was this only the midnight of that day? It seemed so very long, and yet all too short now that it was ended. But it was worth all the suffering and danger in the storm, just to know there was one such family on the earth today.

As the numb flesh thawed out, their blood began to flow in its natural course again, and the warm food renewed their strength. The young men revived perceptibly.

"Well, I feel pretty good after all," said Alan, lifting first one foot and then the other as he slowly, cautiously arose from the table. "I didn't think I'd ever be able to use these arms and legs again, did you, Lance?"

"Well, no," responded Lance, "I thought we'd have to have artificial ones if we ever lived to need them."

So they laughed and joked about their recent peril, and the family devoured them with thankful eyes, and tried to smile, but the anxiety was too recent to warrant of much mirth about it for them.

"Well, now," said Mother Devereaux, looking round radiantly upon her family circle, "the next thing on the program of course is to hang up the stockings, but if you boys would rather just be tucked into bed first it will be all right. The girls can hang up the stockings for you."

"No, indeed!" called out Lance, who had dropped down

into a chair to save his ankle, and now dragged himself to the living room door. "We aren't going to be cheated out of that fun, are we, Alan? That's what we hurried home for, to be in time to hang up our stockings."

"I'd hate to be left out of anything that's going," said Alan pleasantly, "but you know, Lance, I don't belong here. I'm only something the storm blew down on your tender mercies. I don't want to intrude. If you'll just let me lie here on the dining room couch till it's daylight, I'll try to take myself off out of your way."

"The idea!" cried both of the girls. "When we've got your stocking all ready to hang up! Planning to walk out on us! Just like that!"

"Nothing doing, old man!" said Lance, slapping his new friend feebly on the shoulder with his best arm. "If you didn't earn your way into this family, and your right to hang up your stocking with the best of us when you carried me through that blast, I don't know who belongs. Man alive, if you hadn't stuck to me and dragged me in I'd have laid down in the snow and given up. I was all in, and that's the truth. When that ankle doubled under me the pain was something awful, and sickened me. You saved my life, boy, and you talk about not belonging!"

It was Father Devereaux who was beside the stranger instantly, with his hand upon his shoulder.

"Friend," he said earnestly, "*son,* you're welcome, and you're one of us. We shouldn't be happy to let you go till the Christmas is past, unless you have someone who has a deeper claim upon you, and who would be grieving at your absence." He peered into the young man's eyes with something like a searching question in his own.

"I haven't!" said Alan huskily, shaking his head. "My folks are all gone. Just friends left, but they wouldn't care a picayune whether I came or went. I'm free as far as that's concerned, but I couldn't think of butting in where I don't belong."

It was left for Mother Devereaux to answer that, and she came over and put a gentle arm around the young man's broad shoulders, and laid soft lips against his cheek and kissed him.

"Of course you belong," she said tenderly. "We couldn't think of letting you go! We want you!"

Alan was deeply touched. His eyes filled with sudden tears.

"That's wonderful of you," he said huskily. "I appreciate that, and with all my heart I'll stay. But you must promise not to upset any of your plans. If you'll just let me park on that couch I'll be perfectly comfortable. I heard someone say you were expecting another guest and I couldn't think of crowding him out."

Instinctively his eyes sought Daryl's, and he saw the deep shadow come suddenly into her eyes, and her lovely lips set in a thin sharp line. She lifted her chin just a little and a proud, tired look came and covered the sorrow in her eyes. As if she felt that he had addressed his remarks to her she answered:

"The fr—, the *guest* who was to have occupied that room didn't come!" She managed a gracious smile to cover the bleakness in her statement, and suddenly Alan remembered the telephone conversation he had heard just outside his door while he was dressing for the expedition in the storm. And all at once he longed to comfort her.

"And may I be substitute guest?" he asked. "At least until the other man can get here? He'll be coming later, I imagine."

"No," said Daryl quite decidedly, "he won't be coming later." She shut her lips thinly again. "At least, if he does, he won't be staying," she added with finality, and Alan found himself strangely glad that she felt that way.

But Lance looked up in surprise.

"What's that, Daryl, Harold not coming? That's hard lines. The storm keep him back?" His voice was very polite, but they all remembered that Lance had just got in from a six-hour battle with the storm, on foot, while Harold had a car and reasonably good highways all the way.

"No," said Daryl quite calmly, as if she were facing the truth and did not wish to hide it, "he went somewhere else!"

The mother looked up.

"Why don't you explain, dear, that his employer had a gathering at which he expected his presence?" she said apologetically.

Daryl opened her lips to speak and then closed them tightly. Alan could see that she did not want to talk about it.

"Well, then," he said cheerfully, "if you're willing to accept me as a substitute guest I'll be happy to endeavor to fill the assignment, but I still suggest you let me sleep on the couch and not make extra trouble for you."

"Man, don't you know this house has rooms upon rooms, and they're always in a perpetual state of being ready for guests? My mother just loves company. Don't get difficult. That room you dressed in is yours as long as you'll stay. Am I right or not, folks?"

"You're right of course, son," said Father Devereaux. "You'll find all your things from your car there, Mr. Monteith. I took the liberty of getting Bill Gates to tow your car into the village for repairs, and we brought your suitcases and packages in so you wouldn't have to go out in the storm to get them when you got back."

"Say, you're kind," said Alan Monteith, greatly touched. "It's like having a father again and being taken care of. I'd almost forgotten how that felt!"

"I hope you'll let us recall it to you often after this," said the old man genially.

"Well, I certainly would like to," said Alan heartily.

"Okay, that being settled, let's go!" said Lance. "Where are the stockings? Let's get to the next act, or I'll fall asleep again."

Lance limped over to the living room with Ruth, his hand resting on Ruth's shoulder, and her eyes were shining and happy as she looked up to him. Alan watched them a second, caught the stricken look on Daryl's face, and drew himself up from the chair, hurrying stiffly over to her side.

"Say, what is this stocking business? You'll have to induct me into its principles. I haven't hung my stocking up since I was a little kid and Mother helped me pin it on the wall over the register, which was the only chimney we had in the apartment where we lived."

Daryl flashed a sympathetic look at him and welcomed his company with a smile.

"Here's your stocking," she said, affecting a gaiety he knew she did not feel, for he saw the purple depths in her great troubled blue eyes.

He took the long gay striped affair.

"My stocking?" he said, pretending to feel of it and study it. "I don't just seem to remember it. Was that ever my stocking?"

"No, but it is now," laughed Daryl. "See, it's marked 'Pilgrim and Stranger Man,'" she said, pointing to a marker fastened to its top with a safety pin. "We couldn't remember what you'd said your name was so we called you 'Pilgrim and Stranger.'"

"Yes, but that doesn't fit any more," said Alan gravely. "I'm no longer a pilgrim, nor a stranger. We'll have to change that. I've been sort of adopted into the family, but I guess it's a little soon to presume upon that. Suppose we make it 'The Substitute Guest'? How will that do? Do you mind?" He looked up suddenly, keenly, his fountain pen out ready to write, and studied her eyes. Lovely eyes. He never had seen such eyes.

"Mind?" said Daryl. "Why, that's lovely. Of course not."

His eyes lingered on hers for an instant and then he wrote swiftly and handed the card back to her to pin on the stocking.

"Now, where do we go from here?"

Daryl gave a real genuine little laugh and led the way to the fireplace where four other stockings of various lengths and sizes swayed gracefully in the firelight.

Daryl instructed him how to hang it by the loop and he made great ceremony of the act, patting it as it hung long and limp at the end of the row.

"There, little stocking, hang still, and don't be filled with great expectations. You know you only belong to a substitute guest and can't expect much, an apple or a few grains of corn perhaps, but don't let your fancy fly to toy horses and soldiers and that sort of thing. We weren't expected, you know, and therefore aren't in the running. I'll maybe steal in here when Santa is gone and stuff you out with a newspaper I have in my suitcase so you'll look like the others, but don't let on it's a newspaper. You've got to be polite, for it's very nice of them to let us play Christmas with them at all, you understand. Now good night, and mind you be a good stocking till I come back to get you in the morning."

They shouted with laughter over his comical tone, and then they hurried the weary young men away to their rest, with injunctions not to wake up in the morning till they really felt rested and ready.

So Mother Devereaux went to perform a last little rite or two over the turkey, Father to make sure the hens and Chrystobel were really comfortable in the barn, and the girls went laughing up to Daryl's room where they were sleeping together tonight. And the storm raged on, white, white, white, everywhere deep and drifting.

Alan found a bright fire burning in the fireplace, and a nice hot water bag in his bed under the covers. Gratefully he climbed into the warm flannel pajamas he found laid out on the bed, not even considering his own fine silk ones in the suitcase, and got into the big soft bed that smelled of lavender, and was plentifully supplied with blankets. He lay there looking happily out at the wide comfortable room in the flickering firelight, thinking what the other fellow, whose place he was taking, had missed, and why he was willing to miss it; wondering if he wouldn't turn up in the morning and spoil it all; wondering if the girl with the lovely eyes really cared so very much; trying to recall her shocked voice earlier in the afternoon, as she answered to the telephone.

Then sweet drowsiness stole over him, and he fancied he was out somewhere in the storm again, battling his way to this lovely quiet haven, where Christmas was real, nothing seemed hard or artificial, and God still reigned in His heaven.

8

DEMETER Cass was clever. She should have been a detective. And she never gave up until she got what she wanted.

However, her operations with regard to Alan Monteith were somewhat interrupted by the arrival of her hosts, and an influx of guests, which necessitated dressing for dinner. It was half past nine when dinner was over, and then there was dancing, and several new men whom she wanted to try out, and it was not until after midnight that she remembered that she had not yet got into touch with Alan, and that he had not arrived nor telephoned.

They had danced the Christmas in with a queer barbaric sort of dance, having costumed themselves in red with jingling bells and grotesque false faces, though many of them didn't need those, having quite artificial ones of their own. They had danced with their right arms curved over their heads, shaking little carved ivory rattles with tiny silver bells, and had sung Good King Wenceslas and the few other Christmas songs they could remember. They had ushered the day in with a riot, by drinking more than usual. And suddenly Demeter felt that it was time to do something more about Alan.

Carefully she questioned the servants to find if he had telephoned, or arrived quietly, but found he had not, so she betook herself to the telephone again.

It mattered not to her that it was long past one o'clock and that she knew the house to which she was telephoning had serious illness. Nothing ever mattered to Demeter except what she personally wanted, so she put in her call. She got the whole Farley-Watt household out of bed, servants and householders, and disturbed the nurse and even the patient, who woke suddenly and cried out to know what was the matter. And then questioning the frightened old man, who had feared he didn't know what when he heard that shrill ring in the middle of the night, she demanded to know *why* Mr. Alan Monteith had not called her.

Mr. Watt was too bewildered and weary at first to get it all straight and find out what she wanted, but when she finally made him understand he admitted that Mr. Monteith had come and that he didn't believe anybody had remembered to tell him the message that she had left several times earlier in the afternoon.

Demeter Cass minced no words in telling him what she thought of that, and paid no heed to his dignified explanation that his wife was seriously ill, and that their anxiety was such that they hadn't remembered anything else. She went on to demand that Alan come to the telephone at once, and when she was told he wasn't there, had been gone several hours, she declaimed over that. What were they thinking of to let him go out in such a storm? And where did he go? Where was he now? She must get into touch with him at once. It was a most important matter! She made it appear that it might be even a matter of life and death.

"I am sorry," said the old man. "We tried to keep the young men all night, but they refused to stay. They seemed to be anxious to get away at once. We loaned them snowshoes—"

"Well, where were they going?" demanded Demeter.

"Well, I can't exactly say," he answered thoughtfully. "I assumed that they were going to the home of the other young man."

"What other young man? What was his name? Where did he live?"

"If you will excuse me a minute I will get the address," answered Mr. Watt. "I took both of their names and addresses. They were most kind to us in our distress, coming so far in the storm, leaving their own affairs —"

Demeter cut him short.

"Hurry, won't you! I can't wait here all night!" she snapped sharply. "I'm not interested in your affairs. I want to get in touch with Mr. Monteith."

The old man felt as if he had been slapped in the face, but he only blinked and hurried away in his bare feet to get his notebook. When he came back, drawing his bathrobe over his shivering shoulders, he made his statements haughtily:

"The name of the young man with Mr. Monteith was Mr. Devereaux, Lance Devereaux. He lives in the village at the foot of our mountain. The servant tells me that he heard Mr. Devereaux call his home and he wrote down the number. It is Collamer 23-R-2. That is all the information I have. Good night!" and he hung up.

But Demeter Cass did not even know she was reproved. She had all the information she wanted, or if she hadn't she could call Mr. Watt again and ask for more. She rang vigorously for the operator and demanded Collamer 23-R-2.

And so—it was something after two o'clock on Christmas morning—just as Alan Monteith was drifting off into peaceful sleep, conscious of warmth and rest and peace and well-being, he suddenly heard the sound of the telephone just outside his door. It somehow blended with his thoughts before he slept, or his dreams as he drifted into unconsciousness, and it seemed to him it must be that

Harold person once more. But as the ringing persisted he came broadly awake, with the unpleasant conclusion that Harold had come to himself and had started out in the storm to come to the farm, and perhaps he was in distress and needed someone to come to his rescue.

He prodded his weary thoughts until he had reasoned it out. If that Harold had got himself into trouble and someone had to go to his rescue, it would have to be himself. Certainly Lance must not go again, with his lame ankle. Obviously the old man could not go, nor the girls. It would have to be himself! And could he get himself together and face that storm again? Yet he must if there was a need. The man might not be worth rescuing, but the girl with the lovely eyes was troubled about him, and that was enough. Something would have to be done. And yet, how could he? It would require a superhuman effort just to raise himself from that warm bed, just to get his tired limbs into motion again, and get his clothes on!

All the while the telephone bell continued, and he began to think perhaps he should go and answer it himself. Then he heard a soft stirring above, and padded slippers stole down the stairs. The receiver was lifted off, and Daryl's quiet voice answered. It had a frightened note in it. She expected it to be the Harold person, too, and she was afraid! He recalled the drunken voice that had shrilled out to the girl early in the afternoon and listened for it again. He felt a wrath rising in his soul for any brute who would treat such a girl like that! He felt he would really enjoy, tired as he was, getting up and giving that fellow a good sound thrashing! Brute! So he listened for the voice again. He would be able to tell from a few words what had happened, and would get up and slip on some garments and be ready in case the fellow was in trouble and needed assistance.

But it was not a man's voice that shrilled out on the quiet house. It was a woman's, high and petulant, and strangely familiar.

"Is this Collamer 23-R-2?"

Daryl's voice was very low and guarded as she answered, Yes. It seemed to the listener that it also sounded somewhat relieved.

"Well, is Mr. Alan Monteith there?"

"Yes," said Daryl, still more softly. He knew she was trying not to waken him.

"Well, won't you call him to the phone at once?"

There was the smallest perceptible hesitation and then Daryl answered pleasantly, in almost a whisper.

"I'm sorry. He has retired."

"That doesn't make any difference!" said the imperious voice on the telephone. "Tell him it is Crag Mountain calling, the Wyndringhams' place, the Ledge. He'll understand. Call him quickly, please. I'm in a hurry. I've been trying to find him all day."

Daryl's voice was still quiet, but very decided.

"I really couldn't waken Mr. Monteith tonight," she said. "He has had a very exhausting tramp through the mountains in the storm, and barely escaped with his life. If you will give me a message I will tell him to call you in the morning, but he mustn't be disturbed now!"

"Well, really!" said Demeter Cass. "Who are you, anyway? An operator?"

"No," giggled Daryl softly, "I'm Miss Devereaux."

"I never heard of you!" said Demeter Cass. "What right have you to judge whether I shall speak with Mr. Monteith or not? I guess you don't know who I am."

"No," said Daryl with sweet dignity, "but it wouldn't make any difference. Mr. Monteith must not be disturbed tonight. Not for *anything*."

"Well, you're fortunately not in a position to judge. Will you call Mr. Monteith at once? Tell him Miss Cass is calling. Demeter Cass. You'll see what he thinks of you for hindering me from talking with him."

Then Daryl, very gravely, very quietly:

"Miss Cass, you do not understand. Mr. Monteith has been for six hours struggling through almost impassable drifts, on foot, lost on the mountain, and in great danger. He and my brother nearly lost their lives in this tempest. They were almost on the verge of unconsciousness when they finally reached here, and it would not be safe to disturb Mr. Monteith tonight."

"And what business did your brother have leading him off on the mountain in all this snow, I should like to know?" Demeter Cass had a nasty snarl in her voice. "If your brother chose to go on a fool's errand taking medicine to old women, what right had he to drag Mr. Monteith into it? I think this should be looked into. Mr. Monteith had an appointment with us, and was on his way here when your brother held him up to go on this crazy expedition. I understand —!"

Daryl's voice suddenly interrupted the tirade on the wire.

"You understand wrongly, Miss Cass. My brother went along with Mr. Monteith to show him the way. He had nothing whatever to do with the errand. And now, if you will excuse me I will get some sleep. In the morning I will tell Mr. Monteith. Good night!" Daryl hung up the receiver with a decided little click, and Alan Monteith heard little soft scurrying slippers going up the stairs.

Alan Monteith lay still, and in a moment the telephone bell began to ring again. It rang and rang several times but he lay there in the darkness, with the flicker of the dying fire on the opposite wall, and grinned. Every time the bell rang he grinned again. But no more slippered feet came down the stairs and finally the telephone rang no more.

So! This was a side of Demeter Cass he had not seen before.

Demeter Cass on his trail in this out-of-the-way place! How had she found him? He lay and considered it. His mind seemed to have awakened suddenly. He had not heard all she said, of course, but he had heard enough.

Demeter Cass!

And that Harold person! What was he to Daryl?

Wyndringham Ledge and the house party! How far away it seemed! How much more desirable this warm sweet room, and the sheets that smelled of lavender, and the row of stockings hanging downstairs, with his name pinned to one of them. "The Substitute Guest!" Would "Harold" come in the morning and spoil it all? And somehow he would have to face Demeter Cass over the telephone the next day! She would be sure to start on his track again. But there was one thing she wouldn't call early. He knew her well enough for that. She wouldn't waken after a bout such as they likely had tonight until eleven at the earliest, or maybe not till noon. He would have time to make a glib excuse for not trying to come over for the next two days. Or perhaps the storm would be excuse enough. The storm, and his disabled car. He would have the morning, at least, undisturbed, and after that the storm would still be his protection from an onslaught from the crowd. They couldn't come over impassable roads of course.

He fell to thinking of what the morning would be like, those stockings hanging in a row around a bright warm fire! What could he put in those other stockings that companioned the one bearing his signature? He had gifts in his suitcase, extravagant glittering gifts, bought in a rather desultory way, in a sort of wholesale order to the salesman who waited upon him in one of the exclusive shops of the city. He had spent more money on them than he wanted to spend, but he felt he had to. One had to do as the rest did if one went to a party at Wyndringham Ledge. It was the expected thing. And most of the gifts he had bought were for people he did not know personally, a heterogeneous collection of costly trinkets, scarcely considered. Only a very few of the things had he really picked out himself, the rest had been the suggestion of the salesman. The ones he had selected had satisfied his own taste, and he had vaguely hoped there might be someone among the crowd who would appreciate them. Yet he had felt even when he was considering them, that none of them would be just the thing for Demeter Cass. She would be pleased with something exotic, something weird and extremely modern, even something outlandishly ugly, if it were ugly enough to be distinguished. And such things he could not bring himself to buy and present to her. He had been trying to think that Demeter Cass was higher and finer than she allowed herself to seem to be. He wasn't sure himself just which of a number of things he had bought he intended to give her. And now he was glad it was settled for him. If he wasn't there at the party he wouldn't have to give her anything, and he found to his astonishment that he was immensely relieved not to have to decide about her at all now. He was content just to rest, and enjoy this quiet room, this haven in the midst of storm, and think of the pleasant family he was to meet in the morning. Yes, he must think over those gifts and find something suitable for each one, and then he must slip out in the morning before anybody was up and put one in each stocking. Five stockings to help fill! A real old-fashioned Christmas! There must be something among that whole suitcase of gifts that would do! But somehow he felt himself drifting away again. He really mustn't go to sleep yet till he had thought what to put in the stockings!

But sleep came down upon him and enveloped him with peace, and he slept in spite of his best resolves.

It was still snowing when he awoke. He could hear the soft plash against the window pane now and again, but the wind had gone down. The wild roar of it had ceased. There was a quiet sense of being shut in that gave security and a new kind of peace. He wasn't going to feel badly if he had to stay the day out here among these delightful sincere people. He had a feeling as he woke that he was a little boy again waking on Christmas morning, with the thrill of anticipation that he used to feel as a child. It was great. He lay still for a little just to keep that delightful sense of expectancy.

Then he became aware of another sound in the room. The soft burning of the fire, the falling down of a stick that had burned through to a heart of glowing coals. Just out of curiosity he had to open his eyes to look at that fire. Surely it had not kept all night! Not the same fire that was there when he went to sleep! No, it was a big bright lively fire. Someone had been in while he slept and made it up. The room was quite warm. The flicker of the fire was over the walls rosily, playing over the sheer white curtains, dancing over the cretonne roses on the big wing-chair, and the rocker. It was all invitingly pleasant to get up and dress, and suddenly he felt wide awake and remembered that he had to get things ready to put in those stockings out there.

The house was very still. Only the crackling of the fire accompanied the occasional soft plashing of the snow against the upper part of the window panes not already vested with it. It must be that the family were not up yet, unless perhaps they were keeping quiet so they wouldn't disturb him. But who could have fixed the fire? The splendid old father likely. Surely Lance wouldn't have wakened early after his strenuous trip in the snow. And with his strained ankle he wouldn't have tried to make fires yet. Well, he must get up and get active. He seemed to have a strange apathy toward moving. He tested his members cautiously, but beyond a stiffness in his joints, and an inclination to lie still, he found himself not very much the worse for his exposure in the storm. Of course his muscles were lame and sore, and he felt as if every movement were an effort, but he was alive and safe, and why growl at sore muscles. He had suffered as much and more after a stiff football game in college.

He arose and stole toward the fire, holding out one foot and then the other to feel the hearty heat. He found a pitcher of hot water awaiting him on the hearth, and he turned to the old-fashioned wash stand and reveled in the pleasant soap and wide lavender-scented towels. But he must hurry now, for there were still those presents. He must do them up and label them. They wouldn't take long, but he had to decide which things were suitable, and that might take time. Gold cigarette cases and ash trays and distinctive decks of playing cards of which he felt sure the salesman had put several into his collection of gifts, would scarcely fit this family. Would there be anything that would?

He dressed hastily in some pleasantly informal garments, sure that there would be no formality of attire in this household, and then stole to the window to see if his surmise about the storm had been correct. Yes, the windows were still shrouded with snow, and it was still coming down steadily, but not so fiercely as last night, and with almost no wind at all. A glance at the distance showed depth of whiteness in every direction, and he gave a sigh of satisfaction. It might begin to clear around noon, but for a little time at least he was snowbound, and he was glad. Nothing as pleasant as this had befallen him for a long time. He did not want to go to that house party where he was due, and he wondered why he had ever considered it. All thought of Demeter Cass and her after-midnight call had been forgotten. He was all eagerness now to find the right gifts among his collection.

So he spread them out on his bed, and counted them over, unwrapped and compared them, discarding at once the articles that were incongruous and utterly impossible for his use here. He wondered why he had been willing to give such things to anybody. A gift was something that expressed oneself to a large extent, wasn't it? And most of those things he had been intending to use for gifts at the house party were utterly foreign to himself. Well, the man had said he could return any that he did not use and he decided that a lot of them would go back as soon as he reached the city.

So, the ash trays, vanity cases, decks of cards, and cigarette cases went into the discard, and narrowed down the lot quite considerably. Among those that were left he had much ado to please himself. For he suddenly discovered that he would like to give something very nice indeed to everyone in the house. There were among his collection two handsome wallets with key-cases to match, one in pin seal and one in hand-tooled leather. Those would do for the two men of the household. He drew a breath of satisfaction, tied them up carefully in the wrappings that had been provided by the store, and wrote the names of Lance and his father on them. But the women would be harder.

He knew which of all his gifts he would like to give to Daryl, but of course he couldn't. She wouldn't likely accept it if he did. It was a lovely pearl pin of exquisite workmanship, set in platinum, the pearls flawless. It was quiet and lovely, yet very distinctive. He had selected it half tentatively for Demeter Cass, knowing it could be returned if he decided against giving it to her. It was in a way symbolic of what he would like to think the handsome Demeter was like, and yet all the while in his heart he had known she wasn't. He had had a passing thought that perhaps he might make it a test of her. If she liked it she must have the true fineness of soul he had sometimes fancied he saw behind the veneer of sophistication that the times demanded. If she did not, then she wasn't what he wanted. He had almost come to the point of letting that pin make his decision about Demeter, whether or not she was the girl he wanted in his life. He was still doubtful as to whether Demeter as he knew her would ever count it a treasure among her possessions. That was why, now, he could consider the pin as a gift to another.

Strange how he felt about that pin. As if it were a thing with a personality that needed to be appreciated. Now take this other girl—or either of the two girls in the house for the matter of that. There would be nothing incongruous about either of those girls wearing a pin like that. Even on a plain dress it would seem at home, though it would grace a royal garment anywhere.

And how he would like to give that to Daryl. But he mustn't, of course. Girls like Daryl and Ruth did not accept jewelry from strangers. Not even from strangers who had played some small part in saving a brother's life—after he had put it in peril for his own needs. And besides, a gift like that might likely make trouble for her with that Harold person, though he found himself wishing fervently that it might.

But then a pleasant thought came to him. There was no reason why he couldn't give it to Daryl Devereaux's mother, nor why she shouldn't accept it. She had put a motherly kiss upon his forehead that he would never forget. He would like to give the pin to her! It would be lovely fastening the lace about her neck, it would set off her sweet face under her wavy white hair. He would give the pin to the mother, of course! What a pleasure that would be! And now he suddenly saw that to subject that pin to the test of a Demeter Cass was being unfair to it. He liked the pin for itself, because it was something he would have liked to give to his own beloved mother if she had been alive. And he suddenly knew definitely that Demeter never would have liked it, and probably wouldn't have even taken the trouble to dissemble enough about it to make him think she liked it. It wasn't unlikely that she might have screamed out with merriment, in that half-childish way she had sometimes, and called the crowd to laugh over the gift, saying he had gone puritan on them—yes, and kept it up all day as a good joke, and then asked him at night to please take it back and change it for jade.

He knew now that he had never really meant to try her out with that pin, not unless some miracle occurred that would put her to the test before she ever saw the pin. He couldn't have exposed that pin to ridicule. It was too exquisite.

Yes, he would give it to Mother Devereaux! That was settled. Sometime perhaps Daryl would borrow it and he would see her wear it, and that would give him pleasure too.

So he wrapped it carefully and labeled it.

He looked over his remaining property, perplexed. What could he give the girls? He finally decided on two lovely scarfs, made of some rare wool, soft as kittens' ears. He had bought them dubiously, as he had bought all the things he really liked, feeling that in a mixed company such as a house party there would surely be one or two people who would appreciate their beauty. Also the salesman had assured him that they were exceedingly smart. He might have to return them, but he had enjoyed buying them.

He decided that he would give the blue one to Daryl. Blue and white it was, with exquisitely blended colors, and it seemed like the blue of the girl's wonderful eyes. The crimson and white and black one would be gorgeous on quiet little Ruth with her brown hair and dark eyes.

He drew another sigh of relief as he finally folded them and put them back in the pretty gift boxes and wrote the girls' names on them.

He gathered up the other things that he had discarded—"junk" he called it as he stuffed it grimly into the suitcase,—and registered a resolve never to be guilty of buying anything like those again.

He opened his door most cautiously and tiptoed across the hall into the living room. All was quiet in the house. He hoped no one was about yet, though there was such a comfortable air of living and peace about the room that it hardly seemed possible, and that was certainly the aroma of coffee he smelled.

He went over to the fireplace where a brisk fire was crackling, giving good evidence of somebody having been on the job since last night, and there he carefully inserted his packages into the right stockings, or tied them on the outside when they were too large to go in. Somebody else had been to the stockings before him. Every stocking was lumpy and bulging. Even his own was filled to the brim and didn't need the newspaper he had promised it to keep up appearances. It touched him to think of their kindness. This was a great family. How they took a stranger in! And a stranger whom they didn't know about beforehand!

He turned away and looking toward the tree saw packages there piled beneath the branches. Ah! There was another chance! There must be more things among his collection that he could add. There was some fine perfume, he knew, and a lot of handkerchiefs, pretty ones. He had bought those afterward for fillers in case there were more people at that house party than he knew about. He could put several in a box. Perfume, and handkerchiefs, a gold pencil, a small pocket compass. Oh, he could do very well and hold his own with this dear family.

So he hurried back into his room and tied up and labeled a few more things, feeling like a boy again, and having the time of his life.

9

ALAN had just finished placing his second installment of gifts under the tree when he became aware that someone was standing in the doorway, and turning he saw Daryl in a green dress that matched the holly leaves, and a white apron with little red bows of ribbon like holly berries. She was smiling and called out: "Merry Christmas! We were keeping still, hoping you would have a good sleep, but it seems you have stolen a march on us."

"Oh, I had a wonderful sleep!" said Alan. "There must be some magic about that room and that bed. The morning came all too soon."

"But why did you get up? Why didn't you sleep later? We told you to sleep as long as you could."

"I know," he said, "but I was like a child! I never could sleep on Christmas morning. I wanted to see what had happened to the stockings. I should say a good deal has happened!" He grinned as he looked toward the mantel, and then glanced down at the motley array of packages under the tree.

"Isn't it fun?" said Daryl. "I just love Christmas! Even when we were little kids Mother always let us make things for each other, and we always enjoyed the surprises so much. It didn't matter what they were. I made Father a pair of woolen gloves one Christmas out of a piece of brown flannel. I ripped up his old ones and got the pattern. They were all crooked and cut the wrong way of the cloth and the stitches were funny and uneven, but Father made a big fuss about them, said they were the best gloves he had ever had, and wore them every cold day that winter, though I know they were awfully crooked and misshapen. Oh, some of the dearest memories I have are connected with Christmas. It is the best day of all the year."

"I haven't had a real Christmas since my mother died ten years ago," said Alan wistfully. "That's why I'm so pleased that Fate dropped me down here and shut me in so that I could decently stay a little while and get a glimpse at one."

"Don't say 'Fate,' say 'Our Father,'" said Mother Devereaux, appearing in the doorway. "We are glad to feel He sent you to us. Our Christmas is going to be happier because you came. Now, will you come out and have a bit to eat? We're not having a very elaborate breakfast this morning because it is so late, and the children are in a hurry to get to the stockings."

They went out to the dining room and Alan was surprised to find Lance there ahead of him, coming in from the woodshed with his arms full of wood.

"What, you up?" he said. "I thought you would play the part of invalid this morning and I should have all the honors. How is your ankle?"

"Fine!" said Lance, smiling. "Mother did it up in arnica last night and it seems to be all right this morning. Of course I'm saving it a little, but it doesn't pain me any more. I think we came out of that scrape pretty well last night. Are you all right?"

"Fine!" said Alan, "only a little stiff in places, but I fancy I'm not in training as much as you are these days. However there were times last night when I thought we had come to the end of this life down here, and I must own I was ready to give up. If it hadn't been for you I would have."

"Boy! You were great!" said Lance with kindling eyes. "You feeling as low as that, and then bucking up and taking me on too!"

"Well, you needn't praise me too much. I can tell you it was some power beyond myself that helped me keep going at the end. I am sure it must have been your mother's prayers."

"Of course!" said Lance with a reverent glance toward his mother.

"Well, I certainly am glad you're able to be up this morning," said Alan as he pulled out Daryl's chair for her at the table.

"Up!" said the father, coming in just then. "Lance beat me up for once. He fixed all the fires, and then he went out and milked Chrystobel."

"And who, pray, is Chrystobel!" asked Alan mystified.

"Chrystobel is the cow," explained Daryl with a twinkle.

"Oh," said Alan sorrowfully, "then I've missed that! All my life I've wanted to milk a cow, and I never had a chance! And now to have come as near as this and have missed it. How often do you perform that rite, Mr. Devereaux?"

"Twice a day," said the old man, smiling. "I'll let you have a try this afternoon along toward dark."

"Delighted, if you'll let me stay that long," and Alan cast an anxious eye toward the window still white with snow.

"I rather think you'll be compelled to stay," said the elder Devereaux, "unless you want to hitch-hike home. They told me they couldn't do anything about your car until Christmas was over, so many of the men are off celebrating. And we hope you'll be a good sport and stay by us through our good time here. I know the whole family feel as I do, that it will be a great privilege to have you with us."

"Well, you are wonderful!" said Alan. "Just wonderful! You may be sure I'll stay. Nothing could drag me away till I just have to get back to my work in the city. I feel as if I had found the first real home since my mother died."

Daryl lifted her beautiful eyes and looked at him as if she were trying to be sure he meant it, and that look stayed with him. His eyes met hers, and he wondered if she really wanted him, or was only hiding a deep trouble of her own, and wished he were away. Suddenly she smiled, a shy sweet smile, and something happened to his heart. It gave a queer little twinge and seemed to turn over. He told himself it was the unusual exertion yesterday that made it behave so queerly, but he really knew that it was Daryl's smile that had started it.

Simple breakfast, Mrs. Devereaux had said.

There was wonderful oatmeal, steamed all night until each grain stood out softly and separately, with Chrystobel's cream to eat on it, cream almost as thick as the oatmeal. Eaten in old Haviland china saucers with sprigs of forget-me-not on them, and a silver spoon so old it was almost paper thin. Then there were hot rolls and doughnuts and coffee! Simple breakfast indeed!

After breakfast there was family worship. That was an entirely new experience for Alan. His father had been dead a good many years, and while his mother had taught him to say his prayers when he was a child, she had been a shy woman, and had never established the habit of family worship in their small broken home. Alan listened to the scripture reading, and then the prayer with reverent bent head, and thought he began to see some of the reasons why these children had grown up to be so unusual. He knelt with the rest and heard himself prayed for. Heard the Lord thanked for sending him here, and for what he had done toward saving the son of the house, and for all the wonderful ways in which the Lord always worked and made the wrath of man and devil to praise Him, and then heard himself numbered with them as "beloved," not only to them but to God Himself. Alan had never thought of himself before as being beloved individually of God. He wondered as the prayer went on whether that wasn't going to make some difference in the way he lived, if he found he really could make himself believe that God loved him in any personal way.

And then in just a sentence he heard the whole way of salvation mentioned as the fact of all others for which to be thankful: that the Son of God had laid aside his kingly estate and come down to earth to bear in his own breast the death penalty with which all were condemned, that all who would accept His death and life as their own might be free to live forever in the presence of God.

Alan Monteith felt when he rose from his knees as if he had been in the very presence of the Most High. Never before had he realized that God could be as real to any human being as he seemed to be to the old man who had prayed that most unusual prayer.

They had a gay time opening the presents. Alan Monteith couldn't remember ever enjoying an occasion so much since he was a child, and every moment increased his liking and respect and admiration for every member of the group.

They sat around the fire in a semi-circle, each one in an easy chair, and took down their stockings first. It was all cozy and lovely, with the lights of the Christmas tree brightening the room that would otherwise have been a bit gloomy with no sunshine, and that great white blanket of snow obscuring the light from the windows. Father Devereaux, just before they began, had lighted two tall candles in the sconces over the mantel, so that the room glowed with candles and tree and firelight. It was pleasant to feel shut in from the world, with nobody likely to interrupt them. It was like being shut in on a desert island for a time with the very nicest people in the world for companions, and plenty of stores to last indefinitely. It seemed to Alan Monteith like a little bit of heaven below.

Lance handed out the stockings to their owners and they took turns taking out something. Mother Devereaux came first. There was a box with a lovely collar of fine lace in the top of her stocking, so she opened that first. It was from Daryl, and she made her put it on at once around the neck of her gray wool dress, where it dignified her costume, and made her look a bit more fragile and delicate than she really was. Father Devereaux said he really would have to kiss her she looked so sweet. There was a charming bit of verse on a card that Daryl had written for her mother. It was better than reading a story or looking at a picture to be thus let in on the happy intimacies of this charming family life. Alan almost wished he might take notes so that he could treasure always everything that was said and done.

And Daryl was so pleased with her scarf when she opened it first of her presents because it was too large a box to go into the stocking and had to be tied on the hook. She exclaimed over its softness, and said she had always wanted one of those lovely things, but she never could afford it. Her cheeks grew pink with pleasure as she threw it about her shoulders, and her eyes, Alan saw, matched it exactly. They all noticed that too, and spoke of it. "Why, Daryl, it's made out of one of the glances from your own eyes!" her brother said. Alan was delighted. He could see they were all pleased at the present.

A minute later Ruth opened her box and flung her crimson scarf about her where it matched her glowing cheeks and brought a sparkle of pleasure into her dark eyes, as she thanked him shyly.

"Say, now, old man," said Lance, when he found his wallet and key-case, "I'm beginning to suspect you. This is a put-up job. You pretended you were stalled in front of our house yesterday, but it is becoming more and more evident that you had this all planned and meant to spend

Christmas with us, else why would you have selected these gorgeous gifts that are each just what we wanted? See, Dad, you've got one too! The package is just the same size as mine. Open it quick! Say, this is great! But you needn't try to tell me you didn't plan to come here from the start. Only what gets me is how you found out just what we wanted?"

Alan sat there grinning and sheepish and happy, and the packages multiplied, till they were all over the floor around their chairs, and on the little tables that were near at hand; and wrapping paper and ribbon made a bright confusion everywhere.

Alan had not been forgotten by any means. The truth was the family had been so uncertain about, and rather afraid of, the new element which Daryl seemed about to introduce into the family, that each had secretly provided more than one article that *might* serve as a gift to him. They had intended to select the most appropriate one when he arrived and they saw how well they liked him. Their one desire had been to please Daryl by what they gave him, and not to disappoint her. So they had a stock from which to draw when the stranger came among them. But the strangest thing about it was that not one of them shrank from giving any of the things they had bought to Alan Monteith. They felt as if they could not give him enough. And whereas they had been most troubled about Harold's acceptance of some of the things they had chosen, there wasn't a thing they had but they felt would be appreciated by this stranger.

Lance gave him a queer little gadget to fasten to his windshield by suction which would give him the points of the compass; the father, a quaint old book of Scotch sayings and witticisms, in a rare binding, a book that had been handed down to him from his forebears. He hadn't consulted his children about it apparently, for they seemed surprised, and Daryl silently commented to herself that her father would never have ventured to give that to Harold.

And if he had, Harold would have cast it aside as worthless. As she watched Alan Monteith handle and open the little old book with deference as if he understood its value, and turn the pages interestedly, she could not but contrast him with the other guest who was to have been there. She could fairly see the bored look on Harold Warner's face even though he was not present. He probably would not even have bothered to open a page. Reading of that type would never have appealed to him, and the ancient rare binding would have been to him as so much outworn trash. She tried to get away from the thought, but it lingered and hurt her, even while she was telling herself that she was not being fair to Harold. He was a different type, young and gay. But then would come back his light laugh over the telephone last night, his jumbled incoherent talk, and she shuddered.

"Are you cold, dear?" her mother asked, noticing the quiver of her shoulders.

"Oh, no, indeed!" she answered lightly and the quick color stole into her white cheeks. Alan, happening to look her way, thought how lovely she was, and yet marked the faint blue lines under her eyes, and wondered if he knew what made them.

Ruth had made several hand-hemstitched handkerchiefs of lovely sheer linen in preparation for the festivity, and during the long anxious waiting for the two pilgrims to return, she had tucked handsome initials in one corner of each with her skillful needle. There were two of those in Alan's stocking.

Daryl's gift to the stranger had cost her quite a struggle. She like the rest had been a little uncertain about Harold, and had provided more than one possibility. Among other things she had bought a handsome leather case for collars and a matching one for handkerchiefs which she had been sure he would like, not only because it was obviously the best of its kind and therefore costly, but because it was something she had heard him covet. Yet her heart had wanted to give him something finer, more poetic, something that would appeal to heart and brain, rather than just to the material senses. She had even indulged this longing so far as to purchase an exquisite etching of the wise men and the star. She had spent much care on its framing and had taken joy in it when she brought it home, but then she found she could not bring herself to give it to Harold. She wasn't even sure he believed in that star. When she thought it over she was afraid he would not be able to see even the beauty of line and thought in the picture, and so she had hid it away. There had been a book of poems, also, beautifully bound in soft blue leather, tooled delicately in gold. They were poems that she loved, and would so enjoy reading with the ideal Harold whom she had set up in her mind. But those, too, she had hidden away.

It was only at the last moment that she had made her quick decision, feeling strong gratitude to the stranger-guest for his help in the saving of her brother. She had brought forth the picture and stood it up under his stocking. Later, when he came to unwrap it, the last of his things about the fireplace, she liked the look in his face. Harold would scarcely have glanced at the etching. Art and religion did not interest him. But Alan's face lighted up with a glow of real appreciation.

During the morning there was an intermission when Mother went out to the kitchen a few minutes. Daryl had been thinking over the lovely gifts Alan had given to her and her family, that exquisite little crystal bottle of costly perfume for her, the tiny enamel pencil, the wonderful pin he had given her mother. Now she realized that her simple etching seemed far too little to give to the stranger who had poured out his treasures upon them. So with her lovely blue scarf about her shoulders and a dab of the perfume on one cheek, she slipped away upstairs and got the blue leather poems to put under the tree for him. But just as she was hurrying down again she met her brother on the stairs.

"Daryl!" he said softly, "haven't you got something else I could give to Alan? I'd like to give him something really nice, and I don't quite like the other things I bought. They don't seem to fit him. He's such a wonderful fellow!"

Daryl gave Lance one startled look, and then she went back into her room and brought out the leather cases. After all, she might as well make a clean sweep of everything.

Lance was delighted and promised to replace them as soon as the snow would let him get into town, but Daryl said, No, sharply. "There won't be any need," she said with finality. "I shouldn't use them now under any consideration!"

Lance gave her a quick searching look, and went downstairs, wondering if that wasn't being a little hard upon even Harold, just because he did not come to spend Christmas in a storm like this. But he thanked his sister and made no further comments.

"I'll pay you for them, anyway," he said, smiling brightly, "and no end of thanks for helping me out."

So the opening of gifts went on, and Daryl's fair plans for the lover who did not come, broke harmlessly on the shore of the family pleasure, and obliterated some of the sore hurt feeling, enabling her to enter into the Christmas fun without too much agony. Her mother looked on with much surprise and gradual relief as one by one these gifts came forth that she knew her daughter had bought with Harold in mind. Well, at least there would not be a lot of offerings ready for the repentant prodigal when he came, as he undoubtedly would. And it was right that there should not be. If the young man didn't come when he had said he would, he did not deserve Christmas gifts. It would have been different if he had felt the storm prevented his getting there! But to frankly say he had gone somewhere else at the last minute was unforgivable. Anybody, even a cruel boss, would have understood, if Harold had said he had a previous engagement. Especially when it was with the girl whom he seemed to be expecting to marry.

But it was Mother Devereaux who brought out the crowning gift for the guest, just as he had given his loveliest gift to her.

Early in November she had been to the city with Daryl, and had purchased among other things a beautifully bound Bible, soft real leather in a very dark blue, without the divinity circuit edges, a trim, neat fine binding that made the mere handling of the book a pleasure. It was quite distinctive and had been rather expensive. Daryl had wondered when her mother bought it, but when she found out that she had thoughts of giving it to Harold, Daryl gave her a startled look, opened her lips to protest and then closed them again. Nevertheless, the mother had sensed that Daryl was not pleased and at the last minute had delegated her daughter to select two very handsome neckties for the young man. It was these neckties that had been among the first things that Alan had found sticking out of his capacious stocking.

But when Mother Devereaux found her gorgeous brooch, she was so overwhelmed with shy delight that she, too, during the turkey's interruption, slipped up to her room and brought the Bible down, sliding it furtively under the other gifts beneath the tree. And so it was the last gift opened. Alan was almost embarrassed when it was handed to him. He felt that he had already received more than was his due as a casual intruder.

But when the package was opened and Daryl recognized the box, she gave her mother a quick startled look, and then shot a keen, almost defiant look at the stranger. How would he take the gift of a Bible? If he took it as a joke she was ready to defend her mother with fire in her eyes, but she secretly wished that her mother hadn't done it! And then she saw the look on his face as he took out the Bible and her fearful heart was flooded with admiration for this stranger man, for there was what seemed to be genuine pleasure in his eyes as he looked toward her mother.

"I thank you," he said, almost reverently, as he opened the flexible covers, and touched the pages gently. "Mrs. Devereaux, this is the crowning gift of all. It is not only a Bible de luxe, but I guess it is something I really needed. Do you know, I haven't any Bible except a tiny copy I acquired in Sunday School as a child. It is very fine print and I haven't ever read it. In fact the only Bible reading I ever got was when my mother read me Bible stories when I was a little kid. But now, I'm going to read this one! I'll promise you that I will read it through!"

Then deliberately he got up with the Bible in his hand and coming over to her he stooped and very reverently kissed her forehead just at the parting of her pretty silver hair.

Sudden tears came smarting into Daryl's eyes and her heart leaped up with longing and dull ache. If only Harold had been one like this! But Harold would never have taken it this way. He would likely have roared out with laughter at the idea of his receiving a Bible, and told some silly joke that would have hurt Mother. Was that really the kind of man she had chosen for a friend? Did this stranger have to come to them just now in his absence to show her the contrast? She gave a little shiver and turned away quickly, springing up to pretend to fix a log in the fire that had fallen down. Then of course Alan sprang up too, and took the tongs from her, to fix it. Did he also catch the glint of tears as she tried to wink them away and ignore them? If he did he gave no sign, and the pleasant morning went on, breaking up now into gay clatter of thanks and admiration for the various gifts. Everybody hurried around picking up tissue and bright wrappings, and rolling up red ribbons for Ruth who said she wanted them for her kindergarten plays. They were a happy family, and the two outsiders did not feel in the least like strangers. They were having a grand time. It seemed like home to them both, who no longer had any real homes of their own. And the family felt that they really belonged, too. Even Daryl thought, as she went about setting the living room to rights again after the orgy of gifts, how amazingly well the stranger fitted into their life. Almost as if he had been born to it. And there was none of the stiffness and anxiety she had expected to feel if Harold had come. It was heartbreaking to have to own that, but it was true. Harold just wouldn't have fitted. He wouldn't *ever* have fitted. And it wasn't Mother's fault either. It was Harold himself. He *was* different!

But there wasn't any time now to be thinking about such things. The turkey began to make an outcry from the oven that it was done and wanted to get out, and suddenly everybody was hungry. How could one help being hungry with savory odors like those coming from the oven? And they discovered that time was well on into the afternoon. Mother Devereaux called upon them all for help. The table must be set in a hurry. Lance and Ruth did that, while Mother was making the gravy, and creaming the onions, and scooping out the Hubbard squash, and keeping the candied sweet potatoes from burning. Father was delegated to beat the mashed potatoes and turnips. Daryl and Alan went to the pantry for cream and butter and cranberry sauce, and pickles and celery hearts. Then they cut the bread and the cheese and made the coffee. Alan acted like a boy out of school, eager about everything, interested in all they were doing, especially interested keeping a watch on the glass percolator, to lift it off at the right moment when it began to "perk."

Suddenly just as they were about to sit down Daryl remembered and a blank look came over her face.

"Oh," she said, turning toward Alan, "I forgot to tell you. A person called up last night and wanted you to call her the first thing this morning! I never thought of it till now! She said her name was Cass, I think, and she had a queer first name. Even queerer than mine. It was something like Scimeter. I'm so sorry I forgot to tell you."

Alan grinned.

"Demeter," he supplied. "Demeter Cass."

"Well, you'd better call her now before you sit down. I don't know what she'll think of me. She thought I was an operator at first."

"That's too bad," said Mother in dismay, casting an anxious glance toward the turkey, velvety brown on the big china platter that had been in the family for a hundred years or more. It was as if she feared the turkey might be offended.

But Alan shook his head.

"No hurry," he said, "Demeter will keep. She hasn't been up so long herself. This would be quite near to the first thing in the morning for her. She hasn't been long away from her breakfast tray, I'll warrant. I'm too hungry to talk to her now. That certainly is the most wonderful turkey I ever saw! Let's forget calling up for a while."

So they sat down to the table and Father Devereaux bowed his head for the blessing.

It was just then the telephone rang out clamorously, insistently, and kept it up all through the blessing.

"There!" laughed Lance when the blessing was over. "You might as well have called when Daryl told you, and got the credit of it!"

10

DEMETER Cass would have called long ago if she hadn't had something more interesting to do. A new young man had appeared on the scene at the house party and she was trying him out. Also it was true that she hadn't been up very long, for the gaiety of the night before had lasted far into the morning ending with scrambled eggs for every-body, and they had slept late as Alan had known they would do. And then there had been a hilarious breakfast at noon. That took time.

But now for a few moments there was a cessation of amusements and Demeter had returned to the fray.

Alan arose reluctantly with a frown of annoyance. He didn't want to be interrupted now. He didn't want to talk to Demeter Cass. She was a false note in this perfect harmony.

The family hushed their gay clamor when he went to the telephone lest they would annoy him, and so they could not help hearing his short replies:

"Yes? Oh, is that you, Demeter? Merry Christmas! . . . Yes, I got your message but I thought you'd just about be getting up. I didn't get up very early myself. I had a long

hard hike in the storm last night. . . . Why didn't I telephone? Well, to tell you the truth I hadn't thought of it
yet. I had too much else on my mind. And then you know
I told Mrs. Wyndringham that I wasn't sure I could come.
I told you that too. I thought you would understand on
account of the storm. . . . I was going to call up sometime
this afternoon to offer my apologies to Mrs. Wyndringham
and wish you all a Merry Christmas. But I hardly expected
you would be wound up and going yet, so early in the
day. . . . No, it's impossible, Demeter. The storm is too
heavy! I couldn't make it! . . . No, even if I dared try I
couldn't. My car is broken down and it will be a day or so
before it's in shape to travel. . . . Oh, you needn't pity me.
I'm having the time of my life! . . . Yes, they're friends. *I'll
say* they're friends! . . . No, I don't think you have met
them. . . . No, you mustn't think of sending for me. No,
indeed! Why should you even if you *could?* . . . What?
Somebody you want me to meet? Well, I'll be delighted of
course, but I shall have to postpone the pleasure. . . . Why
is it so urgent?"

There was a long pause this time while the voice at the
other end talked earnestly, persistently, and the listeners in
the other room looked at one another silently and wondered. Would he go? If there was a way, would he go?

They glanced out of the window where still the snow
was steadily beating down, and dreaded to think that
perhaps he would try. There was no telling what a man
with his courage would think he ought to do, or, for all
they knew, *wanted* to do. And after all he was a stranger.
These people who were calling him likely had a much
stronger hold on him than they, the chance acquaintances
of a day! Yet how quickly had their hearts begun to knit
with his heart! How they would hate to see him go!

Then suddenly the crisp clear voice in the other room
said: "Why should you especially want me to meet that
man? . . . Oh, of course I'm always glad to make new

contacts. . . . Well, of course I'll be glad to listen. Suppose you come into my office some morning next week. . . . No, not the apartment, *my office,* I said. I imagine I'll be pretty well tied there next week after my vacation. I'll be very busy. . . . Yes, I'm sorry to have disappointed you all, but I'm sure you'll have just as gay a time without me. Please remember me to all the party. Good-by!"

He came back to the table looking thoughtful, a little frown between his pleasant eyes. Was it disappointment that he could not be with his own friends, or annoyance, or what? Daryl studied his face furtively and wondered what kind of girl this Demeter Cass was. She hadn't received a very good impression of her last night over the telephone.

For a little time after Alan came back to the table there was a quietness over them all, as if that telephone call had somehow reminded them that they were of different worlds. But presently Alan seemed to come out of his brown study, just as if he had willed to shake off whatever it was that was perplexing him, and was his merry self again. After all, whoever this stranger was that she wanted him so much to meet, who seemed to be important both to his business career and to Demeter's happiness, he didn't have to face that question for at least two or three days, and he was going to enjoy this Christmas time to the very limit of every moment. So his eyes were soon full of light again, and his remarks kept them all in a gale of laughter.

Lance secretly drew a breath of relief. He had been afraid Alan was going to go native on him and he didn't want this happy time to be spoiled that way. He wanted Daryl to see that there were other young men besides that flip Harold Warner. Also his experience yesterday in the storm had taught him that here was a prince among men, and he didn't want him to fail in anything. Neither did he like to think that any girl anywhere had the power to dim the light in those pleasant eyes, and silence the merriment on his lips. In fact Lance had fallen hard for his new friend and he wanted to keep him. He resented another girl. Especially a girl who could bring worry.

But the generous helpings of turkey went their rounds, and warmth and good cheer in the old farmhouse soon were uppermost. Everybody was hungry and everybody ate heartily. Alan took second helpings till he was ashamed of himself, and told Mother Devereaux he never had eaten such wonderful cooking.

And then came the dessert. He and Daryl took out the plates and brought in the pies, mince and pumpkin. And though they had thought they couldn't eat another bite they managed the pie nicely.

There was something cozy and homelike in all hands washing the dishes afterward. Alan enjoyed it. He felt as if he were a boy again in a big nice loving family of his own.

He watched Daryl deftly wiping a pile of plates, polishing glasses and setting them in rows upon the shelf. She seemed to make a fine art of dishwashing. And yet this girl had a college education, and could hold her own among intellectual people. Still, she didn't seem to be trying to get out of the round of daily household duties that so many girls shirked.

He tried to fancy Demeter Cass wiping dishes and washing out nice linen dish towels as this girl was doing, and almost laughed aloud at the thought. Demeter with her languid airs, and well-polished crimson finger tips. Demeter with her too-red lips and her pearly complexion accentuated by faint blue shadows under her eyes. Why couldn't he have met a girl like this Daryl Devereaux before he ever saw Demeter Cass and her crowd? Before Daryl knew Harold.

He felt a sudden distaste for all that Demeter represented. He wished he had never involved himself in her social round. He recalled invitations ahead to which he was half pledged, which would involve him still further, and a wave of dislike arose in his heart. He wished he could stay forever in his present environment and not go back to the world of fashion and folly, of chasing the latest will-o'-the-wisp fad. Of course he had never done that. He had only stood on the outer edge and looked on, so far, and thought to lure the girl who had tried to fascinate him, back into a sane sensible path. But he recognized that from his position of looker-on it was only a step inside that clique to where he would be a part of it. This house party to which he had not gone had been in a sense the dividing line. A bid to it was equivalent to being accepted and sought after. Good for his business perhaps, but not so good for himself, for his inner self, the part of him that lived and moved and had a spiritual being.

If he had only known a girl like Daryl Devereaux when he first came to the city how different things would have been. But as he watched her he felt more and more that there couldn't be many girls like this one. And she was interested in that insufferable cad whose voice he had heard drunkenly on the telephone last night! He was sure she was. He had watched the shadow in her eyes all day. Well, he thought wistfully, he was glad he was having this little glimpse of a real Christmas with real folks, anyway. It had acted like a sort of mental bath, or a spiritual one, perhaps, to cleanse his soul from the mad whirl of follies toward which he might have been drifting. Perhaps his eyes were open now and he would know better how to make decisions. Perhaps the spell that Demeter Cass had been casting over him was broken by the vision of this other clear-eyed girl. Girls! For there were two of them, of course. He could see that the girl Ruth was lovely also, and he took pleasure in seeing her with his new friend Lance. What a couple they would make, interested in the same things, deeply devoted, each finding joy in the presence of the other! It somehow restored his faith in life and love and true simple living just to watch them. He was glad he had come. Even if he had not seen Daryl, even if she was entangled somehow with a person who had the power to bring sadness to her lovely eyes, he was glad he had come.

When the last dish was in its place, when Mother and Father had slipped away to their room for a bit of a Christmas nap, and Lance and Ruth were bent over some plans of their own for a little log cabin they meant to build for a summer home some time in the far sweet future, Alan looked at Daryl brightly and put out a comradely hand.

"Come on, let's go read my new book of poetry," he said. "I have a fancy for reading it the first time with you." He smiled and she gave an answering smile, and slipped her hand in his, letting him lead her over to one of the big chairs by the fireplace. Then he drew up another near by and brought the book.

"Now," he said, as he settled back to watch her, "read me the one you like the best. I'd like to start with that."

As he sat there watching the sweet face of this cultured lovely girl, listening to her pleasant voice as she read, noting her eyes light with appreciation of some of the beautiful thoughts she was reading, he tried to picture Demeter Cass reading poetry to him. He was not able to conjure up such a scene, with Demeter as the center. In his fancy he could hear her peals of laughter at the thought.

"Oh, Darling! *Poetry!* How Victorian! Just fancy anybody today stopping to read sweet stuff like that!"

He turned from the thought impatiently. Why did Demeter Cass have to intrude into every pleasant thing today?

They had a rare time for over an hour discussing the poems, Alan marveling at the clear logical mind of Daryl, enjoying every moment of their talk together.

Then Father and Mother Devereaux appeared with the coming of the dusk, looking like two fresh daisies, and the talk grew more general. The Christmas tree broke out in its lights again, and the fire was built up afresh.

"How about getting out a picture puzzle son?" suggested the old man. "I wouldn't mind taking a hand in one myself after I get done the milking."

Lance sprang up from his corner of the couch.

"I'm going to milk tonight, Dad," he said. "I was just going out. No, I'm all right. My ankle doesn't hurt at all now."

"And I'm going also—not that I'll be much help," laughed Alan, "but at least I can cultivate the acquaintance of Chrystobel. I really don't know many cows, and I think it would be a pleasant experience."

So the boys went out to the barn, and Daryl and Ruth got out two low tables, and arranged the lamps so the light would be good, and when the boys came back the place looked so cozy and pleasant that Alan's heart suddenly thrilled again with joy at being a part of this dear home for a time.

Lance went to the old chest of drawers in the dining room and got out a large puzzle which had been one of his Christmas gifts, and as he opened it and emptied the pieces out on one of the tables he said:

"The wind is changing, Dad. I think it will be clearing before morning. The snow is much lighter already."

Alan had a quick passing shade of sadness. When the storm cleared this pleasant interval would be over and he would have to move on. But he would not think of that. He would just enjoy every minute while it lasted.

So they settled down around the tables, turning over and sorting the colored bits of polished wood, and parceling them out, a color to a person.

Daryl was sitting next to Alan and all the blue sky was handed over to them. They worked away together, Daryl showing Alan how to hunt for outside edges, and how to tell by the grain of the wood which pieces would be top and which side. They talked about the quaint shapes into which the pieces were cut. Alan was new at them. He hadn't had much time for such things since the days of his childhood when picture puzzles were scarce and expensive.

"Am I to believe that this jumble of pieces will eventually become a picture?" he asked comically, gazing hopelessly at the clutter on the table.

"Of course," said Daryl enthusiastically. "It does look hopeless though, doesn't it? But you'll see it will come out beautifully when it is done. The name says it is a picture of Washington at Valley Forge. It seems just like the Bible."

Alan looked up in astonishment.

"Like the Bible? Well, that's one on me, young lady. Since when was Washington a Bible character?"

"Oh, I didn't mean that," giggled Daryl. "I mean that sometimes, at first reading, the Bible does seem like a jumble of unrelated writings, especially to an unbeliever. But if you believe it is the Word of God, and so have patience to go on and learn how to divide it and put it together, you soon see that each part fits into the rest without discord or contradiction and the whole presents a perfect portrait."

Alan had stopped working and was watching Daryl intently, obviously amazed.

"Well, that's about the most surprising statement I ever heard!" he said. "It's rather sweeping, too, and yet you speak with conviction. May I ask where you got this information?"

Lance glanced up quickly, alert to catch any note of scorn on his new friend's face, hoping it was not there. He was relieved to see only genuine interest and thoughtfulness in Alan's face.

"In the Bible itself, of course," said Daryl. "But not all by myself. We had a wonderful teacher before we went to college. And there are textbooks to help you study. I have one we studied if you would like to see it. But I do think that if a person went to the Bible patiently and believingly, he would soon be convinced, even without a teacher, that it is the Word of God."

"Yes, *believingly!*" said Lance suddenly, as he swung a

finished tree across the table and slid it into place in the sky Alan was working at, "that is the point, believingly!"

Alan looked up again astonished, noting that Lance evidently held the same view as his sister. Was it the Bible, then, that made these people so different from others he knew?

"Well, that sounds interesting to me," said Alan seriously. "I'd like to see that textbook sometime. It would be worth a great deal to me to know without a doubt what you seem to know."

Then suddenly he held up a little piece of puzzle and said half jokingly:

"Now, here, for instance, is a fish! Am I to suppose that this picture we are doing contains a portrait of Jonah entering the whale?"

They all laughed, but Daryl suddenly sobered.

"There!" she said, "that's just what I've been trying to tell you. You think that's a fish, but it's only the shape of a fish. See where it fits? Right there in that pink cloud at your left. It isn't a fish at all, it's just a part of the high light on a cloud. And that's just the way people make mistakes when they read the Bible. They pick a verse out from its context, and go out and say the Bible says so and so, and that that is a contradiction of something else it says. But if you keep the verse in its setting, and compare it with others, you see what it really did mean. Look at your fish now in its own place. See! The fish itself, though still a fish, is no longer important as a fish. It is lost sight of as you look at the picture as a whole."

"Well, that's astonishing!" said Alan, staring at the fish which had taken its place in a cloud.

"Well, if this picture we're doing is going to turn out to be a picture of George Washington, of whom then is the Bible a portrait?"

He asked the question almost idly, hardly expecting a definite answer.

"The Lord Jesus Christ!" answered Daryl reverently, and a little hush fell on the group.

"Wonderful!" said the young man gravely. "I never thought of the Bible as that."

After an instant Daryl went on quietly:

"And it is marvelous how every story and even every Jewish sacrifice and ceremony is needed to make it a complete picture of Him! Take that incident of Jonah for instance. Did you know that it is referred to by Christ in the New Testament, and used to present a picture of His death and resurrection? He said that no sign that He was the Messiah would be given to unbelievers except the sign of Jonah. For just as Jonah was three days and three nights in the whale so He would be three days and nights in the earth."

Daryl stopped breathless, suddenly embarrassed that she had done so much of the talking. But Alan kept on with questions for sometime, Daryl giving keen answers that amazed him.

"Well, perhaps I begin to see," he said at last, holding up two small pieces of the puzzle. "Here for instance are a cat and a fiddle. I in my uninstructed state would naturally suppose that our whole picture was to illustrate 'Hey-diddle-diddle, the cat and the fiddle,' and I would immediately begin to look around for a cow and a moon to finish it with; but since according to you the things in the Bible that sound like nonsense to the uninitiated are heavenly truths, I begin to grasp the idea, and behold! Look here!"

He fitted the fiddle neatly into a delicate green tree, and found a place for his cat right in the middle of another cloud.

"An A plus for you, Johnny, you're learning fast!" laughed Daryl.

"It's due to my excellent teaching!" Alan bowed dramatically.

They all laughed heartily with Alan, but he soon grew serious again.

"Go on, please! I want to hear more," he said.

"Oh, you should ask my brother about it," said Daryl, suddenly flushing consciously as she realized that the room was very still, and everybody had stopped talking but herself and Alan. "Lance has been to a wonderful seminary where they make a specialty of studying these things. He can tell you all about it much better than I can."

Alan looked at Lance surprised.

"You don't say! Are you getting ready to be a clergyman, Lance?"

Lance looked up smiling.

"Oh, no," he said, "I'm just getting ready to be a Christian farmer, like Dad. But I want to be able to give my Christian testimony in the very best way, and I think every Christian should understand his Bible, and be ready to tell anyone how to be saved."

"But he does preach, though," said Ruth shyly, looking at Lance with proud eyes. "He preaches in the mission in Collamer every Sunday night."

"Just talk," said Lance crisply. "Say, you folks are getting your sky done in great shape, aren't you?"

"I want to hear you," said Alan studying the strong young face across the table from him. "I'm coming to hear you soon. And I want to talk with you more about this Bible. It sounds interesting."

"It is," said Lance quickly, "the most interesting study in the world. Say, Daryl, how about a little food? Weren't there some doughnuts? I seem to forget all about that turkey we had this afternoon."

"Yes, I'll get some," said Daryl, getting up, and Alan promptly arose to follow her.

"Get some apples too," called Mother Devereaux. "And, Father, where are your butternuts?"

"Yes, I'll get those. I cracked a lot of them yesterday,"

and he too arose and went to find his big wooden bowl of butternuts.

Daryl filled a platter with big sugary doughnuts and got out some plates and napkins.

"The apples are down cellar. I won't be a minute," she explained to Alan. "You can carry in the plates."

"Oh, but I'm coming down cellar with you. I'm sure I can get the apples if you will tell me where to find them," and he smilingly possessed himself of the willow basket she had picked up from the pantry shelf.

Daryl snapped the cellar light on and they went down into the wide clean space that was as tidy and uncluttered as if it were a parlor. Alan saw the rows of shelves filled with canned fruit and vegetables, the bin of potatoes, and barrels of apples, Northern Spy, Grimes Golden, Baldwin. Daryl pointed them all out.

"Why, you could stand a regular siege if you had to, with all these stores," he said, looking about him in admiration. "I certainly picked my place to get storm-stayed!"

Daryl smiled up at him happily, and for the moment the shadow seemed to be gone from her eyes. She was enjoying the evening as much as he was! A gladness went through him that was new and pleasant.

They had filled their basket and were turning to go back to the foot of the stairs, when Father Devereaux, returning through the dim kitchen, noticed the crack of light from the half open cellar door, and stopped in passing to snap it off, thinking somebody had forgotten it.

"Oh!" giggled Daryl. "They don't know we're down here! Wait, I'll turn it on again. There's a switch at the foot of the stairs. Come, I'll guide you."

She caught his hand and turned swiftly to take a short cut to the stairs, forgetting that Lance the day before had brought down a crate of oranges just arrived from Florida, and set them across a couple of substantial beams to keep them from contact with the floor. Suddenly she pitched forward, her hands outspread widely. And Alan, his apples rolling in every direction, groped wildly for her and lifted her in his arms, unconsciously drawing her close, and putting his face down to hers.

"Oh, my dear!" he said, and knew not what he had said. "Are you hurt?"

Daryl, startled and shaken, could scarcely get her breath to reply. So there he stood in the dark with her in his arms, suddenly conscious that she was very sweet and precious.

"Are you hurt?" he asked again more anxiously, and his lips touched her forehead. He felt her soft hair in his face, and the dearness of it thrilled him.

And Daryl, hearing that word in her ear, "my dear!" lay still in wonder for just an instant, filled with a sweet ecstasy. It seemed that something wonderful, something holy and beautiful, had come upon them and put both their hearts in a joyous tumult. For just that little space of time while the darkness lasted it seemed that heaven had come down to them. As if they scarcely dared breathe lest they would interrupt the precious moment.

Then suddenly the shades of two voices on the telephone swept harshly into their consciousness, the echoes of Demeter Cass' possessive demands, and that drunken voice calling out "Darling!"

And just then Father Devereaux, going into the living room with his butternuts, discovered their absence and hastened back to correct his error by snapping on the light.

The lamp just over their heads blazed forth garishly, even as those ghostly voices on the wire rang in their ears, and they came to themselves suddenly.

Daryl gave a little gasp and tried to laugh.

"Oh, I'm quite all right," she burbled.

He set her down gently, slowly, reluctant to give her up, his arm still lingering about her supportingly.

"You are sure?" he said, and looked at her earnestly. He had a sudden longing to fold her in his arms again and lay his lips upon hers. Instead he stooped and began to pick up the apples. And Daryl helped too. Once or twice they reached for the same apple there in the shadows of the cellar floor, and their hands touched. They laughed like children as they scrambled after one that rolled away from before their feet, till at last they had them all and started for the stairs, Alan reaching for her hand and holding it in a warm clasp.

"I'll have to hold on to you," he laughed. "I can't have you falling again."

She let her hand lie in his for the moment till they reached the stairs and went up slowly, keeping step. Daryl reproached herself for the thrill that his touch gave her. He meant nothing by it of course but common courtesy. He was just solicitous because she had fallen, as any gentleman would have been, and that "Oh, my dear!" was just a frightened exclamation when he thought she was really hurt. It didn't mean a thing! Look at the way people called each other darling today when they were just common acquaintances. What was she to make so much of all this? She, who had looked forward to Harold's coming, to fancy things like this! Her nerves had been shaken, that was all, by that sharp blow across her shins when she fell. It had unnerved her, made her hysterical. It was nothing more of course. Alan Monteith belonged to Demeter Cass, or at least her voice had made it seem that way; and she at least for the present, was somewhat obligated to be considering Harold Warner and her relation to him. This sweet strange thing that had come to her down there in the cellar was a figment of her excited imagination. It hadn't happened! It was only in her thought. It wasn't real at all, and she would not think of it again. Like an evil thought she would stamp it out and put it from her.

They arrived at the head of the stairs, still hand in hand. Daryl snapped the light out and closed the door behind them. Then Alan turned and looked frankly in her eyes, as if he was challenging her to recognize what had just come to them. After that deep look he softly pressed her fingers, then, bearing the apples, he followed her into the living room.

Daryl's cheeks were bright, and her eyes a little starry in spite of her best efforts. She meant to take herself in hand at once, but she could not quickly put away the memory of those strong fingers clasping hers.

Daryl tried to cover her tumult with joking her father for turning the light out on them, and they settled down to their picture puzzle again, everybody eating apples and nuts and doughnuts.

But Alan as he worked silently was casting furtive glances at Daryl, noticing the lovely color in her cheeks and the soft hair disarranged over her forehead, framing her face so sweetly.

And then, suddenly, the doorbell pealed forth in several loud rings, one upon the other, and the knocker began to clatter as if the visitor couldn't depend upon just one summons.

"Who in the world?" said Daryl, starting up and looking wildly toward the door, her face suddenly growing white. "At this time of night!"

"That's probably Warner!" said Lance, rising and giving his sister a quick searching look. "He's done well if he's gotten here through all this tempest!" His tone was like one who was doing his best to give the devil his due.

But a pall fell upon the little company that had been so happy together until this moment, and they sat back from the table and waited while Lance went to the door.

II

BUT it was not the debonair Harold whom Lance brought in out of the cold outside world. It was only a farmer boy who lived on a neighboring farm, and worked winters in Collamer. He came stamping and puffing in, bringing the breath of the storm with him, and bearing an enormous box in his arms that obviously came from a florist's.

"There she is!" he exclaimed as he handed it over to Lance. "Flowers fer your sister! I didn't know one time as I was goin' ta make it. There was a drift in the way mighty near as high as my head, and I didn't see as any doggone flowers was wuth my bargin' inta it, but I mosied around an' found a place where the wind had swep' it clear, and I managed it; but say, ef I had ta do it over again I would tell Mr. Blaine 'nothing' doin'.' Course he offered me two bucks to bring 'em, an' course it was right on my way home, but it was hard enough navigatin' myself, 'thout carryin' a great enormous baby like that along! Blaine he said the man what ordered 'em made him promise he'd get 'em here afore the day was done, an' he'd been tryin' all day ta find somebody would tackle 'em, till I come along, so I'm glad I got 'em here at last, even though I am most froze."

They brought him up to the fire and fed him. Mother Devereaux made him a turkey sandwich and Daryl hurried out to make hot coffee. They dried his mittens and Father Devereaux suggested he would better stay there all night.

"That ud be okay with me ef it want fer my mother. She's alone over there on the farm an' she ain't sa well, an' I ain't sa sure she's got 'nough wood cut ta keep her good an' warm all night. Guess I better toddle on. Thanks jus' the same! But say, ain't ya goin' ta open up them babies, after I brung 'em all this way?"

Daryl's face suddenly flamed but she tried to smile.

"Why, of course, Bud," she said, "and you shall have the first one. Ruth, you open them, won't you, while I run up and get Bud a dry pair of socks. Those he has on are steaming. He'll freeze his feet if he goes out with wet socks on," and she turned and hurried upstairs.

Now what did she do that for? Alan pondered it as he watched Ruth shyly cutting the strings and opening up the great red Christmas roses. They were wonderful roses. There was no question of that. They exclaimed over them as Daryl came back with the socks.

"See, Daryl, aren't they wonderful? And to come out of a storm like that and not be hurt! Whoever picked those out has good taste."

"Yes," said Daryl coolly, "Mr. Blaine has wonderful taste in roses!"

"Yes," said Bud, taking another large sugary bite of doughnut, "Blaine said the fella ordered pink; he said he was very pertickiler they should be pink, but he didn't have none left. Anyhow he figgered red was more 'propriate fer Christmas, an' he wasn't goin' ta lose the ten bucks the fella promised ef he got um here afore the day was over, so he sent these. I guess you like 'em just as good, dontcha?"

"Yes, indeed! *Better!*" said Daryl enthusiastically. "Now, Bud, put these warm stockings on. And don't you want to telephone your mother to say you are coming?"

"Sure thing, ef ya don't mind."

"Yes, and when you get home you call us just so we'll know you're all right!" said Father Devereaux.

"Okay," said Bud cheerfully.

Daryl snatched up a handful of the lovely rosebuds, and a sheet of the green wax paper, wrapping them hastily.

"Here, Bud," she said gaily, "if anybody deserves some of these flowers you do. Take them home to your mother."

And that was all the attention she paid to the wonderful roses that had come to her through the storm!

Bud grinned and buttoned them inside his coat and started out again.

The moon was coming out from behind a weak cloud as Lance opened the outside door for Bud. There seemed to be only a few flakes skimming down the silver night. The backbone of the storm was broken!

Daryl had gone back to the picture puzzle with her back turned to the roses as they lay open in their box on the big table near the tree.

They sat down to the picture and began to speculate as to how soon the roads would be passable after the snow ceased. They spoke of Bud and his widowed mother, and his cheerful willingness to breast the storm again for her sake.

"But aren't you going to put your flowers in water?" asked Ruth apprehensively.

"Oh, I guess I'll just leave them in their box tonight," said Daryl. "They've stood so much, I guess they'll be all right."

She had cast the little envelope containing the card on the table after a mere glance. Alan wondered what this indifference meant. Lance looked at her now and then and wondered also. After all, Harold *had sent* the flowers. He had *tried* to do something nice! Lance was always fair to everybody.

They finished the picture and stood together admiring it. Then Ruth turned to the piano and began to play "Silent Night, Holy Night," and they all gathered around and sang Christmas carols for a while, but still the roses lay in their open box on the table unnoticed. They were there yet when Daryl went upstairs with Ruth, and after all it was Mother Devereaux who went to them at last, bent her head to get a lovely breath from their crimson muskiness, folded them softly in their wax wrapping and took the box into the cool pantry for the night.

Alan went to the quiet guest room and lay watching the flicker of the fire on the wall, and thinking. What a day he had had! What a Christmas! Strange how he had started out the day before wishing for a real Christmas and then had driven straight into one, the best ever! There hadn't been a minute all day when it had not been delightful. He thought it over from the early morning. The tree and the stockings, and the dear friendliness that had taken him right in as if he were really one of them. He was even glad for the terrible experience of the night before that had showed him the strong true dependability, the generous heartiness of the young man whom he was going to be so proud to call his friend!

He let his thoughts hover over the high spots of the day, little things that had touched his heart, a word of Mother Devereaux's, the heartiness in Father Devereaux's voice, the twinkle in Lance's eyes when he got off some comical phrase, the shy look of Ruth as she watched Lance with loving pride,—and then, the loveliness of Daryl!

He came to that last because he was fighting shy of the memory of that moment down cellar when he had had such a revelation of himself, such a vision of the dearness of the girl he had held for an instant! Since those beastly roses arrived he had been afraid even to think of it, lest somehow the glory of that moment would shine from his face and be seen. And he knew it was something that must never be seen. The fact that the roses had arrived almost as soon as they got upstairs again, was a sign that he ought not to harbor any thoughts about that girl in his heart. She belonged to another man! Hadn't Lance as much as said they were engaged? Well, he had implied that. Hadn't he himself seen the shadow in her eyes? Hadn't he heard her eager voice when she talked over the telephone? He wasn't worthy of her, of course, a fellow that would disappoint her for any boss' party, Christmas too, and then telephone her when he was *drunk!* Even drunken men had a little sense.

And it wasn't in the least likely that his being drunk would permanently separate them. Girls were such fools. They always believed a man when he promised he wouldn't drink! Of course she was angry now! He could tell by her voice last night that she had been shocked, and the shock hadn't worn off. Even the roses hadn't made her forget that thick incoherent speech! But it would pass. The roses would eventually get in their work, as the rascal had known they would. And later when it was convenient, he would arrive and call her darling a few times, and it would all be healed! His blood boiled as he thought it over. A girl like that! And he tried to forget how it had thrilled him when he held her in his arms. It had been almost as if he held an angel there! Wonderful! That delicate sweet child, with her lovely eyes, to be tied up to a drunken fool! How did things like that come about? How could a rare girl like that be deceived and give her heart to such a man, a trifler?

Then it came to him to wonder if he had not been on the verge of doing something of the same sort himself with Demeter Cass? Yet he was half startled to realize that the thought of Demeter and the perplexing problems she had hinted at over the telephone had grown strangely dim and meaningless since afternoon.

Somehow he could look at his own case in a very cool-headed way tonight. He had never seen things quite so clearly, except the night when he had first met Demeter at a dinner at the home of one of his clients, and had come home and dreamed his mother came and put her cool hand on his forehead and said quietly: "Not that girl, my son! She is not for you!" And he had waked and thought it over, and decided to have nothing more to do with her. But Demeter Cass, or Fate, had willed otherwise, and more and more he had been drawn into situations where he had to meet her, until he had actually started for that house party yesterday with the idea of considering whether he wouldn't ask her to share his life! Well, why didn't he feel that way tonight? Why was it that he had had even a passing annoyance when she had interrupted the program at dinner time by insisting on a long telephone conversation when he wanted to get back to the table? Was it just because he was hungry? Why was it that he had laid aside all idea of going to that house party even tomorrow, supposing it should clear and the roads be passable? He had to admit to himself that he really did not want to go now. And why was that? Was it because of that moment in the cellar when he had held that precious child in his arms, and heaven's gate seemed to open just a tiny bit and let out some of its ecstasy?

Because if it was that it would be better for him to get right up now and wade out in that snow and go and find Demeter Cass than to let any such notions get into his head about a girl who was promised to another man!

Of course it was all wrong for a girl like that to marry a man who wasn't worthy of her, and when he thought of it it was like stabbing a sword into his heart and twisting it in the wound. Nevertheless it was not for him to interfere between even an unworthy man and his girl! He despised men who did that. He did not care to win even heaven for himself at the expense of another, even if the other were unworthy.

And who was he to count himself worthy of her? Oh,

he didn't drink, of course, he didn't do a lot of the things that men of the world did today. He had his mother to thank for that! But did that make him any more worthy of a girl like Daryl? No, his honesty told him promptly that he was as much of another world from hers as this Harold who seemed to have won her. Perhaps even Harold might be a nominal churchman. There were such, outwardly observing Christian forms but under testing weak to resist temptations. If that was so she would forgive and forgive and go on loving him.

But as far as the atmosphere of her life was concerned he himself was no more fit to mate with her than the other man. What did he know of her Bible and her God?

He thought of the atmosphere of reverence that pervaded her home. The background of sanctity that seemed to set the keynote for everything that was said and done. Not that he had been irreverent toward God and the Bible. He had simply not thought of them at all. They hadn't been a factor with which to be reckoned. He believed in a God in a way, because he knew his mother had done so, but how active her belief had been he did not know. She left him when he was barely out of his childhood, and the years of school life had not helped to deepen any impression of religion she might have left him. But he hadn't been arrogant toward God, nor actively hostile to religion. He had even gone to church on occasion when he was in the company of those who did. But he just had not had time for anything outside his scheduled plan for his life, and that schedule had been preparing himself to be a success in his chosen profession, and getting to himself as much happiness as was consistent with that ambition. The fact that his idea of happiness had been fairly sane and clean, and did not include many of the things that the world today professed to enjoy, did not blind his eyes to the difference between his standards and those of the Devereaux family. He knew that even if Daryl were free, he was not the ideal man who ought to be her companion through life. But—couldn't he change? Couldn't he become the kind of man she could enjoy? That would involve something deeper than perhaps he now understood, but it seemed well worth looking into. On the other hand, was he even as much fitted to be a mate for Demeter Cass? Looking squarely into the eyes of truth there in the middle of the night he was forced to admit that her background was as much alien to his own as this Christian household where he was now a guest. The daily round of the Demeter Cass crowd was not in the least to his taste. How had he supposed he could ever bind himself to a program of eating and drinking and making merry in ribald play. He wouldn't enjoy that. How then had he dared consider Demeter as the one to be closer to him than anyone else in the world? Was it that he wanted her merely to help him get on into the success he coveted, wanted to wear her as his, like a ring upon his finger, that the world might see him a success as it counted success? Or had he in his secret heart hoped that he might be able to change her, to bring her to desire the things he desired, a quiet home and family, little children's voices, and something to come back to from the world of work?

But insistently, no matter how long he put it off, the thought of Daryl kept coming back, and he knew he had to face that brief startling revelation of himself and learn exactly what it was going to mean in his life. Strange he had to trail off here in the snow, face death, and spend Christmas, to find the only girl who ever really stirred his heart this way. And it was just his luck to find her practically pledged to another!

Over and over he had to tell himself that he must stop thinking about her, must wipe out the memory of that moment when he held her close in his arms and felt that he would like to hold her so forever. He must forget it or all self-respect would be gone. But just as soon as he turned over, resolved to go to sleep, back would come the thought of her so close to his heart, her hair touching his face, her breath upon his cheek, and thrill him anew.

"I am a fool!" he said wearily, staring into the quietness of the room. The fire had died down, the snow outside had ceased to fall, and tomorrow would be another day. The roads would clear up and he would have to go home. Perhaps he would never see her again! And that fellow Harold would hang around, likely, and marry her some day, and make her miserable ever after. Why hadn't he found her first? He'd be willing to devote his whole life to trying to make her happy. He'd even be willing to give up his worldly ambitions if he could have a home with her in it!

He tried telling himself that this was glamour, that he had known her but a day, and it was ridiculous for him to feel as if he had lost the whole universe and life were not worth living. This was the middle of the night and he had eaten a huge piece of mince pie the last thing before he went to bed. That was all it was of course. Things would be sane again in the morning.

Ruth was asleep long before Daryl, though Daryl lay tense and still, not stirring. The developments of the day seemed to sweep over her as if she were experiencing them all over again. Slowly she went step by step from one thing to another, taking note of little things she had not had time to take in thoroughly while they were happening, seeing them now in the light of later happenings. Until she came fully upon that moment when Alan had looked into her eyes in the kitchen after they had come up from the cellar. There had been something in his look that called to her, something that her heart had leaped up and answered in spite of all her admonitions to the contrary. And it was this thing that she was really set to examine before she slept. It was as if by that look he had said to her: "You and I have suddenly been set apart from others by something deep and sweet and breath-taking. What are we going to do about it?" That was what she had to face and answer before she slept.

Over and over she had to go, trying to explain away that ecstasy that had come to her as he picked her up in his arms and held her for that instant. Again and again she told herself that it had not happened at all, that she would not recognize it, only to feel anew the thrill of joy at thought of this stranger whom she had known but a day.

Perhaps her struggles were made even worse by the arrival of those Christmas roses from the recalcitrant Harold. Minute by minute she tried to rouse a hope that Harold would come tomorrow and be able to explain it all away and make things right between them. But somehow joy had departed from that thought. She blamed herself and shed a few silent tears at her own state of mind. Then for the first time she had a chance to really face what Harold had done; to shudder over his drunken voice as he talked to her over the telephone, to recall his very words and phrases, and to feel the hot waves of mortification and despair and shame pouring over her face at thought of it. Harold, to whom she had imputed nothing but strength and fineness and honor. Harold, who had promised her he would never touch another drop of liquor if that was her desire, that he didn't care for it anyway. She remembered his light airy promise: "Certainly, sweetheart, if that will be any comfort to you, I'll give it up. I never cared in the least about drinking, only did it because everybody I knew drank. No, it won't be the slightest trouble for me to go on the water wagon. Of course I think you're a bit fanatical about it, but anybody as lovely as you are has a right to a few whims and fancies. But just to prove it's nothing to me, I'll never drink again!"

How easily she had believed him—because she wanted to so much. She saw that now. He had seemed so noble and self-sacrificing to her when he promised so easily. It had only seemed to prove to her how much he cared for her. And he hadn't drank since! Four months ago! Or—*had* he? How did she know? He had taken care that she shouldn't see him drinking anyway. The few times that he had taken her out among his friends where they were drinking he had waved the waiter away with a gay hand and said comically, quite openly, where all could hear him: "No, I'm on the water wagon!" And they had laughed at him, but he hadn't seemed to mind. Now, she wondered—! Were they only laughing *with* him *at her?* And again the blood rolled hotly over her weary young face as she lay there in the dark and faced the possibilities ahead of her.

But at least while she was thinking about Harold she was not thinking about this interesting stranger, who did not belong to her in any sense, and whom she just must not think about nor be interested in. It was all her foolish imagination anyway. Likely he hadn't noticed anything. She would consider it that and just go on facing her own problems. She *must!* What a horrible mess this Christmas was making of itself! When she had thought it was going to be so wonderful! And yet, suppose the stranger had not come? How desolate it would have been, with Harold acting that way!

And suddenly all quietly, the tears poured down upon her pillow! Oh, God, why couldn't Harold have been all right? Why did he have to go off with another crowd? He didn't even have the grace to blame it on the storm. He had gone still farther than the distance to Collamer.

But at last she slept, worn out with trying to straighten out her little world.

They all slept late that morning, the world was so still and white outside, so well padded from all sounds. Even the dogs on the next farm seemed to have their howling voices muted, or perhaps the world was too well insulated with snow to let the sound travel properly.

Father and Mother Devereaux wakened first, and Father Devereaux stole a march on Lance and got the milking done, and quite a space cleared from the side porch to the garage, before Lance awoke.

The sun was shining brightly with such a blazing glory that it was amazing when Daryl opened her eyes and found Ruth nearly dressed. Somehow the perplexities of the night had vanished and hope stood there smiling. It was morning, the storm had ceased, the sun was shining, and Christmas was still here. No telling what delightful thing might happen!

She sprang up and began to dress hastily, putting on a hand-knit dress of bright cherry color that she had knit herself. It was not new, but it went on quickly and always looked well. It gave her somewhat wan cheeks a little reflected color and the tiny line of black edge around the neck and cuffs and pockets set her off to advantage, although she didn't even know it. She was too intent upon getting down to help her mother with the breakfast.

Ruth came down with her, all in dark blue with a little trimming of squirrel fur around the neck and sleeves. Alan thought how nice both girls looked as he came out to breakfast at the call of the bell, and thrilled again at sight of the girl he had resolved last night not to think any more about. What lovely girls they were! What made them so different from the girls among whom he had been mingling recently? He did not realize before what a difference make-up made in the character of a face. And yet there was no lack of loveliness here without it. He had a passing wonder how Demeter Cass would look without her lipstick? Did she have a clean healthy complexion of her own underneath all the decoration? One ought to be able the better to discern the character of a girl by seeing her without an artificial mask.

There were buckwheat cakes and sausage for breakfast and Alan felt he had never tasted anything quite so delectable in his life. Then the three men hurried out to deal with the snow.

"I've phoned down for some more snow shovels," said Lance as he left, with a grin for the girls. "Bill Gates will bring them when he gets up with the plow sometime this morning. When they come, you girls can come out and help if you want to."

"You needn't think we are going to wait for shovels," said Ruth with a toss of her head. "There are plenty of brooms, aren't there? Well, when we get these dishes done we'll be out and show you what the broom brigade can do. You break down the big drifts and we'll do the fine fancy work on the walks."

So they went out into the wonder-world of whiteness and spent two gorgeous hours doing real hard work in the snow. And it was no child's play either, for the snow had packed itself firmly down and settled into impenetrable walls.

Alan worked away with an old long-handled coal shovel, and Lance improvised a snow shovel from boards hastily nailed together. They made the father take the only real snow shovel they had.

"After the snowplow goes through I'll take the car and ramble up the road and retrieve the shovels we left at the foot of the mountain," said Lance, as he plodded on with his unhandy tool.

By the time the snowplow came through they had the front path and sidewalk cleared, and the driveway to the garage in fairly passable state. But they seized on the two new shovels Bill Gates brought with him and went to work again with renewed vigor.

They had paused in their actual work for a little to make an enormous snowman at one side of the path, with a clothes prop for arms. They dressed him in an old red sweater, and put a cap on his head, then took time to engage in a game of snowballing. Suddenly the sound of sleigh bells smote the air gaily, and looking up in astonishment they beheld coming down the road an old-time double sleigh packed with people wrapped to the eyebrows with handsome furs. The fact that the gaily caparisoned horses were only farm horses and not used to all this hilarity did not detract from the impression of the equipage. There were red paper Christmas bells tossing gaily on the ancient harness as well as a string of real silver bells, and they came on as majestically as a circus parade and drew up with a flourish before the Devereaux house.

"Do you know where a family by the name of Devereaux lives?" asked a supercilious passenger from the back seat, peering condescendingly out under golden lashes from her gorgeous furs.

Just then Alan Monteith came around the house with a broom in his hand and a pair of red mittens that Mother Devereaux had sent out for the snow man. He stalked gravely over and adjusted the additions to the effigy before he turned to see what had appeared in the road. Then he suddenly heard a familiar voice and turned sharply, seeing the horses and sleigh for the first time.

"Oh, for heaven's sake, Alan! Is that really you? What on earth are you doing? Hurry up and brush the snow off and get in! We've come to rescue you. Where is your luggage? Get it quick and make it snappy! We're half starved and want to get back to lunch!"

Alan Monteith stood still for a full second and stared till he had identified Demeter Cass and some of her friends, and a strange guilty feeling came to him as if somebody had caught him stealing, as if it was all up with him now.

The other three young people stood and stared also, blinking at the sudden appearance of the strangers.

Daryl recognized the voice at once as the one that had come over the telephone so petulantly. So that was the girl that would have it appear that she owned Alan Monteith!

Daryl had almost forgotten her fears of the midnight watch. They had had such a good time out in the snow, like a lot of children, throwing snow in each other's faces, trying to take each other unaware, doing real work at making paths. Alan was as good fun as if she had known him always. And now this!

"Gosh!" said Lance in dismay to Ruth who was never far from his steps. "Now I suppose this is the end of our good times! Can you beat it? A lot of high-hats!"

"For heaven's sake, Alan," called the imperious voice of Demeter Cass again, "this is a rescue party come to take you off your desert island. Don't you know a rescue party when you see one?"

Then Alan grinned and called back jovially:

"But suppose I don't want to be rescued? What then?"

ALAN came forward then genially, pulling off the red woolen cap that Daryl had hunted out for him, and greeting them all in his free friendly way. The hearts of his three erstwhile companions sank as they watched him.

"For goodness' sake, he's going to fall for it," said Lance under his breath. "He's just lapping it up!"

"I don't see that he is," defended Ruth. "He has to be polite, you know. Didn't you hear what he just said, 'Suppose I don't *want* to be rescued'?"

"Oh, that's a lot of hooey! You watch! You'll see him sailing off with them in about three minutes. That'll be the end of *him!* That's tough! I thought he was going to be different."

"Wait a little," said Ruth wisely. "Maybe not!"

Then they heard Alan's voice loud and clear ringing out:

"But you'll come in and get warm before you go. I'm sure my friends would want you to. Folks!" and he turned back to the three standing in a dismayed huddle halfway up the walk, just as if they were his own family. "Lance, Daryl, Ruth, come on and meet these people! Tell them to come in and get warm before they go back!"

The three thus adjured had nothing to do but come forward, although there was nothing they desired so little to do.

Alan made the introductions gracefully, his red cap in his hand, his hair standing on end in curly confusion, his garments powdered thoroughly with snow. He still held the snowman's broom in his hand.

The introductions were acknowledged coolly on both sides, the two groups eying each other hostilely. Then Demeter took the stage.

"Alan, what a sight you are! Hurry and get your things and we'll get you back to civilization again!"

"Nothing doing, Demeter," said Alan. "I thought I told you yesterday that I couldn't make it this time."

"But that's absurd! You couldn't make it! And then I come here and find you out making a snowman like a child!"

"Well, that's an innocent enough employment, isn't it, in between other things?"

"Other things? What other things, for instance?" and Demeter's eyes went sharply, contemptuously, around the group in the snow.

"Well, several things," said Alan sweetly. "You might not understand, you know!"

Demeter's eyes narrowed as she studied him.

"Come, aren't you all coming in to get warm?" said Alan, looking toward Lance hopefully.

"Yes, come in," said Lance eagerly, now that he saw the attitude Alan was taking.

"Why, certainly, come in," said Daryl graciously, rising suddenly to the occasion. Who was this arrogant creature anyway that she should stand in awe of her? They certainly owed it to Alan to welcome his friends. She smiled, and her rare dimple flitted into sight and out again. Daryl hadn't any idea how charming she was with that high color in her cheeks from the exercise, her brown curls blown wildly about her shapely head, and her eyes starry. Demeter eyed her speculatively, and licked her lips with the tip of her tongue. It seemed to Daryl there were yellow lights in her strange green eyes under her golden lashes.

Then suddenly a look of determination came into her face.

"Why, of course I'm coming in," said Demeter. "I'm coming in and pack your things for you, and while I do it we are going to talk. I told you, you know, that I had some very important business to consult you about, Alan."

"Yes?" he said with a courteous lifting of his eyebrows as he helped to pull her out from the fur wrappings, "and I told you, lady, that I was on vacation, having the time of my life, and we would transact the business in my office after we got back to the city. But come on in and get warm!"

But Daryl had turned and fled into the house by the back way, and when Alan and his troop of guests finally arrived at the front porch Daryl stood within to open the door. In that brief time she had slid out of the skiing costume and donned her red dress, and she stood there in as dainty array as any of that pampered company could boast, her hair rippling smoothly back from the two or three strokes she had given it as she passed the mirror in the hall.

They trooped in staring around them as if they were sightseers in a foreign land, having left what good manners they had at home. But Mrs. Devereaux was just inside the door also, and met them with a graciousness that surprised them. Nevertheless they swarmed around the room and examined everything, conversing freely about them among each other. They went to the Christmas tree and took ornaments off, declaring they were going to take them home for souvenirs; and they helped themselves to Alan's big box of candy that he had just remembered and brought out that morning; and then they stood around and shouted at Alan to hurry, that they had to get back.

Steadily Alan refused to go, and only grinned when Demeter demanded to know where his room was, insisting she would pack for him.

At last Demeter drew Alan aside into the hall, back by the telephone behind the stairs. Daryl had gone upstairs to get something for her mother and coming down heard their voices, Demeter's most excited:

"Really, Alan, you are acting perfectly absurd about this. You've simply *got* to come back with us at once! It is most important! What do you suppose I've turned heaven and earth to get this team and come after you for, if it was only a matter of social contacts? It's business of the most imperative type! It involves large sums of money, and means a lot to you and me both!"

"Look here, Demeter, I wish you would tell me exactly what you mean? I'm tired of this hinting around. If it is business it will keep till I get back to the city, and I certainly am not involved personally with any very large sums of money. You might as well speak out and tell me in a few words what it is all about. This speaking in mysteries doesn't get us anywhere."

"I can't tell you here!" she said sharply. "I must be where no one can overhear. Besides, it's a long story, and you wouldn't understand unless you heard the whole."

"But what is the nature of this thing that is so important? You can surely tell me that. And why does whatever it is have to be transacted during a holiday at Wyndringham's house party?"

"Because the count is there."

"Well, what on earth has he got to do with it? If the count wants to see me on business can't he come to my office in the city? He surely would understand that a man does not want to do business while he is on a vacation. Demeter, you don't understand that this is holiday week, and there can't be any such pressing business. I really don't see my way clear to going up there."

"Alan, you are simply *impossible!* I thought you were a man and wanted to get on in this world. I thought you were my friend, and wanted to help me when I need advice and protection. And here you are acting like a great child! Staying around in a country house playing Christmas tree and hanging up your stocking with a lot of hicks!"

Daryl had come downstairs softly and slipped inside the living room door just behind the Christmas tree, reaching up to unfasten some trifling ornament that one of the unwelcome invaders was demanding as a souvenir, and though she had not tried to hear, Demeter's voice was most penetrating! All in the room could have heard if they had not been engaged in their own chatter with one another. Daryl's fingers fumbled with the glittering bauble and the frail thing slipped and went tinkling to the floor smashing in a thousand fragments. But Alan's voice came clear and stern:

"Will you kindly remember that you are speaking of some of the dearest friends I have in the world?" he said. "As for advice, you wouldn't take mine if I gave it, I'm sure, and I can't imagine Demeter Cass needing protection. If there were no other way I am sure you could prevail upon the same company who brought you here to take you to your home. But as far as I am concerned I have definitely decided that I cannot come up to the house party at this time."

There was silence for an instant, and Daryl, trying to reach another silver bubble on a higher branch, heard their footsteps coming toward the doorway where she stood. Then Demeter's voice, quite changed, full of distress and tender appeal for sympathy. Was it real, or just expert acting?

"Alan, why have you changed so? Why won't you come back among your own kind?"

They were standing just within the door frame now, and Daryl had slipped around on the other side of the tree. She could see them perfectly, and hear them too, although they apparently did not see her. Demeter was looking up earnestly into Alan's face and he was looking gravely, thoughtfully down into hers. His voice was very serious as he answered.

"I'm not so sure they are my own kind," he said.

The girl stared at him with wide contemptuous eyes:

"You want to get on and be a success in the world, don't you? You want to meet the right people who will help you rise quickly, and help you grow wealthy, don't you? You certainly don't think these people are the kind to help you to rise, do you?"

She cast a scornful look around the room.

"That depends on where I want to rise to," answered Alan quickly. And then almost sternly he added:

"You seem to forget that these people are my very dear friends. You call them farm people, but do you know that they are every one college graduates?"

"Oh," said Demeter, with a toss of her handsome head, "that doesn't mean a thing in the line you should take!"

Suddenly she brought out a gold cigarette case and lighted a cigarette, taking a long puff at it and watching him with her green eyes narrowly.

"I wouldn't!" said Alan sharply.

"You *wouldn't?*" said Demeter with a scornful laugh. "Why not?"

"Because Mrs. Devereaux won't like it, and you are a caller in her house. It isn't courteous."

"Oh, *yes?*" said Demeter with an amused lifting of her eyebrows. "What will she do about it?"

"We won't give her a chance to decide," he said, and suddenly he reached over and took the smoking cigarette from Demeter's surprised hold, opened the front door and flung it far out into the snow.

"Well, really!" said the young woman. "Just how did you figure out you had a right to do that?"

"I didn't have the right," he said without smiling. "I took it." And with that he walked across to the people in the living room and began to talk to the rest of the party who were wandering around helping themselves to candy and examining the books on the table. They seemed particularly astonished by an open Bible that Lance had left lying there when he went out to shovel snow.

"What a pretty binding!" said one girl picking the Bible up and feeling of its beautiful leather. "What is it?" She glanced at the heading. "Mercy! It's a Bible! I didn't know they did them up so artistically! What a waste!" and she dropped it as if it had burned her.

"A Bible!" screamed another girl. "That must be what's the matter with Alan, he's gone pious on us! Is that why you won't go back with us?" She turned in mockery to face him.

But Alan only smiled.

"I might consider that as a reason," he said.

Suddenly Demeter Cass whirled toward the door.

"Come on, folks! Let's go! No use to hang around any longer. Alan's completely daffy."

"I want you to know that I appreciate your coming over for me in that delightful sleigh," said Alan, courteous to the last, and including the whole visiting party in his smile. "I appreciate your thoughtfulness a lot, but I couldn't make my plans fit in this time!"

"I'll see you in town," called back Demeter as she marched down the path past the snow man. "At my apartment, please! I'll call you up. I hate offices!"

Alan did not reply. He closed his lips in a firm line and stood with his brows drawn in thought as they drove noisily away. But Daryl disappeared into the kitchen and made herself very busy for the next half-hour, helping to get the lunch on the table.

She could see Alan and Lance in the other room sitting together with the Bible in their hands. She wondered what they were discussing. How much of those quick answers had he meant when he replied to those impudent callers? Was he really interested to know more of the Bible, or was he just being courteous to Lance? But what concern of hers was it, anyway? She had done her witnessing to the faith that was in her, and that was all her responsibility in the matter. She wanted to like him, to believe in him, even though she might never see him any more after he went home. But after all he did belong to another world, in spite of all that he had said to that girl in the doorway. He was just talking, likely, to see what she would say. Maybe they had had a quarrel and that was why he hadn't gone with them to the house party.

Yet back in her heart without in the least realizing it, she was hugging the thought that he hadn't gone. He had *chosen to stay here!*

At the dinner table he apologized for staying.

"I suppose I ought to have taken myself out of your way when they came for me," he said ruefully, "but there were some things I did want to ask Lance before I left, and you all had been so very kind I didn't like to leave, not that way anyway. I wasn't in the mood for a house party, not of that sort. I find my sojourn with you has spoiled me for things of that sort. But you mustn't think I'm going to stay indefinitely with you. I called up the garage just before we went out shoveling, and they said my car ought to be ready late this afternoon, and they thought the roads between here and my city were pretty well broken. I ought to be able to get through tonight, part way at least, so I won't presume upon your kindness much longer."

"Where did you get that presuming business?" growled Lance. "Didn't we ask you to stay? Don't you know we *want* you? Don't you know our hearts were in our mouths when that outfit came barging along after you, for fear you would go and leave us?"

Then the whole family joined in with protests and told how glad they were he didn't leave them, and how of course they wouldn't think of letting him go that night, even if his car was finished, which they heartily hoped it wouldn't be, even if the roads were reported to be open again. He must certainly wait until it was surely safe. They would worry about him. He was one of them now, and whether he liked or not he couldn't get away from their friendship.

Then Alan grew eloquent in telling how much he hated to leave, and during the talk Daryl looked up with glowing cheeks and eyes that carried a sudden starry look, and said quietly that his being there for Christmas had made it a very happy time for them all. Alan's eyes met hers, and suddenly both their hearts went into a joyous tumult which neither of them could control.

All the rest of the day Alan kept watching Daryl, their eyes now and then meeting, each thinking that the other did not know that something strangely pleasant and happy and exciting was between them, something they had bidden be crushed, but which both were glad to know had not died in spite of their best efforts.

They went sledding in the afternoon when the dishes were done, on the old bob-sled, down the hill back of the barn, and all of them forgot the cares and perplexities of their young lives, and were wildly happy, cheeks tingling with the cold, eyes shining, hands clasping helping hands, strong arms holding on the swift beautiful way down the hill.

After the delicious supper which they all got together, just as if none of them were company at all, they had a little Bible study together before they did another picture puzzle.

And when the puzzle was put away Ruth sat down at the piano and Daryl brought her violin, and they had lovely music again. Alan, as he sat back in the comfortable chair, watching the lovely face of Daryl as she played her violin, thrilled anew at the charm of her. After all, that

Harold person hadn't turned up all day, and his roses hadn't been in evidence. They seemed to have forgotten them completely. Was he so much to her as they had made him feel?

And then, right in the midst of the lovely strains of the most exquisite part of the Messiah, there came a loud knocking on the front door, a screaming of the doorbell and a thumping with the brass knocker. The music stopped suddenly, while they gave startled looks at one another, and came swiftly back to earth, considering what possibility was before them now? Daryl's first thought was that Demeter Cass had come back to get Alan, and that this time she would succeed in carrying him away from them.

But it was Father Devereaux, grave and sweet, who went to the door and ushered in the handsome renegade, Harold Warner.

He came frowning into the room as if they were the recalcitrant ones, and glowered around upon them, selecting Daryl out of the group.

"Hello, folks," he said to them all casually, while looking straight at his girl. "I couldn't get here sooner, Daryl, but I've come after you now! Hurry up and get your togs on! I've got a sleigh out here and I'm taking you to a dance. It's swell. Get on your best bib and tucker and be snappy about it! It's miles away, and I don't want to miss anything."

It was Ruth who slipped out to the refrigerator room and gathered the crimson roses from their seclusion, putting them into a great silver pitcher, and sliding them unobserved into the room on a little table near the dining room door. Ruth did thoughtful things like that.

But Daryl didn't even know she had done it. She was staring white-faced, wide-eyed at the young man who had been her lover, seeing him as she had never seen him before.

13

ALAN had not needed the belated introduction to tell him who this good-looking, arrogant youth was. He had recognized the voice at once, and suddenly the evening and all its quiet delight was dashed in a thousand pieces. He wished he had gone home, gone anywhere, even out into a snow-drifted world, so that he might have missed meeting this young man.

Then he looked at Daryl and his heart was wrung. She stood there white and unsmiling, looking steadily at the young man.

"Hurry up, Darrie!" commanded the young autocrat. "I'll give you five minutes!" and he pulled back the sleeve of his handsome fur overcoat and glanced at his wrist watch. "Can you make it in that?"

Daryl's chin was lifted just the least bit haughtily, and her voice was very cool as she answered:

"No!" she said. "Even if I wanted to, which I don't. I have guests here, Harold!"

"Guests?" His quick eyes went swiftly around the room, passing over Ruth and fastening on Alan. His brows drew down in a frown and he flashed Alan a contemptuous, annihilating glance.

"Guests?" His eyebrows lifted questioningly. "I'm quite sure your guests would be willing to excuse you. This is an unusual opportunity for you to meet important people, Daryl, and give you an entree into a new circle. But you'll have to hurry. I promised I'd be right back."

"Promises have been broken before this." Daryl managed a light laugh. "No, Harold. It is quite impossible. I really don't care to go, even if I could. An entree into that kind of a social circle wouldn't interest me in the least."

"But you don't understand," said the young man vexedly, flashing a glare of annoyance at Alan. "For sweet pity's sake, isn't there some place we can go by ourselves for a minute? I want to explain!"

But he had scarcely finished before he discovered that the others had fairly melted away, and they were alone. Still Daryl did not move.

"You are acting like a naughty child!" said the young man angrily. "I haven't time to argue with you, and I ought to go off and leave you and let you bear the consequences. If it weren't that this means a lot to me in a social way I would. But if you are to be tied up with me"—he gave a quick glance about to make sure no one was listening, and lowered his voice a trifle—"don't get on your high horse just because of a silly fanatical idea you have—"

"Please don't consider yourself tied up in any way," said Daryl haughtily.

"Now, listen, Daryl,—!" He strode over to where she stood. "Don't be a fool! Go upstairs and get into your things, quick! We can talk this out on the way! It's a lot of silly nonsense anyway and you might as well learn now as any time that people have to do as the world does or—!"

"You're wasting your time, Harold, I'm *not going!*"

"But, Daryl, you see this means a lot to me financially."

"Then you'd better hurry along," said Daryl decisively. "I shouldn't be an asset at all in a thing like this. I'm positively not going!"

Angrily he strode to the door, then he paused and gave a quick searching look about, his eyes resting perplexedly on the silver pitcher of crimson roses glowing in the doorway.

"Didn't my roses get here?" He frowned, fairly glaring at her.

"Oh, yes, they came," said Daryl sweetly, suddenly realizing the roses by her side. "Yes, they came Christmas night. The man nearly froze to death getting them here, but *they came!* They're very beautiful! Thank you!" She said it most formally.

"Those aren't the ones I ordered!" he growled. "I told him pink ones. I insisted on pink ones. He promised to get them."

"They couldn't get pink ones," she said, still composedly. "He sent the best he had. He had trouble to find anybody who was willing to bring them out here. His own boy is sick and the drifts were awful!"

"*I* hadn't any trouble getting here. The way from Collamer is perfectly clear."

"Yes?" said Daryl. "But the snowplow has been out here twice since then. Besides, you are in a sleigh. The boy was *walking!*"

"Walking?" he said incredulously. "Seems to me that's not very great efficiency in a florist."

Daryl said nothing and he stood a moment looking at her.

"Come on, Daryl, be a good sport and come! I came all this way after you!"

"No," said Daryl firmly. "I don't wish to come!"

"Mad yet? Oh, very well!" and he turned on his heel and stormed out the door, slamming it after him. Daryl could hear him whistling a jazzy song as he sprang into the sleigh and drove noisily away, the sleigh bells jangling irregularly in thin notes far apart. They were an ancient string of bells with some missing.

The house was very still for a moment after he had gone, as if the rest of the family had suddenly been spirited away, although in reality each individual member was awaiting developments, ready to efface themselves if that seemed the thing to do at that critical moment.

Then Daryl's voice rang out clear and steady, under perfect control:

"Come on, folks, where are you? Are we going to finish this pastoral, or not?" and her violin swelled out in the tender melody:

"He shall feed His flock like a shepherd—"

They all trooped back smiling with relief and took their places, and Mother Devereaux with fine intuition slyly slipped the crimson roses into the dark dining room out of sight.

It was a rare evening, even happier than the day before. All the happier for the events that had threatened to wreck it. Twice that day alien forces had appeared and nearly overwhelmed them, but they had risen above them. Alan, as he stood near to Daryl singing while she played her violin, watched furtively her lovely profile, and exulted in the way she was bearing herself. How she had risen to the occasion and put that fellow in his place! How coolly she had spoken, how clear-cut her sentences! There had been no hesitation. And he hadn't been so cocksure of himself when he went away either! One could tell that by the very slam of the door as he left.

Oh, he would likely come back and make it up. Daryl was too lovely a girl to be dropped so easily! Perhaps he would learn his lesson for a time, perhaps not, but anyway he would make her think he had, and probably get her in the end, more the pity. But tonight, at least, she was theirs, head held high, lips smiling, forced perhaps, but nonetheless lovely, thrilling in the music she was playing! She was riding on the top wave of victory and Alan was glad and proud of her.

This one evening he would have to remember!

He did not stop to think that she might have practically said the same thing of him, and that their experiences had been almost identical that day. Each had turned away an invitation in order to stay by the old farm and the little group, who because they had lived through fear and peril, and almost death together, seemed to have a closer bond between them than any of these others could offer.

The father and mother sitting back in the shadows listening and watching, realized it all, and prayed and trusted as they watched their girl tenderly. Lance as he sang cast now and then a veiled glance at his sister, wondering if she had got some sense at last. His indignation boiled at the thought of the great big handsome bully blowing in there and ordering his sister to get dressed and go with him without a moment's notice, just as if he owned her! He was glad she had some spunk and refused to go. And to a dance, too! When he must know Daryl didn't dance. Maybe she'd got her eyes open at last, and seen that he wasn't the angel from heaven she had supposed. Maybe Alan had been sent here to show her what a real man could be! But then he had a girl too! *Some girl!* Red lips as if they were bleeding! Lighting a cigarette in their house without as much as by-your-leave! Why were people all mixed up this way? Well, Alan had given her the slip anyway. He was thankful for that!

And then his eyes dropped to the pretty brown head just below him. What a prize his girl was! Nobody in the world like Ruth! What a blessing God had given him in her! How every other young man was to be pitied that he didn't have a girl like Ruth!

But nobody knew just what Daryl was thinking as she kept her eyes alight, and her lips smiling, a bit of color, too, in her cheeks, playing on tirelessly whatever they asked her to play, as if she were enjoying it and could not get enough. And now and then meeting the light in Alan's eyes with one of her own! How much was real and how much was forced in it all? Nobody quite knew. They were happy, glad that they were there together, that neither outside influence had prevailed. Loyal friends they were, and this was their night.

It was late when they finally broke up and went to bed. Christmas was over for another year. The morrow would bring changes which they did not like to face tonight. Father Devereaux's prayer was peculiarly tender as they knelt around the fire before saying good night.

Perhaps the watches of the night brought saner, sadder thoughts to some of them, but if so there was no sign on their faces next morning when they gathered for breakfast.

Then after breakfast there was another reprieve. Bill Gates telephoned that Alan's car was not quite ready, as they had been delayed so many times to go to the rescue of cars stalled in the storm. It would not be ready until late in the afternoon.

They tried again to persuade Alan to stay one more night, but he had been in telephone communication with his partner and felt he must go as soon as the car was ready.

So they went sledding again all the morning, a glorious day, with the sun shining sweetly overhead just as if it hadn't been in hiding for a good many hours. The world was dazzling in its whiteness, and out behind the barn the long hill was packed and smooth, a beautiful slide with nothing in the way to break the thrill of the flight.

They lingered long at lunch, pretending that they were not breaking up in a few minutes, dreading the moment when their guest would leave, and Alan dreading most of all to go. He hadn't realized until he was about to leave them how his heart was knit to every one of this dear family. And to think he had just happened upon them!

But at last he tore himself away from the pleasant company and went into the guest room to pack his belongings.

Lance went with him to help and they had a heart to heart talk together. The dusk of the short winter afternoon was coming down and Father Devereaux had thoughtfully built up the fire. Its bright blaze lit up the gloom that was gathering in the corners of the room. It seemed so pleasant and cheery that Alan looked around and sighed.

"I shall never cease to be thankful that I was thrust in here," he said as he looked at his new friend wistfully. "Not alone because you did the most wonderful thing a man could ever do for another; or because you have the most delightful family on earth and I love you like a brother; not altogether either because I've had the most wonderful Christmas I've known since I was a child; but because I've found something here that I didn't know existed. I don't know just what to call it. Perhaps it ought to be named Faith. I was at a critical time in my life, I know now. I had reached a stage where I wasn't sure I quite believed in anybody or anything, and what was the use of trying to follow a thing you called conscience? Yet I knew I was terribly hungry for something. Then I came here, and heard you all talking to God as if He were real, and trusting in Him, and reading His Book, and I got a new vision of what life might mean. I can't say I know much about it yet, but I'm determined to find out, and I can never thank you enough that you started me thinking about these things."

Lance's face lighted with radiance.

"Well, brother," he said earnestly, "why not just accept the Lord Jesus as your Saviour, and settle the question once and for all now, tonight?"

"Is it as easy as that?" Alan asked wonderingly.

"It's as easy as that for us!" said Lance reverently. "But it cost Jesus Christ everything to make it so!"

Alan sat thoughtfully gazing into the fire for a little.

"Do you think one ought to make a decision like that in haste, knowing as little as I do about it? I've not been living in the atmosphere that you were brought up in. Suppose I'm not able to keep it up?"

"Keep what up?" asked Lance, his bright eyes holding the other's glance.

"Well, suppose this feeling doesn't stay with me when I get back into my life again, and mingle with my world? Suppose I get over wanting to be good." Alan laughed embarrassedly.

"Thank God we are not saved by our feelings!" breathed Lance fervently. "Admitting the fact that we are natural born sinners and deserve to die, we are saved by accepting the death of Jesus Christ in our place, recognizing that He took upon Himself not only the penalty of our sins, but the sins themselves."

"I understand that."

"Well, if you are saved by His death, and not by your own life, suppose you do lose this feeling of wanting to be good, as you say. Does that take away the fact that Christ died for you?"

Alan's face lit up.

"Why, no, of course not!" said he. "But, is it all in what He's done, then? Haven't I anything to do?"

"It's all in what He's done! The finished work of the Cross. Your part is to receive it!"

"That's great!" he said slowly. "But, still, I don't quite trust *myself*, Lance. Why won't that feeling of assurance make me feel as if I can go out and do as I please? I don't feel that way now, but I might when I get away from you all. I just want to understand it thoroughly. It seems too good to be true, the way you put it."

"It isn't the way I put it, it's the way God Himself puts it. See here!" and he pulled out his Testament that was always in his pocket. "See this verse. Mark it down and read it whenever you get to doubting. See, it's John 5:24. 'He that heareth my word, and believeth on Him that sent me, *hath* everlasting life, and shall not come into condemnation; but *is* passed from death unto life.'"

Alan took out his notebook and wrote down the reference.

If Lance had warmed to his new friend before, he felt now as if his heart was knit with this other one who so humbly and sincerely laid his pride in the dust.

"You see, brother," he said eagerly, "there's a mighty good reason why you won't feel like living as you please. It's because, if you truly take Christ as your Saviour, you're born again. That is, you have a new nature into which God puts His own Spirit. And the Spirit of God doesn't feel like sinning. Of course you still have your old sinful nature too, as long as you're down here in a mortal body, and it will always have the desire to sin, but the Spirit of God in your new nature is stronger than the desire to sin in your old nature. As you choose deliberately to let the Spirit of God do what He will with you, the old nature is constantly defeated and you do not practice sinning, sins don't crop out in your life. It is Christ living in you that keeps you."

Alan looked into Lance's eyes steadily for a moment. Then he got up and walked to the window looking out for a long time. At last he came back and sat down by the fire again.

"That's pretty wonderful!" he said gravely. "How do I go about accepting Him?"

"Your very desire to do it is known to Him," said Lance gently. "But why not tell Him straight out?"

Lance knelt down and Alan knelt beside him.

Quietly Lance spoke as to One in the room with them:

"Father, thou hast saved me, a sinner, by Thy grace, through the blood of Thy Son. Here is another who wants to be saved—"

Lance paused, and after an instant Alan spoke out clearly:

"O God, I accept Jesus Christ for my Saviour!"

It was very still in the room, only the soft flaring of the fire, as the two young men remained with bowed heads, while the solemn decision was registered above.

Then Lance's voice broke the stillness again:

"—let it be according to Thy Word to the glory of our Lord. Amen!" he finished.

Neither spoke for a minute after they arose, but Alan gripped Lance's hand. Then he said in an apologetic voice: "I'm glad you made me do it. But—I don't feel any different. Should I?"

"A baby isn't conscious that it is born, is it? It's the parents and the rest of the family who feel glad. Our Father is rejoicing over you this minute. That's something you take on faith, though, and learn later when you get to studying the Word. But I'm rejoicing too, brother!" Lance's voice was husky with feeling and he took Alan's hand in another strong warm clasp. "We are really brothers now, do you realize that? Both children in the family of God, both born-again ones."

"That's wonderful!" said Alan warmly. "I like that. It's great to belong to something—to Some *One!*" he added with a reverent lifting of his eyes.

Then they heard Alan's car driving up to the house, and they hurried out.

Alan had just a minute alone with Daryl. As he took her hand for farewell, he said with a kind of triumph in his voice:

"I'm really in the family now, Daryl. I've just taken your Lord for my Saviour, and I'm going back to begin my life all over again. Will you pray for me?"

Daryl lifted her lovely eyes filled with real radiance and said with unmistakable joy in her voice:

"Oh, I am glad, *glad!* And of course I will pray for you! May He give you great joy and blessing!"

Her voice was low and sweet, and suddenly as he held her hand and read the real gladness in her eyes, he felt again that great longing to take her in his arms and lay his lips upon hers. For just an instant something flashed from eye to eye and then Alan turned quickly to the rest. There were no words further that he might speak now. But he went over to Mrs. Devereaux and kissed her hand, and said:

"Mother Devereaux, you've been wonderful to me. May I come back again sometime and visit you?"

And Mother Devereaux patted his hand and told him he was welcome whenever he would come. The rest of the good-bys were quickly said, with eager invitations for a return visit, and he drove away into the dusk.

As Lance came back from a last word at the car, and stood with the rest on the porch while they watched their guest away, he said in a tone of quiet triumph: *"He's saved! He accepted Christ just now!"* and there was a look on Lance's face as if he had just had a glimpse of heaven.

"Yes," said Daryl softly, "he told me!" She said it very quietly, and her brother looked at her and smiled, but wondered in his heart.

Alan, as he drove away into the winter sunset, had a strange feeling that he was not alone. He had a Saviour who was to be with him constantly, within him. He need never be alone again! And suddenly a great joy went singing through his heart.

And all the way home through the white starry night, that sense of a Presence traveling with him remained.

But how would Demeter Cass fit in with all that?

14

DARYL was lonely after Alan was gone. She wouldn't admit it to herself that he had anything to do with her loneliness. He was only an incident of course, though a pleasant one. She blamed her state of mind on Harold. And of course he had a good deal to do with her restlessness.

Ruth was still with them, like a sweet sister, but Ruth and Lance had a great deal to talk over together, and they were so all-in-all to one another that Daryl couldn't help feeling alone sometimes, though she never let them see it. She entered into all their plans, and she and Ruth were like two sisters, bright and happy, going about and doing things together. They went sledding too, and later when the snow was cleared from the creek below the hill they went skating. It was all very jolly and nice, but there was a decided realization that the true holiday was over.

They had asked Alan to come back for New Year's, but he had said he couldn't, so soon, that he had a number of engagements that must be kept, especially a dinner on New Year's Day at the home of his partner, which he could not very well cancel. Daryl didn't know of course how hard it had been for Alan to say he couldn't come. He had even weighed the matter of calling off that engagement in spite of his promise to Mr. Meredith. But he had decided against it. It was not only the fact that New Year's Day would be a very likely time for Harold Warner to come back and try to make his peace, and Alan didn't want to be there when that happened. But he had a strong conviction that if he stayed longer, or went often to that blessed home, he was going to have a very hard time to keep his resolve not to think of Daryl continually. So he had firmly refused the eager invitation from the whole family, and held himself resolutely to the engagements he had made in the city.

Harold did not come on New Year's Day either. He stayed away purposely, perhaps, to teach his young lady a lesson. Let her spend the day alone for once without word from him and perhaps the next time she wouldn't be so high and mighty about her refusals. And then, perhaps New Year's Day was a time when there were plenty of other things to do, and he didn't miss his quiet sweet Daryl so much.

But he came down for the week-end the next Saturday, came in a beautiful borrowed car, looking handsome and sleek and prosperous, and bearing a very nice ring in a velvet case in his pocket, in case he should feel it wise to use it.

Daryl was cool in welcoming him. In fact the whole family were rather formal with him, but that disturbed him not at all. He blew in exactly like a son of the house who was condescending to them all to waste valuable time in the country to humor them.

Daryl was just clipping off the tips of the stems of some very gorgeous yellow roses that Alan had sent down by express to her for New Year's Day, and arranging them in two tall crystal vases when he came, and she went right on with her work after she had greeted him. He eyed the roses savagely as he took off his hat and coat and hung them familiarly in the hall. He did not want to say anything about them. He wouldn't give her the satisfaction of asking about them, but as she went steadily on with her work somehow he couldn't resist.

"I suppose that ape that was here Christmas sent those!" He glared at her, but she did not look up.

"Oh, did you think he was an ape?" she asked sweetly.

They did not have a good morning together with that beginning. There were long arguments, most of them on the subject of drinking. Now and then a discussion regarding broken promises, and parties given by the boss' daughter, though this latter topic was mostly a monologue by the young man, unsolicited by Daryl, mostly in the nature of apology, with charges of jealousy. Daryl closed her lips quietly and let him talk.

"Now, look here, Daryl! It's time we fully understood each other!" announced Harold after he had had a good lunch and managed by his ungracious attitude to clear the living room of all the family. "You know your attitude with regard to drinking is absurd! You can't be a part of the world as it is today and not drink!"

"Well," said Daryl quietly, "I'm not trying to be a part of the world as it is today. A Christian isn't intended to be 'of the world' anyway. We are 'called-out ones.'"

"Oh, that's all very well to talk about," he said loftily, "but you can't do that you know! I'm a Christian myself of course, have been for years. I told you that. I joined the church when I was fourteen, but that doesn't keep me from being a human being."

"No, it wouldn't," said Daryl.

"Just what do you mean by that?" roared the young man angrily. "Everything you say seems to be full of nasty slams, and I don't like it!"

"I mean that joining a church does not keep anybody from living a worldly life," said Daryl gravely.

"Well, of course I understand that joining a church is the outward symbol that you are in sympathy with religion in general," he said condescendingly. "I'm not a child. I don't need to be told that. You are quibbling! That's what a woman always does when she gets her mind set on some one thing. If you don't look out you'll turn out to be a fanatic!"

She only looked at him steadily with sadness in her eyes. Why hadn't she seen this side of him before? She had been so sure that he would be willing and eager to be led to a closer walk with God!

He looked at her beautiful eyes and grew angrier as he looked. Why did a girl with eyes like that have to go and get pious? It was all well enough to have a little religion. Religion was a sort of safeguard for a woman of course, but to be so set in her way, and to have so many queer old-fashioned notions! He opened his mouth and tried again, not looking at the lovely eyes, they somehow made him feel uncomfortable.

"You see, really, Daryl, in my position as a rising business man," he cleared his throat, arranged his necktie, and tried to look stern and important, "I'm obliged to go into society a good deal, and one can't go into society and not do as others do. You know I don't care anything about drinking. I've told you that before. And I promised you, yes, I *promised* you, I know, that I would swear off entirely, but I found it wouldn't work. It just doesn't go down with my friends! When in Rome you've got to do as the Romans do, you know. Doesn't the Bible say that?"

Daryl did not answer. She wanted to laugh but found herself instead struggling with sudden tears. How she was getting her eyes open!

"I don't intend to make a practice of drinking of course," he went on. "That's absurd! What do you think I am? A *drunkard?*"

Daryl lifted honest eyes.

"You were drunk when you talked to me over the telephone, Harold!" She said it solemnly, with utter sorrow in her eyes.

"Nonsense!" he said sharply. "Nothing of the kind! I may have been a bit funny, kidding you, and all that! I had taken a little more than I usually allow myself, but I certainly wasn't drunk. I can stand a good deal of liquor, Daryl. It doesn't effect me easily. But I had had a long cold drive and I thought it would keep me from being sick if I took an extra glass."

He looked at her almost virtuously.

Still Daryl didn't answer, and then a great tear fell down on her hands that were folded in her lap.

"Aw, forget it!" he said in an annoyed tone; and then suddenly he reached out and drew her into his arms embracing her fiercely.

"You silly little pretty Puritan!" he said, half angrily, half passionately, and kissed her again and again on lips and forehead and hot wet eyelids, before she could get free.

For Daryl was fighting him off, struggling from his grasp, pushing him away from her, and she sprang to her feet as soon as she got free, wiping off his kisses with her handkerchief, her face white and excited. She had a sudden revelation that she did not want his kisses.

"No!" she said vehemently. "*No!* You must not do that! You have no right!"

"Right?" said Harold, lifting amazed eyes. "Why haven't I the right, I'd like to know? Haven't you been my girl for almost six months? Haven't I intimated that I was expecting to marry you pretty soon?"

"I don't think you have," said Daryl, suddenly haughty. "But if you had it wouldn't make any difference now."

There was such an utter sadness, a withdrawing in her voice, that Harold was startled.

"Oh, I say, now, Daryl, that isn't fair of you! I came out here with the intention of talking it all over with you. I even brought you a *ring!* Come here and see it! It's a beauty!"

"No!" said Daryl sharply. "No, please!"

But he held the little blue velvet box out on his hand temptingly.

"Aw, come on, Daryl. Forget all this nonsense and come and look at your ring. I didn't say much about it because I wanted to wait till I could get a really fine one. But I decided not to wait any longer. If you and I are going out a lot you should have it to wear right now, so I borrowed the money and got it! Come on, Baby! Come on and look at it. It's a beaut!"

He arose and came toward her, springing the cover of the box open and letting the afternoon sun glitter through the big showy diamond.

"Isn't it a pip?" he said, suddenly throwing his arm around her and holding the diamond in front of her, resting his chin possessively on her shoulder.

But Daryl pulled away and stood back from him.

"Don't!" she said seriously. "I could not wear your ring, Harold! There was a time when I would have been overjoyed at a ring from you, even a little plain one. You would not have had to get me a great gorgeous one like that if everything had been all right. But, Harold—!" She half turned away, struggling with the tears. Then she turned back, her head lifted high, an earnest look on her face.

"Harold, you killed something that I thought was very precious that night you got drunk and talked to me over the telephone. I never, *never* could forget that. I kept trying and trying to think how I could be mistaken, how you would come and tell me that you had only been joking or something—though it seemed a cruel sort of joke when you knew how I felt about it—and then you came and not only didn't excuse yourself, but you are trying to *justify* yourself in doing something that made it possible. Oh! You cannot know how awful it was to me! And then the fact that you went away to another place after planning for our Christmas together, you actually *went* without saying a word about it until you *got there!* Altogether it just broke my faith in you. For two whole days I tried with all my might to build up again the ideal I had of you, but it is gone. I can't get it back. It was a terrible shock, but I haven't any illusions left."

"Aw, applesauce!" said Harold as she paused and gave him a sorrowful glance. "I didn't know you were a sob-sister! For heaven's sake, snap out of it. Don't you know you are spoiling all my week-end? If this has got to keep on I'm leaving the first thing in the morning!"

He whirled about and went and stood staring sullenly out of the window. He was standing so when Ruth came to call them to the evening meal, and Daryl was sitting across the room from him, her face in shadow, but strangely quiet as if all happiness had fled from her life.

The rest of them did their best during dinner to bring about a happier state of things, but Harold remained sullen and silent, scarcely answering decently when a question was addressed to him. After dinner he did not offer to help with the dishes as the others were doing. Instead he took himself off to his room while Daryl was busy. Her mother kept trying to send her back to the living room to keep him company, saying she and Ruth would finish, but she would not go. With a forced brightness she remained till the last dish was put away and the table set for breakfast, and when she finally came back to the living room Harold stalked out of his room and remarked in a tone plenty loud enough to be heard in the dining room where the others were about to take refuge from his company, that it wasn't right that she should have to do menial work when her people were plenty able to hire servants. And that even if she did want to do it she shouldn't have to be tied down that way, especially when he was there, and had only a short time to stay.

Lance heard that and pricked up his ears. Then he laid his hand on Ruth's arm and said in a good clear tone, "Come on, folks, let's have some music," and he marched them all into the living room and established Ruth at the piano.

"Come on, Harold," called Lance politely, "you sing, don't you? How about this quartette? Are you tenor or bass?"

"Baritone," said Harold languidly, "but I don't care to sing tonight! I came here to see Daryl!" he added pointedly.

"Yes?" said Lance with imperturbable good humor. "Well, Daryl sings. Come on and be a good sport!"

"Thanks! No!" said Harold decidedly.

"Well, then, how about a picture puzzle?" offered Mother Devereaux, determined if possible to get a little acquainted with this young man whom she might have to have for her son-in-law some day.

"They're a pain in the neck!" growled the handsome spoiled boy. "I might rise to a game of bridge though, if any of you are good players," he offered contemptuously.

"I'm afraid we'll have to pass that," said Lance crisply. "We don't any of us play bridge. But I could get out the ping-pong table. It doesn't take any time at all to set it up."

"Child's play!" said Harold scornfully. "I have to work hard enough all the week without doing it under the guise of amusement."

"Well, I have it, we'll go sledding then! The hill is fine tonight and the moon is out!" Lance grinned in his most friendly manner at the glowering guest.

"Oh, heavens!" said Harold. "How restless you are! I have no desire to go wallowing around in the snow getting wet and cold. Go if you want to. I prefer to stay here."

So they all settled down around the fire genially and began to talk. Lance distinctly heard Harold say quite audibly to Daryl who sat not far from him, "How long do we have to stand this?" but he went right on telling jokes and laughing with his father at some little local happenings they were talking about, and the whole family sat quietly by just as if nothing at all was going on, just as if everything were perfectly serene and harmonious. Ruth told little incidents of her kindergarten, some childish pranks that were truly amusing. Father told how Chrystobel had nosed under the hay he had brought her and got the apple he had hidden there for her dessert. Lance got off an anecdote of his college days, and even Mother roused to ask Harold about his business, where he boarded, and if he had pleasant surroundings. He answered in monosyllables as far as possible, and looked bored to extinction. Only Daryl sat silent for the most part, though now and then rousing to talk brightly, and then relapsing into sad silence again. But the family were so exceedingly pleasant as if they were trying so hard to stand by her, that she began to suspect them of a plot as she watched them one by one, and then eyes glowed with sudden love for them all, and she came out of her silence and told some bright stories herself.

But still Harold sat in silent gloom, enduring, and waiting for the family to take themselves off, which they showed no signs of doing. They just sat and laughed and talked.

Suddenly Lance said:

"Daryl, get your violin and let's do that Messiah music. Harold wasn't here last week to hear it."

"Oh, Lance!" said Daryl softly, aghast at the suggestion.

"Don't bother, Daryl" said Harold loftily, "I hate to hear girls play the violin. They never do it well, and they always look so extremely awkward, all long arms."

"Oh, but we don't mind," laughed Lance. "Come on, Darrie, we've got to do something to entertain the crowd. Can't waste a whole perfectly good Saturday night like this." He held out his hand to his sister and pulled her to her feet, and then he took Ruth's hand with his other one and pulled them along to the piano.

Daryl's cheeks were flaming, but she rose to the occasion, taking down her violin and beginning to tune it. As she gave a preliminary touch of the bow across the strings she looked up comically at Harold and said:

"Never mind, Harold, if you don't like it you can go to sleep." Then she turned quickly toward the piano and began to play, dashing into the music with a fuller tone, and a truer swing than she usually had, and presently the sweet strains of Handel filled the room, and Father and Mother Devereaux sat back and watched their three proudly, forgetting for the moment the unwanted guest whom they had tried so hard to entertain, forgetting that they had all agreed to rally around their girl and help her out of what appeared to be a most unhappy evening. They had heard the arguments. They could not avoid it for Harold talked loudly. They could not help but know that Daryl was being true to her own standards, although they didn't understand the whole thing of course. But Mother Devereaux was beginning to hope that her girl was getting her eyes open.

The musicians were doing some fine work. They all had good voices; Ruth sang alto and Daryl's voice was high and clear. Lance, adaptable always, took either tenor or bass solos, rearranging the high notes to his range. They all had fine musical appreciation, and had been well taught. There was something in having their backs to the audience too, as they stood by the piano. They were not courting appreciation. They were singing for mere love of it, and perhaps for the glory of God too, and Harold was entirely out of the picture.

He lolled suddenly on the couch watching his erst-while girl with smoldering eyes, and wondering just what line he would take with her? Should he make violent love to her after this farce was over and compel her to wear his ring? Or should he just go away offended, and stay away awhile until she got over her pet and got frightened lest he wouldn't return? He had no question but that this would be the ultimate result. He decided on the latter, unless she showed signs herself of weakening before the evening was over. It would be better at once to let her know that he was master, and that he wasn't going to stand any more foolishness. Imagine marrying a little prude!

When the last lovely note of the final chorus died away and Daryl turned with an air of finality and put her instrument in its case, Father Devereaux arose.

"Well, folks," he said genially, his fine old face shining with pleasure, "that was lovely! And now I guess it's about time we had worship," and he went and got his big old Bible and brought it back to his place by the fire. The musicians came and sat down in their places, and the room grew quiet. Then suddenly Harold arose precipitately.

"If you'll excuse me I think I'll go to bed!" he said bluntly. "I've got a beastly headache."

"Why, that's too bad!" said Mother Devereaux sympathetically. "Can I get you anything? Some soda, or hot water, or a bit of medicine? I noticed you didn't seem to enjoy your supper."

"Better light his fire, Lance," said Father Devereaux as he turned to the place in the Bible. "It's all laid ready!"

"Thanks! I'll light it myself if I need it!" said Harold curtly, and stalked off to his room, making short work of his preparations for sleep. They heard him thump down into the bed during the prayer as if he had flung himself there from a height, and Daryl felt a desire to giggle nervously, in spite of the tears brought by her father's prayer for "the stranger within our gates."

Oh, that prayer! If Harold could have heard it, how angry he would have been to think that anyone supposed that he needed praying for. But even if Daryl had been more in love than she ever had thought she was, she could not have found fault with the tenderness of that prayer.

And when she went to her bed that night Daryl rested her heart down hard on the everlasting God, and went straight to sleep. There were going to be no regrets in her heart when she let Harold and his ring go away just after a late breakfast the next morning, as he did. She had laid all her burden and perplexity in the hands of the Lord to do with her as He saw fit.

DEMETER Cass did not come to Alan Monteith's office the first thing when she got home from the Wyndringham house party. She decided that she could do more with him if she could bring him to be a little anxious about it himself, and make him do the calling up. Perhaps it would come to him that he hadn't been exactly kind to her and if he should be repentant of course she would have a great part of her battle won. It wasn't thinkable that that little country girl with the big angel-eyes had been able to make him forget her. She had her siren ways and knew she could depend upon them. Besides she had great stakes to win, and must go cautiously.

So she let three days go by without a sign from herself, and yet no ring or call, nor even a letter of apology came from the young lawyer, who had been so busy since his return that he had scarcely thought of her.

Then one morning when he came to the office he found a note summoning him to her house at eleven o'clock to stay to lunch.

He had to go over to the courthouse almost immediately, so he instructed his secretary to call her and tell her that it would be impossible for him to come as he had to be in court till four o'clock, but if she could be at the office then, or early the next morning he would give her a half hour.

Demeter had told the secretary she would come that afternoon. But when Alan got back, tired and hungry, for he had been too busy to stop for lunch, she was not there. He waited ten minutes and then there came a ring, and a sorrowful voice spoke:

"Alan, I'm sorry, but it's quite impossible for me to come out this afternoon. The doctor has just been here and says it would be suicidal for me to go out in the cold with this condition of my lungs. It's a bad cold on my chest, you know, and I've been threatened with pneumonia. Now, I'm sorry to ask it, but won't you come over and have a cup of tea with me? It is imperative that I see you this afternoon. I cannot wait any longer!"

With an annoyed look at his watch, and a hopeless thought of the papers he had to go through that night before court tomorrow, he reluctantly said:

"All right, I'll come, but I can't stay more than a half hour, Demeter. I'm rushed to death just now."

"Thank you, Alan!" she said drearily and hung up.

So Alan jumped into his car and went.

He was vexed with himself for going. He felt somehow that to go to her apartment was poor. He had a lot to do and it would be hard to get away. Besides, business transacted in a house was not nearly so satisfactory as in an office where things were formal. A girl like Demeter could use the sentimental appeal to better advantage outside an office than in. But what else could he do but go? He couldn't be brutal and refuse. And she seemed to think it was so important. Well, he would get away as soon as he could. What on earth could it be that was so important, anyway?

He passed a tired hand over a weary brow and sighed. And then he remembered.

Ever since he had left the farm, ever since that quiet

moment when he had knelt with Lance by the fire and surrendered himself to the Lord he had had that sense of a Presence with him. It had wakened with him in the morning and been near by in the offing all day when he was hard at work. Today, even in the busy courtroom where he had had to be alert every moment, he had still felt that there was some One to whom he might turn in perplexity. Some One who was wiser than any judge or lawyer anywhere, and who could guide him unerringly. He put up a quick petition. "O Lord, you know about this. Show me what to do, solve any perplexity. Don't let me do the wrong thing in any way."

Demeter had set her stage well.

The room was spacious and luxurious, done in black and silver, a combination that well set off its owner with her gold hair and strange green eyes, eyes that could melt tenderly into almost blue at times, and then into stormy gray!

There was a fire burning at one side of the wide room and the curtains were drawn reflecting silvery lights from their folds. There was a great black velvet couch with many pillows of black inviting to comfort. It was drawn across the front of the fire, a low tea table at one end. An immense white bear-skin sprawled across the floor in front like a gigantic protector, its glassy eyes regarding him, its great pink jaws menacingly wide open. A lavish wealth of roses, pale shellpink, shed exquisite perfume through the air. Off through a wide doorway the outline of a grand piano gave pleasant vista.

Demeter entered the room a moment later, just giving him time to take in the beauty of the setting, and her entrance was like the rising of a curtain in a play.

She was attired in a lovely négligé of clinging white transparent velvet with glimpses of pastel chiffon that matched the roses and looked like a delicate cloud at sunset. It gave her a frail, almost unearthly beauty, with her gold hair and strange eyes. A single jewel sparkled on her white neck from a thread-like chain and her stockingless feet were shod in silver sandals through which peeped shamelessly her little pink toes with their polished nails stained to match her finger tips. These details did not enter Alan's consciousness at once, but the effect was of an exceedingly intimate costume, and he was startled at the picture she had made of herself. Something suddenly steeled and warned him in his heart. Was this then what God had to protect him against? Or was he mistaken? *Could* anything as lovely as this not have a soul as beautiful?

She drifted in almost wearily like an invalid, and dropped upon the velvet couch, its depth of black bringing out still more startlingly her exquisite little self. She had certainly gone to a great deal of trouble to charm him, but of course Alan didn't realize that. It only seemed that he was being let into her inner circle, the intimacy of a more-than-friend, and he wasn't quite sure that he wanted to be there. In fact he was pretty certain that he did not. But whether he wanted to or not, he was there, and must get through with it as best he could.

God! Are you there?

He greeted her gravely, but did not take the seat beside her on the couch that she indicated.

"I'll just sit here where I can see you," he said easily, dropping into a great armchair across the hearth from the couch.

She did not urge him, but he saw that she did not like it that he had refused.

"So sorry I had to demand your presence," she said coolly, "but my doctor positively refused to let me go out, and my affairs could not wait another day!" There was the tiniest bit of reproach in the words.

"Well, I'm sorry you've been ill," he said, and thought as he looked at her that in spite of her subdued manner she did not look at all sick.

"I'm sorry, too, that I must hurry. But this was the only

way I could have come. I shall have to work nearly all night tonight to be ready for court tomorrow morning. I'm sure you understand."

"No, I wouldn't understand," said Demeter a little haughtily, "but it doesn't matter. You are here and I'll do my best to tell you the business in the time you give me." She sighed gently as if she had been treated inconsiderately, but was willing to forgive.

"We'll just have our tea while we talk," she said.

She touched a bell and a servant appeared with a tray of good things. Alan was grateful for the food, and it was of course delectable. When he was served and the servant had departed he said pleasantly:

"Now, what is it?"

"Well, Alan," she said, looking him directly in the eyes, holding his gaze in spite of his desire to get away from that disturbing glance. "I need a great deal of money at once, and I want you to get it for me! That's the story."

And then she watched him.

He looked at her blankly.

"Money?" he said in dismay. "You surely know I have no money, at least so little that it would scarcely count with you as any."

"Yes, but you have the means of procuring it," said the girl, still pinning him with her glance and watching his reaction to her words.

"The means?" he repeated blankly. "I don't understand you. I have no means of procuring money!"

"Think!" said Demeter. "Haven't you trust funds in your charge?"

Alan laughed.

"Yes, but they are *trust* funds, and I have no desire to spend the rest of my life in the penitentiary for embezzling them!" He tried to speak jocosely, but she did not smile.

"Don't be childish!" she said impatiently. "I'm in earnest."

He watched her, wondering just where this strange conversation was going to lead. Then he answered gravely.

"Suppose you explain. I'm sure you are not so ignorant of business matters as to think that I could hand over trust funds to you because you happen to want some money."

"No, but you have to invest them, don't you?"

"Yes, certainly, but how would that help you?"

"Couldn't I borrow them?"

"You! Borrow them!" He looked at her with undisguised amusement. "Just how would you go about doing that? Have you collateral for great sums of money?"

"Certainly!" she said, and her eyes were glittering now, and strangely they reminded him of a serpent's eyes just before it was about to strike its victim.

"Well, that's extraordinary! Are you going to explain?"

"Yes, presently, when I've told you the rest."

"Oh, there is more?"

"Of course," she said annoyedly. "I have worked this thing out very carefully. You have a trust fund in the name of Bronson MacMartin, I believe, haven't you?"

He gave her a startled look.

"I believe we have, but how should you know?"

"He happens to be my uncle, and a part of that fortune, perhaps the whole of it, will be mine some day. Do you wonder now that I should know about it? And are you surprised that I should have thought of it now in my need, since it is practically mine now?"

"I don't understand."

"Well, Uncle Bronson will never come out of the sanitarium. As far as his money is concerned he is practically dead now. And the only other heir is a distant cousin who has not been heard of for years. He went off to the Orient to live years ago and no one knows what has become of him. So I'm practically talking about my own money, you see."

"Demeter, what in the world are you driving at, and

where could I possibly come into the affair?"

Demeter suddenly melted into smiles and looked wistfully at him.

"Alan, I want that money, and where you come in, darling, is to get it for me. I want you to release it for me, now, within a few days. I know you can do it if you will, and I'll see that you are not the loser thereby."

He gave her a quick troubled look.

"You are talking nonsense, Demeter! The Bronson MacMartin funds are well invested and cannot be touched!"

"Not if you can get a better investment? One that pays a higher rate of interest?"

"That wouldn't be possible, not in these times, not *safe* investments. The place where it now is is as safe as the Rock of Gibraltar, and the terms of the arrangement are very definite. Even if I thought it wise I would be power-less to change it."

Demeter narrowed her eyes.

"I think you can change it!" she said confidently. "I am sure you will do so when you hear everything."

"There is more?" he asked cautiously, giving a furtive glance at his watch. This was going to be more complicated than he had feared, and the time was going fast. He had already been here three-quarters of an hour. O God! Are you near?

"Yes, there is more, and that's where the count comes in."

"The count?" Alan looked around sharply. Was there a count to be reckoned with yet tonight?

"Oh, he isn't here yet, my dear," said Demeter coolly. "I told him I'd keep you till seven o'clock. He couldn't get here any sooner. But you'll stay! After I've told you the rest, you'll stay to hear what he has to say."

Alan's face settled into grim lines of sternness.

"Demeter, look here! If you have more to tell, tell it

quickly. I'll give you five minutes, and then I'm going. I'm late already for what I have to do."

Demeter smiled serenely.

"Well, listen then, but I'm sure you'll stay after you have heard me. I have come on a marvelous fortune, if I can only get funds to develop it at once, before someone else snaps it up."

She watched her victim, but his face was a mask now and told her nothing. His unbelieving eyes watched her narrowly.

"It is simply marvelous!" she went on. "It is in oil and silver, both. And I have bought several large areas of land containing these oil wells and silver mines!"

"You have *bought* them? What with, may I ask?"

Demeter smiled confidently.

"With the money that you are going to get from Uncle Bronson's estate for me!" Alan gasped at her superb audacity.

"You see," said Demeter, "I have it all thought out, every detail. I've even been to see the wells, saw them spouting great streams of oil up into the air, and I have looked down into some of the silver mines. See, here is some of the silver that I brought away with me. I went last fall when you thought I was in California for a month."

She suddenly pulled out a little drawer in the table beside her and brought forth some nuggets of silver in various stages of refinement, also some photographs, and a few papers.

"Here are the proofs," she said sweetly, handing out a bright nugget, and then calling his attention to a photograph. "There is my photograph," she said, pointing to a figure which was unmistakably herself standing in a surrounding of mountains and plains, watching a stream of something shooting high in the air.

Alan took the whole collection in his hand and studied them. There were no marks of real identification anywhere on the pictures, just landscapes with spouting geysers of some kind. They might have been taken of course in almost any oil field. What did it all mean?

"Have these oil wells been examined by experts?" he asked suddenly.

"Oh, yes. The count looks after all that, of course. There are the papers. They vouch for everything."

"But what has the count got to do with it?"

"Why, didn't I tell you? He discovered this land, in both cases, and got the refusal of it before anyone knew there was either silver or oil there, and he is letting a few of his friends in on it, just to get the things started, but we mean to keep the most of the stock in our own hands!"

Alan was silent for several minutes while he examined the photographs and papers in the minutest details. Suddenly he looked up and studied the girl before him.

"Demeter," he said, "you've asked my advice, and said you would take it. Well, then, I advise you to have nothing more to do with this. I'm convinced just on the face of it, that it is a gigantic swindle. Of course you're not aware of it, and I don't know who is at the bottom of it, probably that count, whoever he is, but you would better drop it at once. As for getting hold of your uncle's property, that's absurd. It couldn't be done, and I certainly never would attempt it, even if I could. It would be criminal!"

Suddenly Demeter in all the beauty of her clinging garments, arose and glided over to where he sat, perching lightly on the arm of his chair like a bird, and flinging one warm pink arm across his shoulders, bent down until her lovely cheek was close to his, and her perfumed hair brushed his face.

"Darling!" she said in a most alluring voice, "don't be difficult! There is one more paper you must read and then I'll tell you everything!" and she thrust a legal-looking paper into his unwilling hands.

He glanced down at the paper, almost too angry to take

in what it said, and Demeter raised her lovely arm and ran her fingers lightly through his hair, playing with the short crisp wave above his forehead, in little gentle intimate touches. Then suddenly, with a sinuous motion like a serpent, her other hand came up and lifted his face till it was beside her own, and her voice dripping with tenderness whispered, "Darling, you'll do this for me, won't you?" And then her lips stooped to kiss his, with a long lingering caress.

Alan was taken off his guard for the instant, set around by habits of courtesy. But before her object was accomplished his strong hand came up swiftly, captured the little caressing hands in a grip like a vise, and thrust her from him, with the kiss fairly trembling in the air between them.

"Demeter!" he said sternly, on his feet at once, her hands held at arm's length. "What are you trying to do?" His eyes were scintillating with righteous wrath. "Was I summoned here to a petting party, or is this business? Please sit down and act like a decent woman. I'd like to continue to respect you, if I could."

He led her to her couch and left her, going to the far end of the room and standing up beside a lamp to read the paper he still held.

Demeter was very angry. Little points of fire played back and forth in her eyes, and her mouth was set in a thin vengeful line, but she sat perfectly still and watched him.

When he had finished reading the paper he turned toward her, his face still set in its stern lines. He spoke to her as if she were a very naughty child.

"This paper," he said, "is absolutely worthless. It is utterly illegal as it stands, and would never get by anywhere. The whole thing looks to me like a fraud!"

With swift subtlety Demeter's expressions changed to one of quiet triumph:

"But that, my dear, is where you come in! Don't you understand? You are to put those papers into form so that they shall *be* legal, and then—" she paused an instant with bated breath as if she were listening for someone who was at hand—"and then," she went on, "you are to share with us equally in the enormous profits!"

Alan stood still in the middle of the room and looked at her astounded, his face white, a new kind of rage beginning to look forth from his eyes.

"Do I understand that you are offering me a bribe?" he said, and contempt grew in his voice as he spoke. "Absolutely nothing doing, either now or at any other time! I will wish you good evening!" and he turned and walked out of the room.

Pausing in the hallway to pick up his hat and coat he was at the front door in time to meet a man whom the servant was admitting. A dark man with handsome glittering shifty eyes, and a look of knowing his way about the earth pretty well. He eyed Alan sharply as they passed, and Alan gave him a long look, sure that he would not forget that face. For that must be the count!

When Alan reached his apartment he found that he was still holding Demeter's last paper crumpled in his hand.

He smoothed it out and read it over again, his wrath rising anew at the whole slippery scheme. Then as he went to put it by he happened to glance on the back and saw a penciled note scribbled in a strange hand.

> Dearest:
> Don't show this to your lawyer friend just yet, not till I've got in my work, and don't say anything about the fish already landed. Keep this absolutely on the q.t.
>
> Yours,

There followed a list of names in Demeter's dainty little script. Alan sat staring at it for some time, wondering if there was anything he ought or could do about it all.

Then suddenly he dropped on his knees beside his desk and began, unaccustomedly, to pray.

"Oh, God! I thank you that you stood by me! Show me what next!" and added, "Thank you for being always here!"

Then he arose and went at his work for court the next morning.

16

AS ALAN went on through the busy days that followed there were two things he was trying to forget. One was the revolting thought of Demeter trying to lure him by the force of her physical beauty into something she must have known was criminal. He could not quite bring himself even yet to believe she had known fully what it meant to do what she had asked. He tried to put the matter in abeyance, because he did not have time just now to think it through, to catalogue it in his mind and write a finish to the matter. He wanted to be able to at least think the best of her possible. She was too lovely to associate with women who would stoop to use their physical charms to bend a man to their will.

The other thing to be forgotten was the lovely thought of Daryl Devereaux as she had lain in his arms that moment in the cellar, and he had felt that she was the dearest thing on earth. He had to get away from the memory of that. He couldn't hope to have her for his own, and he must not go through life stricken because of one moment that was not really his.

Sometimes he wished he had time to take a run back

there for a day just to see how things were, and whether that Harold person was still on the horizon. But of course he was, and why make it any harder for himself by knowing about it? Sometime soon he would try to get hold of Lance, make him come down and spend a few days with him, and then perhaps he would get a clearer idea about things. But he wouldn't have time just now to go about with him, and he simply must not think about it. So he put Daryl's letter thanking him for the New Year roses away under lock and key as very precious, and would not let himself take it out and read it over as he longed to do. He must not let his thoughts dwell on her.

There had been several social engagements, made in the early fall, which he had put down on his calendar and quietly forgotten until the day came in sight. Several of these he could cancel, and did, for he had neither time nor inclination for social life. But there were two or three ahead that he could not very well avoid because the invitations had come from clients, and in such a way as to make the acceptance a personal favor. Especially was this true of the debutante party that was to be given for the young granddaughter of Mrs. Martin Bennington. She had paused after a business interview in his office one afternoon and said: "By the way, Mr. Monteith, I am just sending out the invitations to my granddaughter's coming-out party. One will come to you, and I do hope you will make time in your busy life to accept. I like you, and I would like Theodora to have at least a background of fine men among her wild young crowd of modern youth. I hope you will please me in this."

Alan had smiled and said he would be delighted, and had really felt flattered after she left to think of the gracious way in which she had put the invitation, making it really an honor worth going after, as social honors went, and one that could not fail to help him in his business connections.

But the night of the event, about a week after his

experience in Demeter's apartment, when he came face to face with his calendar and realized that he must attend that affair whether he liked or not, he was not so much delighted. For one thing he was fatigued by the extra work of the week, and the sickening length to which a certain legal affair had dragged itself out, and he wanted to get away by himself for the week-end and think things out.

But instead he hurried into his evening clothes after a final interview with his partner which had lasted long beyond business hours, and took his way to the Bennington mansion, wondering just how soon he could decently get away and get some sleep.

He entered the throng of pleasure seekers and went the rounds, down a long receiving line, told Theodora how lovely she was, chatted with one or two of his mother's old friends, a client or two, joined a knot of men who were obviously bored with the scene and talking politics to kill time, refused numerous cocktails, and in due time drifted to the ballroom. His eyes wandered indifferently over the spacious place, selecting a few to whom he must show courtesy, calculating how soon he could courteously get away. There was no one here in whom he was especially interested, and yet he realized that it wasn't long since he had enjoyed scenes like this. What had made the difference?

Then came Theodora, and he danced with her, among the first to claim that privilege. It was what her grandmother had intended of course, to start her off with men she felt were just right. And then he danced with Theodora's debutante cousins, three of them, pretty, modern girls, not especially interesting, he thought. Or was it that he was growing older and could not appreciate young things any more?

He was a good dancer and girls always enjoyed dancing with him. He said a few of the usual vapid things, but when he had done his duty by the third of the cousins, until someone cut in on them and relieved him, he turned away, and there in the doorway stood Demeter!

He had not expected Demeter to be here. This was not her set, yet he knew that she must have the entrée here if she chose. And she had chosen, it seemed. Why?

She was dressed in some pale green shimmering stuff, with a glitter of stones about her neck, and a good deal of Demeter showing down the back, yet somehow she had managed to give a demure look to the costume in spite of its daring cut. It went up high to the jeweled throat in front, and was held firmly together down the back by delicate lacings of jeweled threadlike chains from the shoulders down to a point at the back of the waist.

She stood cool and quite haughty there in the doorway looking straight at him, just as if nothing at all had happened between them. Just as if she were sure of him and herself, and he would welcome her coming as he had done many times before.

"Good evening," she said. "You're dancing with me, did you know it?" and as if he had taken the initiative, she stepped into position and placed her hand in his.

The dancers were crowding behind them, and they must move. There was nothing to do but fall into step, but his face was stern and his lips were set in a thin line. Now, what was she going to do? He wanted nothing less than a season in her company, and he had no intention of allowing her to take the lead, yet he must not make a scene of course, and she had known that and had taken advantage of it for some purpose of her own.

"It is good to see you back in your own environment again," she said amusedly as they moved off with the music.

And suddenly it came to him that this was not his own environment. There was nothing satisfying here for him.

God, are you there? It was a cry his heart had been making again and again through these last days, and always there had been that sense of His Presence, that feeling that he would never be alone again. But now, as he cried, it was gone! He had lost that precious sense that had been with him since he first knelt and surrendered himself to the Lord! What was the meaning of it?

Someone touched him on the shoulder, and looking around he met that cold sinister eye of the man who had entered Demeter's house as he was leaving the other night. He had cut in on them!

The count!

What was he doing here?

He stepped off the floor into the shadow of the window drapery and watched them for an instant as they moved away in the dance. He could not be mistaken. It was the same man. Somehow they were planning something together! It did not matter! He had to find the Presence again. He looked vaguely about the brilliant scene. But God would not be here! Why had *he* come? He stepped through a side door into the wide hall and searched out his hostess, making his apologies. "Oh, must you go so soon?" she said in a disappointed voice. "Theodora will be so disappointed!" and he found himself saying, "I must go. I have lost something and must go and find it!"

Now why had he said that? She would think he was crazy!

"Oh, did you lose it here?"

"No, not here," he answered positively.

"Was it valuable? I hope you will find it?"

"Yes, it was valuable," he said, "but I shall find it. I am sure I shall find it, but I must go at once!"

He got himself back to his apartment with the greatest possible speed, and going into his dark room knelt down and began to pray.

"God!" he said, "I have lost the sense of Thy Presence! I cannot do without it. I do not know what to do to get it back. God, why did Thy Presence leave me?"

He knelt there a long time, and by and by it was as if the

Lord came and stood beside him, laid His hand on his head and spoke to him:

"You went into a place where I could not go with you," He said. "You went into the world that crucified Me! They would crucify me again if they could! If you want to find your pleasure with that world of the flesh you must expect to lose sight of Me!"

"But I don't, Lord!" he cried out. "I care nothing about that world now. I cannot do without You! O Lord, return to me!"

Years afterward he told Lance Devereaux of that experience.

"It was as if the Lord stood beside me again, and said to me, 'I will never leave you, nor forsake you!' It was as if He told me many things that night that I had not understood, nor even *known* before, but afterward I found them all in the Bible! And that's how I learned separation from the world. It was as if He had said, 'I died for you, did you die with Me? Well, then, we must live this new resurrection life together, you and I!' You see, Lance, I was all new at it, and there was no one around who could help me then. I didn't even know how to read His word very well. So the Lord just had to tell me Himself."

And Lance, listening with misty eyes and rapt attention, said reverently:

"That was a very precious way to learn. Most of us are so sure we know what is best that we have to learn by stumbling and falling, and even hurting others in our fall, before we know which way to walk!"

But that night Alan spent upon His knees with God! And when he slept he felt the Lord watching over him, and awoke to find himself rested as he never seemed to have been before.

It was about the middle of the next morning while he was busy at his desk that the telephone rang. It was Lance's voice:

"That you, Alan? Well, we're all coming down to the city Friday night to a meeting we want to attend. One of the greatest Bible teachers of the day is to be there and we want to hear him. We're staying at the hotel overnight, and we thought perhaps you'd like to take dinner with us and go to the meeting afterward. Is your calendar all filled?"

"It is not!" said Alan joyously. "I've just got done canceling every social engagement I had, and if there ever was anybody glad to hear a voice it is I to hear yours. But there's nothing doing on that hotel business. You're all coming here! Yes, I mean it! Dad and Mother too! You're my family, aren't you? Didn't I get adopted after the most approved fashion? Well, then say no more! I'm having you for company. Yes, I've plenty of room. There's an apartment across the hall that I can get. It has two bedrooms and is vacant, plenty of room for Dad and Mother and the girls; and you and I can bunk together. How is that? I expect to talk you to death all night, by the way. And, say, nothing doing about that overnight business. This invitation is for the week-end! I need you and I'm going to have you. You came just in the nick of time! Yes, you can. You can get Bud to come over and feed Chrystobel and the hens, and keep up the fires. I'm going to have a visit from my family!"

There was a pause while Lance at the other end consulted with the family, and Alan waited with his heart beating wildly. Daryl would be there in his own apartment, and he would find out just how things had been going with her. Daryl! Daryl! Darling—!

"Yes? Oh, that's good! What time will you get here? Yes, I'm meeting you at the station. Oh, you're coming in the car? That's better. You won't be tied up to trains. Well, I'll be home about four o'clock Friday, and I'll be watching out the window, but in case I'm a bit late you come right in. I'll leave instructions with the janitor! What time does Ruth get out of school Friday? Two o'clock? And you're picking her up at the school? Oh, then you ought to be able to make it by four-thirty at the latest, at least unless you take the roundabout way by which I first arrived at your house! Say, this is the greatest thing that has happened to me since I left your house! I feel like a four-year-old. I can't wait for the time to come. Good-by till Friday."

He hung up and beamed around upon his stenographer.

He didn't explain what had made him so happy, but he didn't need to. He had fairly shouted into the telephone, and she couldn't help understanding. She smiled sympathetically. She hoped it was nobody related to Demeter Cass that was coming. She hated Demeter Cass with all her heart, and hoped she never would come around or telephone again, snobbish little pest!

But Alan found it very hard to work the rest of that day. He was planning his house party, and a misty dreamy look came into his eyes as it occurred to him to marvel that now that God had separated him from his old life and friends, He was bringing something sweet and precious to take their place.

IT was a quarter to two on Friday afternoon when Harold Warner arrived at the farm again, drove up to the front gate and parked his car, and stormed the knocker and the bell together again according to his usual custom.

"Daryl!" called Mother Devereaux from the foot of the back stairs in a cross between a shout and a whisper. "There's somebody at the front door and I can't go. Can you? I've got to finish packing these mince pies and doughnuts, and I haven't changed my dress yet. Father said that we ought to start in exactly half an hour from now. Can you see who it is?"

"Yes, I'm coming," said Daryl, setting her hat on quickly at a becoming cocky angle and hurrying downstairs with her fur coat over her arm. She flung the coat on a chair in the living room as she passed through and opened the front door. It was probably only somebody to enquire the way somewhere. People often stopped to ask the way. Then she opened the door and there was Harold!

She must have showed her blank dismay in her eyes and voice as she said, "Oh!" for Harold immediately bristled.

"Oh!" he said contemptuously. "Is that all the greeting I get after all this long absence?"

"I'm sorry," said Daryl. "I certainly didn't expect to see you when I opened the door. And even now I can't offer you a very cordial greeting because you see we're just on the eve of going away for a few days. But come in just for a minute, won't you? I've time to say greetings at least." Daryl was coming into good form by the time she reached the end of her sentence. She had lived through a good many stages of her fizzled-out romance since Harold drove away that Sunday morning after New Year's, and she had come to wonder just why she had ever thought he was the only lover in the world. Yet she had rather dreaded seeing him again, fearful lest her first infatuation might return upon her and bring the whole matter back again.

But here he was and must be dealt with.

"Come in? Of course I'll come in, Daryl," he boomed. "You certainly wouldn't think I'd come all this way without coming in, would you? Sure, I'll come in, and stay too. I planned to stay over Sunday. Brought my togs and I'll go out sledding with you, if that's what you want. We've got a lot to talk about, Baby, so you'd better take that hat off and stay awhile yourself. You'll have to change your plans, for I've come on important business, and I don't mean maybe, Darrie." He stopped and tried to take her in his arms and kiss her.

But Daryl wasn't there! She slipped back and looked at him remorsefully. Here he was taking things for granted in his important way, and Lance was already backing the car out of the garage ready for starting!

"Please don't, Harold," she said steadily. "I'd rather you didn't try to kiss me. I told you that, you know, when you were here before."

"Oh, yes, I do remember something like that," he said good-naturedly, "but I knew you didn't mean it. I knew you were only bluffing till you'd get your own way. Take off your hat and sit down and we'll get this thing all cleared up. I came up just to have an understanding, and believe me, I'm going to have it, if I have to talk from now till Monday morning!"

"Well," said Daryl, suddenly dropping down into a chair and looking at her former lover, "sit down. It won't take long to have a thorough understanding! I'm perfectly willing to be friendly, and put aside all the things you've said and done, but we're *not* engaged—I'm not sure we ever really were—and you have *not* the right to kiss me any more familiar than friendliness permits. I am not expecting ever to marry you. Is that clear?"

"Mad yet?" asked Harold, grinning at her, admiring her spirit and her pretty brown suit that was so becoming, thinking after all she was a pretty good-looking girl.

"No, I'm not mad!" smiled Daryl. "I never was mad. I was only hurt. But that's gone now. I discovered that I had been mistaken in a lot of things, and I'm not even hurt any more. Of course I'm sorry that you feel as you do about some things, but it hasn't the vital bearing it had a month ago on my future. So you needn't think I have any hard feelings toward you."

Harold studied her a moment thoughtfully. He hadn't expected exactly this line.

"And now, I'm sorry," she went on as Lance honked the horn and she glanced at her watch, "I'll have to say good-by. We're leaving immediately. If you only had taken the trouble to telephone this morning you would have been saved all this long journey."

Harold's mouth and jaw grew stubborn.

"I'm staying, I told you," he said, "and so are you, little lady! We aren't going to have any more of these tantrums. We're going to get this thing settled up. Let them go on without you. We're staying."

"Oh, but that's impossible!" laughed Daryl. "The fire has been banked, and there isn't a thing left in the house to eat but dry cereals. You'll have to come some other time when I am at home if you want further conversation with me, for I am leaving now."

"Where are you going?" he demanded, suddenly angry.

"Why, I'm going to a house party," she said sweetly.

"A house party! Where?"

"At a friend's," said Daryl quickly, her cheeks flushing prettily.

He studied her with narrowing gaze.

"You are going to a house party when I am here and you might stay with me?"

"Seems to me you went to a house party not long ago when you might have been here with me," she said. "But the case is quite different now. There is absolutely no reason why I should want to be with you any more."

"That's nonsense!" he said. "People don't change as quickly as that. Where is this party? Can't I go too? I invited you to mine."

"I'm afraid not. I'm afraid you wouldn't enjoy it any more than I would have enjoyed yours. We shall be attending religious meetings most of the time and I know that's not in your line. But anyway, Harold, it's useless for us to talk any more. I'm done, and I think you'll discover it's for the best when you consider everything."

"Daryl, where are you?" called Lance.

"Coming," called Daryl. "I'm all ready but my coat."

"Well, hustle up, Daryl, I promised Ruth I'd be at the school exactly at half-past and we'll barely make it now. What in the world is keeping you?"

Lance appeared in the doorway and suddenly discovered Harold.

"Oh, I beg your pardon, Warner. Say, that's too bad! You picked a bad time to come, didn't you, with us just leaving. Sorry, but those things will happen once in a while. But you must come around again when we can give you a warmer welcome. You see the fire is banked and the house isn't really warm enough for comfort. Anything we can get for you, a cup of tea or anything? Mother might manage that if you haven't had your lunch. I could drive down for Ruth and come back and pick the rest of them up."

"Thanks! I have had my lunch," said Harold curtly, and he swung sullenly out the door without a look back and drove away into a world where Daryl did not belong.

Daryl wondered at herself as she sat in the car and watched him go. Just a few short weeks ago her heart would have writhed to have him go this way, and now she was only anxious to have him gone! Was that because she had a fickle heart? No, she was sure it was not! Oh, suppose she had married him and then found out how ruthless and bad-tempered and unloving he could be! Even apart from the drinking which to her mind was unspeakably dreadful, he had not been loyal to her, nor thoughtful of her in any way. He had just lived for his own pleasure and convenience, and now he expected her to give up everything and stay at home and argue with him. O blessed escape! Even if she were not on her way to a delightful time, which included meeting the very nicest friend that could be— only a friend of course, but still a wonderful friend. She was cured of lovers, and she wasn't ever going to think again of that little incident in the cellar; that had been too trifling for a second thought. She was cured of romance forever now. She was going to be heartfree and happy!

Then suddenly a memory of Demeter Cass floated through her mind, and brought a serious expression over her face.

Her mother saw it and put out a tender hand, looking anxiously at her.

"There wasn't any reason why you would rather have stayed at home with him, was there, Daryl?" she asked sweetly. "You know it isn't too late now. We could get out and Lance could drive after him and tell him you had changed your mind. It wouldn't take long to build up the fire and I could whip up a dinner in no time. If it's something that may bring sorrow to you all your life, why —! We could telephone Alan, you know, and make it all right!"

"Oh, Mother dear!" laughed Daryl. "No, no, *no!* I don't want him back, and I wouldn't stay home for the world! Please, Mother, don't rub it in! I was an awful fool of course, and I'm so glad God showed me in time. But please let's forget him now! Lance, let's get started."

"Sure thing!" said Lance, putting his foot on the starter. "You wouldn't think anything could induce me to go chasing after that ill-tempered bum, do you? I thank my lucky stars I'm not going to have him for a brother-in-law. Now, let's go!"

Alan, meantime, had been having a rare time getting ready for his party. He almost neglected his business, thinking and planning for the coming of these dear people who had taken him into their home and hearts.

He saw that his apartment and the one across the hall were in perfect order, with flowers in every room. He arranged with the restaurant on the first floor to serve dinner up in the apartment on Friday evening, and provide perfect service so that everything would move smoothly. He went to the delicatessen down the street and stocked up his refrigerator with all the delicacies he could think of for midnight suppers, and quiet meals by themselves when they didn't want to go down to the hotel dining room. Then he went around and put little touches in the rooms, a picture here, a book there, magazines, a little crystal bud vase with a single yellow bud in it for Daryl's room. He had seen it in the window of a shop he passed and couldn't resist it. He even bought a picture puzzle or two, and wished at the last minute that he had thought to rent a piano and have it sent up. He felt as if he had never been so happy in his life, preparing for his guests. And then he clipped the day short, gave his curious stenographer a holiday, and got home before four o'clock, though he knew they couldn't likely arrive before half-past at the earliest.

On the way home he had stopped and bought a large box of candy, the duplicate of the one he had bought at Christmas. It seemed that he could not think of anything more to do. And then he sat down to watch out the window for their car to arrive. He hadn't thought of Demeter Cass all day. He hadn't once thought of the paper he had brought away with him from her apartment. He had locked it away in the safe in his room and had meant to examine it more carefully at his leisure, but the whole affair had passed entirely out of his world for the time being. It was then that the telephone rang and he heard her voice speaking.

"Alan, is that you? Oh, I'm glad you're there! I'm coming up to your apartment now. I'll be there within five minutes. I'm bringing the count with me. We have something very important to tell you. Are you going to be there all the evening?"

"No!" said Alan shortly. "I'm going to be out all the evening. I'm having guests for dinner who will be arriving at any minute now, and we are going out for the evening. It will be impossible for me to see you now."

"But, Alan, we must! You'll simply have to arrange for us to see you privately for a few minutes at least, perhaps downstairs in one of the private reception rooms. We are in a terrible predicament. We have lost a most important paper and I must ask you if it was one of those I showed you. I cannot tell you over the telephone. I must see you at once! For the love of mercy, fix it up somehow. We are starting at once!"

And just then there were voices outside the door and the bell of the apartment rang loudly.

"I am sorry," said Alan hastily, "I cannot see you to-night. My friends have just arrived. You'll have to excuse me!" and he hung up and hurried to meet his guests.

18

HAROLD Warner drove off down the white road into the white, white countryside. He was more shaken than he had been since the time when his grandmother came to visit when he was seven and took him aside and administered the sound spanking of which he very much stood in need. He drove on and on and couldn't quite make up his mind where to go.

For the truth was he had lost his job that day. He had not merely been laid off for a time with a hope for the future, but he had out-and-out *lost* his job. Been fired, he told himself unbelievingly. He was always unbelieving when he was fired from a job. It wasn't by any means the first time this had happened either! But then, there would be more jobs, he told himself. There were always more jobs. People talked of how hard it was to find a job, but he never had any trouble. He was so good-looking they took him on whether they needed him or not, just to have him around to look at. That was the way he thought about it, when he had to think about it at all. But he did usually find it easy to get good jobs. The trouble was in persuading his employers to keep him when they got to know him. But he didn't consider that part. He generally made enough to keep him in neckties, with a little left over for flowers and candy for girls. But he really was up against it now. His job and his girl lost all in one day! It was hard lines.

Of course there were plenty more girls, too, when one thought about it. But Daryl really had been a peach! Such great eyes! It was her eyes that had got him. And her father was so well fixed! That pleasant home! He had figured on staying there a week or two till he got rested up from his last job and ready to go back to the city and hunt a new one, and it certainly was hard having them go off like that. Fire low and nothing in the house to eat. He had lied about having had lunch, of course. The fact was he had barely enough in his pocket to buy gas, and he had planned on a good meal when he got to Devereaux's. Mother Devereaux was a good cook, and fairly hospitable if she was rather a frost in other ways.

Yes, it was hard lines to have all this happen at once, especially right on top of the boss' daughter giving him the air, just when he had thought he was getting along so nicely with her. If it hadn't been for thinking she was really interested in him he wouldn't have stayed away from Daryl quite so long. That was probably what got her. Two or three days might have been enough to give her a lesson. He had carried the discipline a little too far! She was high-spirited, that girl! A pang of sadness went through him at her loss. Maybe—but no, she had meant it. He could tell that. Just as he had known the boss meant it when he fired him this morning. It was final and there was no use going back and trying it over. Just a waste of time. Of course he still had his good looks, and his college education.

But he was hungry! And the only place he knew where he could get a free meal was home. Home was a long way off. It would take an hour and a half of hard traveling to get there, and every cent he had for gas. Still, if he spent the gas money for a meal he wouldn't have any place to sleep that night and he wouldn't have the gas to get anywhere else. Too bad now he had bought that car, and used his last month's salary for the first installment on it! Perhaps it would have been wiser to have turned it back, but well, he hadn't. He'd better go home and see the folks and get a good meal, borrow a little money from his father, and after he was rested get himself another job, and maybe another girl. There were always as good fish in the sea as ever were caught.

Of course there was Elsie Bracken, in the old home town. She was probably still waiting for him. Good little Elsie! She wasn't so bad either. Had sweet blue eyes, something like Daryl's. Maybe that was who Daryl always made him think of. He'd never figured it out clearly before. Elsie'd been off to school, trying to fit herself for him, he supposed. He hadn't seen her for some time now, and he hadn't written so often either. Of course he had told her he was very busy and all that, and she hadn't made much kick. She had been faithful enough writing herself, had really kept him in touch with the home town. His mother wasn't much on corresponding unless somebody died, or she needed some money. Strange his mother had never been able to understand that it took a lot of money to live in town and keep up to a fine job and go around in good society.

Well, he'd better go home now, anyway, for a day or two. He might look Elsie over again, and if she was all right maybe it would be as well to marry her and have the question settled. Her father wasn't so badly fixed either, and he would probably give her something pretty hand-some for a wedding present. He could tip her off to ask for it in money and let them pick their own. Of course, it would be a little awkward not to have money for a wedding trip and all the fixings. But they had the car. It wouldn't take so much for gas, and they could really have a pretty good time traveling around and seeing things.

They could stay at tourist camps and it wouldn't cost much. Elsie wouldn't expect grand hotels of the kind Daryl and his boss' daughter would rate. But Elsie was a pretty good scout! If she had a bit of money it would be all right. And in case he could work it to get married right away in a few days it would be a pretty good hit back at Daryl, too! The thought intrigued him. He began to plan the letter he would write her. He thought of several phrases that would be good to use. It would be nice to tell her that Elsie reminded him of her, and that she was his oldest sweetheart. Yes, he would go home!

So he turned at last into a narrow, rough, scarcely broken road, and plowed his way through the snow mile after mile, trying to figure out just how he was going to manage to get through a wedding without any money. Of course he could hock the ring, Daryl's ring, but he wouldn't get much for it out in a country town, and the people were always so nosey in a little village like that. They might ask impertinent questions. The only trouble about it all was that the ring wasn't all paid for yet, but that wouldn't matter. They could go to another state and it would be several weeks or months before the lending company that financed it would find him. By that time he would have another job and plenty of money. Of course having a good-looking wife might help him to get on too, and be respected.

Well, that was that. He had lost his job and his girl, but there were plenty more in the offing, and he still had his good looks. When he got something to eat it would be all right! Beefsteak and onions would be good. He would get his mother to fix some up as soon as he got in the house. Beefsteak didn't take long to cook. He would stop at the market when he passed through the village and get the beefsteak, charge it to his father, and save time.

Just then, with the taste of the onions fairly in his mouth and the smell of the beefsteak cooking, he ran over a great rock beneath the snow, nearly upsetting his car, and with a loud bang his rear tire exploded, and went down with a long exhausted sigh like something dying. And he was seven miles from the nearest garage, and no spare tire! He finished the soliloquy he had begun at the Devereaux's with a single phase, as he stood in the snow and glowered at his limp tire:

"Can you beat it?"

Demeter Cass and her count had been having a stormy time. The count had arrived that afternoon, quite unexpectedly, and in a desperate hurry! He demanded all the papers and photographs and letters that he had given to Demeter, and he wanted to know just exactly what she had said to that fool lawyer she had persisted in dragging into the case.

Demeter was used to dominating a situation, but the count was now dominating Demeter. He had gotten all he could out of her, it seemed, and now a situation had arisen which meant that if she could do nothing more for him, he was done with her.

"There is one paper missing," he said cuttingly, and looked at her with his cold prominent eyes that were a cross between milky marbles and peeled onions. "It is the most important paper of all!"

When he was angry or annoyed the count had a strong Spanish accent, though at times he could speak beautiful English. He used the accent now and Demeter lifted her chin haughtily. She did not care for his accent.

"The papers are all there! Everything that you gave me."

"They are not!" said the count. "The most incriminating one of all is missing. Where is it? I demand it!"

"I tell you that is everything I had," said Demeter. "What would be the point in my holding on to one of them? It certainly would not do me any good if you are going away."

"It certainly would not. On the contrary it would do you great harm if this thing came to trial and that paper was found in your possession."

Demeter looked frightened.

"Is there danger of this thing coming to court?" she asked sharply.

"There certainly is, unless we can do something at once!"

"But you told me there was no danger whatever!"

"I told you! Yes, I told you! What I supposed was true! While that man Bryerly stayed in Europe there was no danger whatever. He had bought heavily with us, and whatever he did the rest did. But now he has suddenly arrived on the scene, and he is starting out to investigate these mines and these oil wells, and when he finds they are not there where he thinks they are you know what kind of a storm will be raised! He has money and he will prosecute! He will do more than that! He will hound us to the ends of the earth. He is that kind of a man!"

"Us!" said Demeter resentfully, "where do you get that *us?* I certainly do not appear in this matter except as an owner of stock!"

"You don't, don't you? Whose picture is that on the photo we have been using in vouching for this? Whose signature is signed to some of the letters we have written to your friends? Do you think you can get by and go free if I get into trouble? You are known to be my friend. We have been everywhere together! You have been hand-and-glove with me in this matter! And did you think you would go free if we got caught!"

"But we must not get caught!" said Demeter. "You said —!"

"What I said does not matter. That was then and this is now! We shall certainly be caught if that paper gets into the hands of someone who is interested to search this thing out. We must find that paper if we have to search heaven and hell for it! Where have you been keeping these papers?"

"In my safe as you told me to do."

"And how many times have you taken them out?"

"Only once when I showed them to Mr. Monteith as you asked me to do. I don't like your tone. I'm not a child!"

"No, you are not a child!" said the man sneeringly. "I sometimes wonder whether I should have trusted you as I did. You may be more cunning than I think. But unless you can produce this lost paper which is most incriminating, you certainly will have plenty coming to you."

"I don't know what you mean!" said Demeter, turning white beneath her exquisite complexion. "I have certainly been absolutely true to you, and have done a lot of hard things to get you where you wanted to be. Who else do you think would have got you into the social set where you have been invited? How would you ever have met Mr. Bryerly if it hadn't been for me? And the two old Catmann sisters who bought so much stock? And all that list of names. Wait! I wrote them down on one of those papers! The one that had your note on the back asking me not to show that paper to Mr. Monteith. Where is it? You must have put it in your pocket!"

"I have not put anything in my pocket, young woman! That is the missing paper! The one with the list!"

"Well, it was there! Among the rest. I'm sure it was. And besides, I don't like the way you are talking to me. After I have done everything in the world for you."

"You did it for yourself as well, didn't you? You wanted money yourself, didn't you?"

"Yes, but where is it? I not only haven't seen a dime of all that you have collected, but I gave you everything I had in my checking account as well, expecting returns almost immediately. I am practically penniless, and it won't be time for my next check for six weeks. I'm simply having to charge everything I buy, and it's most inconvenient. If you are going away as you say, I shall have to ask you for some money at once. You promised that money would be forthcoming right away!"

"When we could open the mines, remember I said, *when* we got the mines, and get the oil wells to working."

"But you said they were starting at once!"

"And so they were practically, if we could have laid our hands on the money to start them. You promised to get that fortune that was coming to you from your uncle, you know."

"Well, I probably will yet," said Demeter haughtily, "but I shall not let you have any of it if you act this way."

"You can't get that money, remember, young lady, unless you have papers for collateral, shares, you know. And I certainly shall not look after my part of this matter if you are going to be childish and demand money every few minutes."

"But it was the money that I went into this for. You said it would be a great fortune."

"Exactly so, and it would have been if there hadn't been so many hitches. If you, for instance, had been able to hand over the hundreds of thousands that you led me to expect from that trust fund, if you had worked your young lawyer just right, we would have had it in plenty of time to start the work, and all would have been well. But now that man Bryerly has got wind of something somewhere, and he's onto us. We've got to work fast if we would save ourselves. I didn't anticipate that you would fall down on your job when I promised instant returns. We're lucky now if we get out of this jam and go free. Yes, I mean it. You needn't look so incredulous. And if you don't find that paper for me before another half-hour we're both in a tight fix. I have reason to believe that they are already on our trail. I'm waiting here till dark, and then I'm leaving. If you find that paper and hand it over before I go there may be some hope that I can pull things together, but if it's gone it's all up with you and me both! Isn't there some hope that that fool lawyer took the paper with him?"

"I don't think so! He's not that kind of a man."

"Oh, you don't think so!" said the count contemptuously. "You and your smooth young lawyers! Look here, Demeter, are you in love with that man?"

"Of course not!" said Demeter, her eyes flashing haughtily, "but if I were what business of yours would that be?"

"I would certainly make it my business," he said with a meaningful look. "I don't trust you as I used to do. I know you were dancing with him the other night."

"Yes, and what for? To do the work you had set me to do. And you spoiled it all by cutting in. I had the stage set for a final scene that would have won my point and then you had to cut in! I'm just disgusted with you!"

Suddenly Demeter leaned forward and took a picture from the little pile of papers that lay on the top of the box on the table between them.

"Let that alone!" said the count surlily. "Do you want to lose more valuable papers for me?"

"This is mine!" she said with dignity. "It is my picture. I certainly don't want it to get into any scene in court. I know how to protect myself."

"Oh, you do, do you, Demeter? We'll see whether you do or not, I have the film of that picture, remember, and it wouldn't do you any good to destroy that picture because I could easily print another as I printed that. But you can put that picture back in the box with the rest. I don't intend to have that in your possession. I don't trust you any more, you know too much. That has my picture in it too, and if you should try to turn traitor and tell what you know, I don't intend you shall have any ammunition. Put it down!"

"No!" said Demeter, firmly.

"Yes!" said the man savagely. "As long as you have that incriminating paper in your possession I'm keeping that picture against you. If I get into trouble you'll go along with me."

"Wait!" said Demeter as he came near to take the picture by force. She reached over and took up the telephone from its stand by her side.

"What are you going to do?" he demanded, seizing hold of her wrist and grinding its diamond bracelet into her white arm.

"Stop!" she said furiously. "You're hurting my arm! I'll get your paper for you if it's to be had. I'm telephoning Alan Monteith. If he took it I can make him give it up!"

"Oh, so you think maybe he took it, do you?"

"I just remember he had some paper in his hand, when he left. He may have carried it with him without knowing it. You see, you had just arrived and I was rather upset. I didn't expect you so soon. You said you wouldn't get here till seven."

"Oh, and so you think your paragon may have made some mistake, do you? Or was it you that made the mistake on purpose? Look here, what are you two trying to put over on me, anyhow? You think you can make me believe that he took a paper by mistake, do you, as important a paper as that? Well, I'm not so dumb as you seem to think I am, and you'll have some time getting by me, you'll find out!"

Just then Alan answered the telephone.

"No! Don't tell him I'll be there! You little fool, you!" growled the man standing over Demeter. "Tell him I'm not here! Tell him I'm out of the city! You little fool, you!"

But Demeter had hung up.

"I couldn't!" she said. "He hung up himself. He has a dinner party. They had just arrived. Come, we'll have to go at once!"

"And you think I am going there? I? To a cunning lawyer's house? The very most dangerous place in the world for me to go! Go yourself if you like, but I shall be far away by the time you arrive there! You little fool! You've done for me now. And yourself, too, incidentally. Give me that picture! I'll have that anyway!"

"I won't!" said Demeter, holding it tightly in both hands. "I'll tear it in pieces if you try to get it away from me!"

"Oh, you will, will you?"

Demeter looked up defiantly and found she was looking into the eye of a sinister little automatic.

"Hand over that picture, and don't open your mouth to scream. I'd just as soon shoot us both as not, anyway."

Demeter saw the insane look in the man's ugly eyes and handed over the picture, and just then the doorbell sounded clearly through the room! But the little gun remained pointed straight at her as the man spoke in a low warning voice.

"If that's anyone after me I haven't been here in a week. Understand? Go out there to the door and tell them so, and don't turn around and look back. Remember this gun can reach out to the hall door! Remember I shall be hearing every word you say! And dead women tell no tales!"

Demeter, with every bit of natural color drained from under the rouge in her cheeks, sat staring at that gun, and at a sign and further whisper from the man, rose and went to meet the maid who had answered the bell, conscious of the greatest fear that had ever come into her life.

It did not help matters that when she reached the hall of her apartment she came face to face with a great burly policeman. He was looking at her as if he did not care in the least that she was Demeter Cass, descendant of an old and respected family, possessed of a fine inheritance, dashing member of the smartest set of the city. He looked at her like primitive Justice out to search her very heart and soul, and pierce asunder the joints and marrow of her being.

"I wantta see that count you have here," he said, pinning her with his glance.

She heard herself repeating the words the count had just told her, but they were like water poured upon the ground so far as any effect they had upon the policeman was concerned. He just leered into her face.

"Now, looka here, lady, we know he's here. We saw him come in. No use lying about it. We gotta find him!"

"He hasn't been here for a week!" repeated Demeter like an automaton, feeling herself trembling from head to foot, wondering if she were going to fall, reeling and leaning against the wall.

The policeman strode past her pushing her aside roughly, and she turned with all her senses whirling about dizzily and looked into the room she had just left, expecting to hear the report of that sinister little revolver, and to see a dead policeman lying on her lovely white velvet carpet, with his head on the head of her great white bear rug.

But the room was entirely empty!

The imposing figure of the count holding his little automatic had melted away. Even the box with its papers and photographs, nuggets of silver and sample of oil in a small high bottle, were gone. There wasn't a trace of the count or any of his belongings. And when they searched the place for him they found nothing. Not even a servant had seen him leave, not one would own he had been there. Demeter, too, though frightened almost to the breaking point, stuck sweetly to her story that she hadn't seen the count for over a week. She went early to bed, knowing that the place was being watched, and lay awake planning how to escape from the net that seemed to have enclosed her.

So that was the reason that Demeter and her count did not appear at the door of Alan Monteith's apartment, shortly after his guests arrived, to plant a thorn in Daryl Devereaux's breast and spoil the beautiful evening for them all.

ALAN as he hung up the receiver and sprang to meet his guests had only time for a hurried committing of the whole matter to the new Master of his life by just a lifted heart and an upward look, and then he completely forgot about it, and did not think of it again until they were well on their way to the meeting. Then he gave a passing thought to the wonder of having perplexities solved, and difficulties avoided that had loomed so large. How marvelous it was that God, the great God, had time and thought for such little difficulties in the lives of His own! Whatever had been the reason, God had taken that trouble out of the way for the evening. Would all life be like that if he kept within the will of God? If he had the Presence constantly with him then it wasn't far to the throne. One had but to call. It was wonderful!

The conference was a great experience. Somehow it had never entered Alan's head that there were large groups of people like this who put God first, and loved His Word and His Work above all else. The Christians he had known heretofore had been ordinary formal Christians, who went to church, sometimes twice on Sundays, gave to good causes, were respected in the community and upheld all kinds of good works. That was all. He had never heard one of them mention the name of the Lord except in a most formal way. Their Christianity hadn't been a very vital thing with them.

But these people radiated Christianity, and one knew from the very look on their happy faces that "they had been with Jesus." And some of them didn't look as if they had much else in this world to be happy about, either, if one might judge by the plainness of their apparel.

Alan sat at the end of the pew and looked down the line of happy faces. Mother Devereaux next to Daryl, then Father, then Ruth, and Lance at the far end, and his heart suddenly swelled with happiness. Wistfully he watched them all. If they all could but be his family! Was there any hope? Or was this but a little bright spot that would soon pass and leave his lonely world drab again?

But no, that could never be. His life couldn't be drab again with that Presence constantly near. He would never be alone again, even if these dear new friends had to go another way than his. They had at least introduced him to his Lord, and that was the greatest thing they could have done.

But it was a very happy evening, with Daryl by his side. The dearness of her grew in his heart. The nearness of her was precious. Her beautiful eyes looked up to his as she smiled in enjoyment over the meeting! Just to be holding one side of the singing book with her seemed heavenly sweet to him. This one evening at least he was granted to enjoy her company. If never again through life at least he would have had this.

So they banished the thought of the Harolds and Demeters and just enjoyed the evening together. They would have enjoyed the meeting of course even if they hadn't had each other. Equally perhaps they would have enjoyed each other without the meeting. To be enjoying it together seemed like a little heaven below.

For it was strange how Alan had been able to enter into this new atmosphere and breathe the air of joy in the Lord and feel that it was the fulfillment of all he had been longing for all his life. It came to him to wonder what some of his acquaintances at the Bennington dance would think of this meeting if they could be here. What would they think of him for enjoying such things as these better than all the hectic joys of the world in which they moved? And then he marveled at the change that could come to one on being born again. That was the explanation, he was born again, and old things were passed away!

He looked down at the sweet girl by his side and noted the light in her face, the eager interest with which she was listening to the message that was being spoken, and his heart thrilled anew to think that his interest in these things and hers were one. At least they had this in common, even if he might not hope for anything closer in this life, that they were both children of the Heavenly Father, both born again into the household of God.

The last night before the guests went home to the farm Alan and Lance lay awake far into the small hours talking. Alan had many questions to ask which Lance could answer. Lance in turn marveled at the way the young Christian had grown in the few short days since he had been saved, all by himself as it were, with his Bible and his Lord. His heart thrilled anew with love for this man who had dropped into his life out of the midst of a storm.

"You don't know what it is to me to have a friend like you!" he exclaimed suddenly in the midst of their talk. "I couldn't love you more if you were my own brother!"

"Same here, Lance!" said Alan. "I feel as if God had been wonderfully good to me leading me to you, and setting a seal upon our friendship by leading you to do that great thing for me, going that awful journey through the storm! I can never tell you just what it has meant to me to know a man would go so far for an utter stranger!"

"I thought it was great of you to be willing to go on in the face of that storm the way you did to keep your promise about that medicine," said Lance. "I liked the look in your face when you said you'd staked your life on keeping your promise to that doctor. I knew I was yours till death when I heard you say that, and I knew I was a hundred percent for you, and was going with you even if it meant—well, whatever it meant to me also!"

Silently in the night they gripped each other's hands in a quick warm clasp that men seldom give to one another. It meant a silent life-covenant of more than friendship, of real comradeship forever.

They were still a long time after that, and then Alan spoke again.

"There is more to this than I have told you, Lance! I was at a turning point in my life in more ways than one. I was almost to the place where I was going to ask the wrong woman to marry me. I think I must have known all the time in the back of my mind that she was the wrong woman. But it was the way of the world and it was getting me. I was restless and hungry and there didn't seem to be anything else to satisfy. I wasn't sure she would, but I was almost persuaded to try. And then God stopped me."

"Stopped you?"

"Yes, by letting me see your two girls, your sister and your Ruth. Just to see them in the pleasant intimacy of their home life for a few hours was enough to show me the contrast. If I had never seen them again I would have carried a vision of what a woman could be in a home and in a man's life, a vision that I knew that other woman never could fulfill."

Lance lay still for a minute and then he said thoughtfully:

"It wasn't all on one side, brother. I think we have a lot to thank you for in helping to open the eyes of my sister. We were all kinds of worried about that poor fish who seemed to have charmed her. I don't know how he ever managed it, though of course he is a good-looker in a showy way. But she was pretty well convinced, I think, that she was for him. And then the Lord sent you along to show what a real man could be. I'm sure that went a long way in making her see she might be making a mistake."

"Oh," said Alan hesitantly, "I don't think I figured in that. She wasn't even thinking about me. I was just an interruption. I think, if anything could make her see, it would be the fellow himself." Then he suddenly closed his lips. He mustn't even tell her brother what he had overheard from the telephone.

"Look here, man," said Lance earnestly, "she'd seen him before and it hadn't opened her eyes. No, I tell you it was having a real man in contrast to bring out what was wrong in him that changed her."

"But how do you know she is changed?" asked Alan, hoping against hope.

"Well, I'm sure she is," said the brother happily. "Surely you yourself saw how she refused to go with him. And then day before yesterday —! Oh, you don't know about that, do you? You don't know how nearly we got held up and didn't get here, do you? Just when we were on the minute of starting too."

"No, what was that! I'm glad I didn't know about it at the time. It certainly would have been an anxious minute for me."

"Well, that was what it was for me for about five of them at least. I was so mad and worried I felt like wringing somebody's neck. We were practically on the point of starting. I was out in the garage arranging the suitcases to make as much room as possible. Dad and Mother were doing the last things about shutting up the house, and Daryl even had her hat on, when that bum drew up at the door in a shining new car with two or three suitcases, come to stay the weekend apparently! Say, I was mad!"

"I should say!" said Alan, aghast at what might have happened.

"Well, first I thought I'd just go out there and tell him to go to thunder before Daryl ever saw him. But I knew it had to come to a showdown sooner or later, and perhaps it was just as well for it to happen right away, because I knew Dad and Mother were almost sick worrying about it, though they wouldn't own it. So I waited about three minutes to give Daryl a chance to take a stand if she was going to, and then I backed out the car and honked the horn several times, just as if I didn't know the chump was there; and in a minute I followed it up by opening the side door and calling to Daryl to hurry, that we were late starting already and Ruth would be waiting. After that I marched into the room to beard the lion in his den, and do you know that chump was daring to tell my sister that she ought to stay at home and entertain him because he had come all that way to see her! And after the way he had left the last time, too! He just ignored all his insults and sneers and expected to be taken right in and welcomed. Well, I'm glad to tell you that Daryl talked right up to him, just told him she was sorry to disappoint him but it couldn't be helped, and she had to leave. And then after he was gone and we got started Mother asked her if she would rather have stayed and Daryl told us plainly that she was done with him, and had sent him on his way, said she was glad God had showed her in time or something like that. So I'm pretty well satisfied that she's over that. If I had had to call that poor fish brother-in-law the rest of my life I don't know how I could have stood it!"

"Well, that's great!" said Alan, trying to keep the thrill out of his voice. "I felt that way about him too, but of course I didn't know him at all. It seemed to me that it was a dreadful mistake, your sister is so lovely, and he seemed so—well, different! You're sure he won't come back again and try to win her over?"

"Oh, he may of course," said Lance sadly, "but we're all praying about it. I don't think the Lord would let that happen! But we're going to try to help her forget all we can, and I think this trip is going to do a great deal. Ruth says she told her last night that this conference was the greatest thing she'd ever had in her life, and you can see for yourself how much she has enjoyed being here. You've been a wonderful help, and I can't help thanking God every time I pray that He sent you to us for a friend."

"That's great, brother!" said Alan fervently, and then lay awake a long time thrilling to the thought that perhaps now he might allow himself a chance to win Daryl for himself. The vision of what life would be with such a girl by his side was so breath-taking that he scarcely slept till morning began to dawn.

At breakfast the next morning, which Alan had had served in the apartment again so they might have the last few minutes together, Alan asked Lance about his mission.

"How is it you could leave it over Sunday, Lance?" he asked. "Is it intermittent, or do you have it every week?"

"Oh, it's every week of course," said Lance, "but there's another fellow who is studying in Bible School who takes it for me now and then when I have to be away."

"You going to speak next Sunday?"

"Yes, I'm supposed to," said Lance.

"Well, I guess I'll run down and hear you next Sunday, if you don't mind."

"I was going to suggest," said Father Devereaux, "that you spend next week-end with us, or as much of it as you can spare from your business. You know Mother and I are getting old and we like to have our children around us as much as possible."

"Wonderful!" said Lance. "You needn't make me the excuse. I'm nothing to hear after the speakers you have in the city here, but it will be great to have you come. Could you get down Friday night? The sledding is still pretty good."

"I certainly will if I can get away," said Alan eagerly, and his eyes sought Daryl's face. He told himself that he must go very cautiously. He must not let her know that he loved her yet. It might startle her and spoil the pleasant friendship that he hoped might be growing up between them.

But Daryl looked up with only welcome on her face, and did he fancy it or was it true that the flush on her cheeks and the light in her eyes meant that she was really glad to have him coming?

But he did not realize that he was letting his eyes speak things that he had not even dared to form in his thoughts as yet. Were her beautiful eyes answering his heart's hunger or not? He could not be sure. He must go slowly.

So it was settled that he would spend the next week-end at the farm, and that made the good-bys easier.

"Well, he certainly is a prince of a fellow!" said Lance as they started on their way.

"Yes, he's all that!" said Father Devereaux.

"He's a dear lad!" said Mother Devereaux.

"He's wonderful!" said Ruth.

Nobody looked at Daryl, and she sat quietly by her mother and said nothing, but there was a dreamy look in her eyes and her lips were parted in a lovely smile.

"Have a good time, little girl?" Her father suddenly reached across her mother and patted her on the cheek.

"'Deed I did, Daddy," said Daryl, reverting to her little girl habit. "Had the time of my life!"

"Glad you came?" asked Lance slyly over his shoulder, winking quietly at Ruth.

"So glad, brudder!" laughed Daryl in the way she used to do years ago.

"Glad you sent the handsome brute flying?" dared Lance, growing bolder.

"Double glad, brudder!" and her laugh rang out clear and heart-whole, and the whole family sighed in relief.

They had been so afraid that Daryl would get morbid about having done it, when the excitement of their visit to the city was passed, but this certainly did not sound that way.

So they went happily home, planning what they would do next week-end when Alan came down.

Alan did a good deal of thinking that week, at least nights when he came back to the apartment alone. The daytime was filled with hard work and no room for personal questions. But in one of the watches of the night Demeter and her wild telephone call about a missing paper came back to his memory. He wasn't sure just what she had said, he had been so excited about his guests. But now he remembered the paper he had brought away with him from the last fiery interview. He got up and hunted it out from the drawer where he had locked it away. He spent some time studying it carefully, and wondered if he ought to call up Demeter in the morning. Perhaps he should tell her about it. But it was all a hectic mess and he didn't want to get into it. Perhaps he would better just put it in an envelope and mail it to her.

But in the morning when he tried to reach her he was told that the telephone was disconnected. He hung up and wondered what that could mean, and finally mailed the paper, having the address typewritten.

But the next evening as he idly glanced over a yellow news sheet left beside him on the seat in the subway he saw two items that startled him. One was a racy column of news-gossip, with a sting to it. A name caught his eye, the name of the count.

The article said:

> It is rumored that a certain count who has been making himself unpopular crashing high-class parties in the city, and selling stock in oil and silver to a number of our worthy and gullible citizens, has suddenly disappeared, and taken with him numerous

large sums of money received in payment for said stocks. His disappearance seems to be simultaneous with the arrival from abroad of our old friend J. G. Bryerly who holds a quantity of these stocks, and had come over to investigate them. Rumor has it that there are no oil wells in the location described in the certificates, and that the silver mines are empty. If so the shareholders are to be pitied, but not nearly so much as the count who has been wise to disappear.

It is said that a certain golden-haired woman's smiles have aided and abetted the sale of these shares, and that she would perhaps be wise to disappear as well until the oil wells can be resurrected and the silver mines restocked. But all this is of course hearsay.

The article raced on to attack another character or two, but Alan read and re-read the first part, and wondered what had become of Demeter, and if she were really in trouble. Wondered again if it were true that she had actually known how utterly worthless that stock was, and had yet gone on trying to delude people into buying it.

He turned the page over with a troubled frown, and then a news item in the social column caught his eye.

Miss Demeter Cass, a prominent member of the city's social set, and active in the Junior League, has closed her apartment for the winter and gone to southern California to stay with an elderly relative who is ill and needs her companionship. Miss Cass will be greatly missed in her own circle of friends, but it is hoped that she will return in a few months to her native haunts.

Alan paused, and had to smile over the idea of Demeter Cass allowing herself even for a few hours to be the companion of an elderly invalid relative. It was so unlike

Demeter. And then he threw down the paper and sat staring off into nothing, startled at himself. That was his present quick judgment of Demeter, and yet he had been so blind, so completely crazy not so very long ago, as to consider whether he might not marry her! How good God had been to him to save him from such a terrible mistake!

When Alan arrived at the farm in time for dinner Friday evening, there was as much joy over his greeting as if they all had been separated for months.

Ruth was there for over Sunday as usual, and they all acted as if they were blood relatives who liked nothing better in life than to be together.

The time passed all too swiftly, there seemed to be so many nice things to do, singing and reading and talking, skating and sledding, and doing little homely pleasant things about the house together, catching up for all the years they had not known one another.

And after they had spent a long delightful evening together, suddenly Alan looked up at Daryl and said:

"Daryl, why don't we go down cellar again and get some apples? Come on, I'm hungry for an apple," and Daryl smilingly arose and led the way.

Lance almost offered to go, and then thought better of it and closed his lips, watching them away with a pleased look to his eyes.

Alan went and found the willow basket they had carried down before, remembering where it hung on a nail in the pantry, and Daryl snapped on the cellar light.

When they started down the cellar stairs Alan surprised Daryl by slipping his arm about her waist and walking down the stairs in step with her.

"Now," said he, as they reached the bottom of the steps and glanced up, "do you suppose if we stayed down here long enough some of them would come and turn the light out on us? I'd mightily like to recapture the moment we had together before down here, and go on from there if I might. It seemed to me it was the sweetest moment of my life. Daryl, look up!"

He took her face in his two hands and lifted it up so that he could look deep into her eyes, and then suddenly the moment returned to them, the thrill, the joy of being together, the dearness of each other! Alan drew her within his arms and held her close, stooped down and whispered, "Daryl, I love you!" and Daryl yielded to his embrace, a flood of joy breaking forth in her heart.

"And I love you!" Daryl whispered back. "Oh, Alan! I never dreamed there was anything as wonderful as this!"

"My precious!" he said, and suddenly reached out and snapped off the light, catching Daryl up in his arms as before, like a little child, and held her face close to his own. They felt again the ecstasy of that other moment they had tried so hard to put out of their memories. Oh, the joy of knowing that the other cared in this wonderful way!

And after all it was just for a minute, again, for they could hear footsteps above, and Mother saying,

"Why, where are those two children? Do you suppose Daryl didn't know where you put the barrel of apples?"

Alan gave her one tender clinging kiss, and set her down, for they heard Father Devereaux's steps coming toward the kitchen. In a minute he would discover that the light was turned off. Alan reached out and snapped it on, and they were both giggling softly as they took hold of hands and stole over toward the apples.

"But wait!" whispered Alan in a low tone, "I've something for you. I didn't know whether I would ever have the chance to give it to you or not, but I thought I'd have it with me in case I dared!"

He took out a little white velvet box from his pocket and took something from it. Daryl could not see clearly in the dim cellar but she suddenly realized that a wonderful stone was catching the garish little cellar light and flinging it all around the place.

Alan drew her hand up into his and fitted the ring on her finger.

"Is it big enough?" he asked anxiously, "because I told them I thought it would be the smallest size for you have such little, lovely hands!" and he laid his lips down in the palm of one and kissed it tenderly.

"It's perfect!" said Daryl. "Oh, it's a beautiful ring. See it sparkle! Oh, Alan, how could you get such a perfect fit?"

"Well, I'll have to confess. I stole one of your gloves when you were up in the city."

"Oh, so that's where my new gray glove went! I thought I had lost it in the store!"

They were having a wonderful time down there in the cellar. They almost forgot the apples, till Lance called out:

"Say, you two, aren't you ever coming up again?"

And then they hastily gathered their apples and hurried up the stairs.

"Well," said Lance, sharply eyeing their innocent faces, "you were gone long enough to grow a tree and pick the apples. Did you find anything besides apples down in the cellar? I was just about to organize a search party and send out for you."

"Yes," said Daryl, holding out her hand, her eyes sparkling in company with the gorgeous ring she was wearing. "I found something. I found this. How do you like it?" and she held her hand out shyly for them to see.

It was a wonderfully happy time that followed. They were all so delighted. Father and Mother Devereaux were touchingly glad. Lance cut up all sorts of pranks, teasing them and telling them how pleased he was, and Ruth went over and kissed Daryl tenderly.

They hardly got to bed at all that night there were so many things to say, so much to talk over. Father Devereaux's prayer when they finally knelt for the evening worship was so tender and full of thanksgiving that God had sent them a new son that the tears came to Daryl's eyes, and Alan who was kneeling beside her reached over and pressed her hand tenderly.

But they did get to bed at last, too happy to go to sleep right away, with so much to think over and be thankful for!

It was Saturday noon that the special delivery letter arrived.

They had just come in from skating, hungry as bears, and ready for the nice lunch that Mother Devereaux had prepared for them.

They all heard the car stop in front of the house, and a quick look of apprehension went around the table. What invader had arrived now?

Lance, with a quick protecting look toward Daryl, pushed back his chair and went to the door, and they all sat utterly silent while he was signing for the letter.

"It's for you, Daryl," he said, trying to sound natural, but he couldn't help knowing that handwriting. There had been too many letters during the last few months coming to Daryl, written in that hand.

It was only Daryl of them all who seemed unconcerned.

"A special delivery for me?" she laughed. "Now who on earth can it be from? My best friends are all present. Which of you is guilty?"

Then she glanced at the big bombastic script and knew of course. But her hand did not tremble, and she did not turn white. Her cheeks were still rosy from the exercise in the cold air.

"Excuse me if I read it, and we'll get it out of the way," she said, and opened the letter.

They tried not to seem to watch her. They talked a little about the ice, whether it would last another week for skating. Father Devereaux sharpened the carving knife unnecessarily long and noisily. But they all cast furtive side glances at her and were relieved to see her face remain placid. Then suddenly she startled them by bursting into a clear gurgle of laughter:

"Listen to this folks. You might as well hear this now and set your hearts at rest. It won't take but a minute and I know you've all been worrying lest Harold is coming back again."

Then she read:

> Dear Daryl:
>
> I feel that it is due you that I should let you know at once that I am married to an old sweetheart of mine. Her name is Elsie Bracken. We went to school together and have corresponded more or less through the years.
>
> I am sure that you will understand that I could not go on waiting for you to make up your mind, but I thought it right to let you know at once so you will not entertain any more false hopes.
>
> We were married this afternoon, a very quiet wedding since we are leaving at once for the far west where I expect to take a new position. Elsie is a very nice girl and well fixed, and I find that she has grown even more good-looking than she used to be. You were right when you told me that you and I were not suited to each other. I feel this is very true. Elsie is more pliable than you, and I feel that I can mold her character, and we shall have a very happy life together. But I shall always have a friendly feeling for you in my heart. You certainly have beautiful eyes.
>
> Yours as ever,
> Harold
>
> P.S. Don't bother to send wedding presents. It might make Elsie jealous and interfere with our happiness.

Daryl was laughing a bit ruefully as she read and when she had finished she laid the letter down on the table. Then she looked shamedly up at them all and smiled:

"I feel as if I ought to cry out, 'Oh, what a fool I was that

I ever thought there was anything to him!' I am so ashamed of myself. Won't you all forgive me, dear folks, and won't you forget that we ever knew him? I feel as if I never can thank God enough for saving me from a life with that man, and for—" she lifted shy loving eyes toward Alan—"and for sending me somebody so fine and wonderful! I didn't deserve it!"

Then suddenly Mother Devereaux, her dear eyes filled with joyful tears, got up from her chair, threw her arms about her girl and kissed her, and one by one they all followed suit. Father Devereaux came with the carving knife still in one hand, and then Lance, gravely, dragging Ruth by the hand, laughing. And last of all came Alan, solemnly, with a great light in his face, and kissed Daryl there before them all.

"Now," he said comically, "I can truly say that I am happy, since I know that I shall not have to contend with this gay Lothario who erstwhile aspired to your hand. It certainly relieves my mind. Tell him he can send *me* all the wedding presents he wants to. I won't ever be jealous again!"

"So, that is that!" said Lance at last when they all sat down to their belated lunch. "And now may I please have my lunch? I'm all caved in!"

The morning after Alan went back to the city he had a call from Dr. Sargent.

"I haven't heard from you since I sent you off to what might have been your death, in the worst snowstorm of the decade, and I thought I'd better look you up and apologize. Also I wanted to see if you needed my ministrations. I hear from the Watts family that you arrived in the nick of time, and the lady is on the mend in great shape. But they expressed great doubt as to whether you were yet alive, so I called to see!"

Alan welcomed him eagerly.

"Oh, you needn't thank me," he said, his face radiant. "You did me the greatest service a man can do for another.

You were the means of my finding two of the most precious things in life. I not only found a wonderful girl who has promised to be my wife, but I came to know the Lord Jesus Christ as my Saviour. Don't thank me. Let me thank you!"

The doctor was still a moment staring at him. Then he said:

"You would be as lucky as that, wouldn't you? A lot of men find wives, but I didn't know a mortal man could know the Lord."

"Well, he can!" said Alan assuredly. "Not only find Him and know Him but feel His Presence with him guiding and keeping day by day. It's wonderful! I want to tell you about it."

The doctor studied his friend for a minute and then he said:

"All right! I'll be glad to hear. You always were different from anybody else I know. But just in passing, let me say that my only regret at the news is that we shall probably now not have your company at Christmas next year as we had hoped. You'll likely be having a Christmas of your own. But I wish you joy! Now, tell me all about it!"

About the Author

Grace Livingston Hill is well known as one of the most prolific writers of romantic fiction. Her personal life was fraught with joys and sorrows not unlike those experienced by many of her fictional heroines.

Born in Wellsville, New York, Grace nearly died during the first hours of life. But her loving parents and friends turned to God in prayer. She survived miraculously, thus her thankful father named her Grace.

Grace was always close to her father, a Presbyterian minister, and her mother, a published writer. It was from them that she learned the art of storytelling. When Grace was twelve, a close aunt surprised her with a hardbound, illustrated copy of one of Grace's stories. This was the beginning of Grace's journey into being a published author.

In 1892 Grace married Fred Hill, a young minister, and they soon had two lovely young daughters. Then came 1901, a difficult year for Grace—the year when, within months of each other, both her father and husband died.

Suddenly Grace had to find a new place to live (her home was owned by the church where her husband had been pastor). It was a struggle for Grace to raise her young daughters alone, but through everything she kept writing. In 1902 she produced *The Angel of His Presence, The Story of a Whim,* and *An Unwilling Guest.* In 1903 her two books *According to the Pattern* and *Because of Stephen* were published.

It wasn't long before Grace was a well-known author, but she wanted to go beyond just entertaining her readers. She soon included the message of God's salvation through Jesus Christ in each of her books. For Grace, the most important thing she did was not write books but share the message of salvation, a message she felt God wanted her to share through the abilities he had given her.

In all, Grace Livingston Hill wrote more than one hundred books, all of which have sold thousands of copies and have touched the lives of readers around the world with their message of "enduring love" and the true way to lasting happiness: a relationship with God through his Son, Jesus Christ.

In an interview shortly before her death, Grace's devotion to her Lord still shone clear. She commented that whatever she had accomplished had been God's doing. She was only his servant, one who had tried to follow his teaching in all her thoughts and writing.